Praise for *The Worst Wom*

"*The Worst Woman in London* is the kind of historical [romance] I've been dying to read. . . . Certainly it's one of the most complex and satisfying explorations of the idea that everyone is the hero of their own love story—even the villains."

—Olivia Waite, *The New York Times*

"A refreshing, generous tale that tells two love stories as it explores the abhorrent impact on women of divorce law in the Victorian age. . . . Romantic, feminist, and shimmers with intelligence. Let's hope Ms. Bennet keeps writing—we need more historical romance just like this!"

—*All About Romance*

"Bennet brings off what many historical authors try but fail to achieve: she gives us characters who feel historically accurate but with a modern sensibility. . . . With gorgeous, period-appropriate prose, appealing characters . . . it's a great example of the best of historical romance. It's also angsty and emotional without falling into melodrama. HIGHLY, highly recommended!"

—*Plot Trysts*

"I loved it so much. Why? First, the writing was beautiful. . . . The plotline Bennet chose . . . allowed her to create characters that were, or became, open-minded without seeming anachronistically modern, [and] the growing affection between Francesca and James . . . felt natural and believable. And hot. And most importantly, there were no good or evil characters in this book; only human ones in various shades of gray."

—*Guiltless Pleasures*

[illegible] the Street Woman in London

[illegible]

THE WORST WOMAN IN LONDON

THE WORST WOMAN IN LONDON

Julia Bennet

UNION SQUARE & CO.
NEW YORK

UNION
SQUARE
& CO.
NEW YORK

UNION SQUARE & CO. and the distinctive Union Square & Co. logo are trademarks of Sterling Publishing Co., Inc.

Union Square & Co., LLC, is a subsidiary of Sterling Publishing Co., Inc.

Originally self-published in 2022

ISBN 978-1-4549-5448-4

Library of Congress Control Number: 2023051925
Library of Congress Cataloging-in-Publication Data
is available upon request.

For information about custom editions, special sales, and premium purchases, please contact specialsales@sterlingpublishing.com.

Printed in Canada

2 4 6 8 10 9 7 5 3 1

unionsquareandco.com

Cover illustration by Vi-An Nguyen
Interior design by Kevin Ullrich

To anyone whose Prince Charming turned out to be a venomous toad.
You deserve better and I really hope you get it.

CHAPTER ONE

London, 1872

The Thorne marriage was doomed from the start.

Of course, James Standish didn't know that yet, as he sat on a bench in the shade of a plane tree, waiting to meet the bride-to-be.

Impulsive, headstrong, hideously romantic Thorne was getting married. Never mind that six and twenty was far too young an age for any man, even a less impetuous one, to sacrifice himself on the altar of matrimony. Remarkable the things that went on when one's back was turned.

By the time James knew anything about it, the matter was entirely settled. The wedding would take place in August, before the grouse shooting started on the "Glorious Twelfth" and lured the fashionable set to the country.

"Standish." Thorne loped across the grass, golden hair flopping into his eyes as always, his mouth curved in a sheepish grin. "Not late, am I?"

James rose and smoothed the lapels of his new black morning coat. "Not at all."

"Hope you haven't waited long. Thank you for coming all this way to stand up with me."

No need to let Thorne know how little he relished being here. "You know me," he said, trying to sound jovial. "Any excuse to escape Shropshire. I spent the entire season dancing attendance on Aunt Miriam."

"Poor you." Thorne clucked sympathetically as he led the way through the sunlit square toward the Palladian townhouse where his intended, Miss Francesca Heller, resided. The gracious white stucco towered over them, devoid of ornament, elegant in its simplicity.

Thorne bounded to the door, rang the bell, and stood tapping his foot on the stone step.

"Steady on." James leaned one shoulder against the doorjamb. "If you don't calm down, Miss Heller's aunt will think you're a collie and refuse to let you on the furniture." Despite his words, he always found Thorne's enthusiasm rather endearing. Whenever James sank into one of his sporadic bouts of ennui, his friend always somehow managed to encourage him out again.

Thorne stopped tapping but smoothed imaginary wrinkles from his gloves instead. No more than ten seconds passed before he lifted his cane and rapped on the glossy black-painted panels.

James smiled and shook his head. "They won't thank you if you scratch the paint. I've never seen anyone so keen to put their head in the marital noose."

Just then, a footman opened the door on behalf of an elderly butler who stood ready to welcome them. "Hello, Walters," Thorne said. "Mr. Standish and I are here to see the ladies."

"Of course, sir. They're waiting in the parlor."

They relinquished their toppers to the footman and followed the butler across the checked tile of the entry hall. A wide, curving staircase led them up to the first floor and the principal receiving rooms.

Thorne's hand shook as he reached up to brush a lock of hair out of his eyes. He approached the parlor with the air of a supplicant entering the Holy of Holies.

James stifled the urge to tease. With Thorne in his current agitated state, it would be too cruel. Besides, new husbands often pruned their less respectable acquaintances after the wedding, and he didn't want to end up among the deadwood. They were close friends now, but all that might change once Thorne had a wife and in-laws to consider.

"Mr. Thorne and Mr. Standish, madam." Walters bowed out of the room.

The door closed, entombing James with an overexcited Thorne, two ladies he'd yet to meet, and nothing to console him but tasteless sandwiches and weak tea.

A woman rose with a rustle of wheat-colored skirts and came forward with hands outstretched to Thorne. "My dear Edward, it's always a joy." Then she turned her dazzling smile on James. "You are very welcome here, sir."

James stood, utterly confused. Alluring she might be, but surely this woman was too old for Thorne.

"Thank you, Mrs. Lytton," Thorne said.

Mrs. Lytton? *This* was Miss Heller's aunt? How fortunate Thorne answered for both of them, because James couldn't have uttered a word.

All the aunts he knew, including his own, were old spinsters or matronly battle-axes. Mrs. Lytton didn't look much past thirty. Generally, aunts didn't have plump, kissable lips, or breasts that strained the confines of their tea gowns. If someone put a gun to his head and forced him to pick a wife, Mrs. Lytton was the sort he'd choose, a woman who looked like she knew a thing or two.

He stood there, like a hungry lion sizing up an impala, until Thorne cleared his throat and gestured to a girl standing just beyond Mrs. Lytton. "Standish, this is Francesca—I mean Miss Heller."

Lord, he'd almost forgotten why they'd come.

The girl stepped forward.

Ah. This was more like it. If James had noticed her before, he'd have known immediately which lady was which. Miss Heller was perhaps ten years younger than her aunt and just the type of girl he'd been expecting.

According to Thorne, she possessed fortune, breeding, and beauty excelling even Cleopatra's. In the flesh, she was pretty enough, but too short for such high praise. The top of her thick, dark hair—fashionably if fussily curled—barely reached James's chin. Her gown did little to flatter her small stature; rows of white ruffles covered her from neck to ankle, obscuring her figure. Altogether, with her sweet smile and fair complexion, she reminded him of a doll gracefully posed in a shop window.

Not his sort of woman, though he understood why his friend admired her; she was a perfect debutante. Girls like her thronged the ballrooms of London during the season. If James one day discovered they assembled them in a factory somewhere, he'd feel only mild surprise.

"There," Thorne said. "The two people dearest to me together in the same room at last."

"It's a pleasure to meet you, Mr. Standish." Miss Heller spoke the commonplace sentiment with just the right degree of eagerness. Any less and she might appear cold. Any more would be vulgar.

James smiled and bowed, but inwardly he groaned. He loathed chitchat and foresaw half an hour's worth. Still, three more days and his part would end. He'd watch Thorne marry this thoroughly appropriate girl and wave them off on their wedding journey. No doubt their chances of rubbing along happily as man and wife equaled any other couple's.

The ladies sank gracefully onto a blue damask upholstered settee. Thorne, the poor fool, crammed himself into the elegant Queen Anne near Miss Heller. His back would ache like the devil before he'd drained his first cup. James tried not to look smug as he selected a plush armchair and settled in.

Mrs. Lytton poured tea into a floral-patterned cup. "Milk or lemon, Mr. Standish?" she asked, and added lemon at his behest. He resisted an uncouth urge to graze her hand with his thumb as she passed him a side plate.

Once she'd furnished everyone with tea and scones, the inanities commenced.

First, they talked about seating plans. Then they moved on to flower arrangements. By the time they got around to those inconsiderate souls who RSVP'd at the eleventh hour, James had started fantasizing about leaping through a nearby window.

Thorne frowned at him. "You're looking a bit green, Standish."

Mrs. Lytton sighed. "Oh, poor Mr. Standish. How tiresome you must find us. Let's talk of something else."

"Have you seen the latest *Fortnightly Review*?" Thorne asked. "Everyone's talking about this serial they're printing called *The Eustace Diamonds*. It's about an adventuress. I read the first installment, but I don't understand why it's so popular. I refuse to believe women like this Lizzie Greystock character exist."

Mrs. Lytton gave a sage nod. "It's extraordinary what passes for amusement these days."

"Why would anyone want to read about a heroine like that?" Thorne said, toying with Miss Heller's fingers.

The need to play devil's advocate got the better of James. "Why on earth wouldn't they? She sounds like fun."

Thorne glanced at him. "Well, she isn't ladylike."

"Oh, I see. You're one of *those*. When you read *Vanity Fair*, I bet you preferred Amelia Sedley to Becky Sharp. Tell the truth." James himself was by no means certain that he'd prefer an adventuress like Becky to dull but virtuous Amelia as a wife, but he knew which sort he'd rather take to bed. His friend, on the other hand, probably didn't distinguish.

Thorne furrowed his brow. "Of course I preferred Amelia. She *is* the heroine. Actually, she rather reminds me of Francesca."

On cue, Miss Heller's cheeks turned rosy.

Mrs. Lytton set her cup down on a gilt-edged end table. "I don't have a great deal of leisure for books myself. Of course, one must try to keep up or find oneself quite left out of the conversation. I daresay I wouldn't bother otherwise. Not like Francesca." She smiled at her niece. "Though I believe, in her heart of hearts, she prefers history."

Thorne threw back his head and laughed. "Truly? I assumed she'd prefer novels and such. Don't tell me I'm marrying a bluestocking."

"I read novels too," Miss Heller said. Her smile, when it came, wobbled slightly, as though she didn't quite mean it.

No one else seemed to notice or, if they noticed, they didn't attach any importance to that telltale tremble, but James had caught a glimpse of something else in her clear, leaf-green eyes. Was it sadness? He felt an unexpected pang of sympathy. Despite her frills and flounces, why shouldn't she like history best?

"Really, Thorne," he said. "It's hardly a shattering revelation."

A shrug in response. "No, of course not."

James leaned forward, interested for the first time since he'd sat down. Nothing could be duller than an engaged couple billing and cooing like turtledoves, but he wondered if these birds might not be a tad misled as to their suitability for long-term nesting. From what he'd seen so far, they didn't know the first thing about one another. After a brief acquaintance and a five-week engagement, here they were poised to pledge their lives to each other. Such indecent haste and the bride wasn't even with child. And if he saw trouble brewing after observing them for all of two seconds, what else might be going on beneath the surface?

Thorne smiled at Miss Heller like a father indulging a little girl. "Perhaps once we're married, we might read together sometimes."

A scene sprang to mind. Thorne, in an easy chair, reading aloud from the improving works of Rousseau or Richardson while his wife perfected her embroidery. It was enough to make any right-thinking person nauseous.

Mrs. Lytton took the opposite view. "What a charming idea, Mr. Thorne. A husband should act as his wife's guide if she wishes to educate herself. I think it unseemly, women attending university like men. All those stocky, plain-faced girls one sees at Benslow House. Pioneers they call them. It makes one shudder."

James hadn't given any serious thought to the notion of female education but, as a general rule, he favored anything that shook things up. "Oh, I don't know. Surely one's wife should know how to converse intelligently on subjects other than hat trimming and the relative merits of plumes versus blooms."

Miss Heller didn't say a word. Perhaps she didn't agree, or perhaps she agreed but was too polite to say so. James found himself eager to know which, but before he could ask, Mrs. Lytton distracted him.

"More tea, Mr. Standish?" As she leaned forward to pour, her impressive breasts threatened to spill from her bodice. The square-cut neckline, though not precisely immodest, tested the limits of tasteful afternoon attire. He snapped his attention back to the left where Miss Heller sat.

Their eyes met.

She didn't blush and look away. Instead, she regarded him calmly, a faint crease showing in her brow. Was that disapproval? He wanted to laugh, but he kept his face carefully blank. Whatever he did, he must try to make a decent impression on these women for Thorne's sake. He bit the inside of his cheek, but he couldn't prevent a slight twitching of his lips.

Miss Heller lifted her eyebrows. Just when he thought she was about to rebuke him, her frown melted away. Her green eyes lit with unexpected humor, and her commonplace prettiness bloomed into beauty. The transformation lasted two seconds at most before she smothered the smile. Clasping her slender white hands in her lap, she stared at them as if they fascinated her.

He might almost believe he'd imagined the whole thing, but then her shoulders began to shake. Heaven help him, she'd caught him ogling Mrs. Lytton's bosom and she found it funny. His own laughter threatened to burst out, but he pressed his lips together and averted his gaze. If only mirth were not so contagious.

Two things occurred to him at once.

First, Francesca Heller was nothing like Amelia Sedley from *Vanity Fair,* whatever Thorne said. She might never make a decent adventuress like Becky Sharp, but she had a ribald sense of humor and the brains to hide it from a fiancé who wouldn't approve. Thorne might seem like a fellow worth the sacrifice, but would she still feel the same in a year? In two? How long could she keep pretending to be other than she was?

Second, James realized he liked her. In fact, he liked her tremendously.

The other two remained oblivious, still deep in discussion about the evils of female education and the women's movement. Miss Heller composed herself and rejoined the conversation, her expression serene, and that one moment was all it took for him to understand what no one else seemed to grasp; she wouldn't do at all.

Miss Heller simply wasn't the right girl for Thorne. James knew by the way she hid her laughter, by her sadness when Thorne patronized her, and by a dozen other insignificant details. If the ceremony went ahead in three days, it might prove the worst mistake of her life.

If it were any other man, the two might marry, realize their mistake, and make the best of things, but Thorne was a romantic and he'd rhapsodized at length on Miss Heller's delicacy, her girlish ignorance, and sweet compliance. When he realized she wasn't the girl of his dreams, his spirits wouldn't just plummet, but crash. When people tumbled from their pedestals, as they generally did sooner or later, Thorne didn't hesitate to cut them out of his life. Even his own father.

The girl didn't understand, not consciously, and Thorne hadn't a clue.

Perhaps James ought to say something.

He imagined all the wedding guests bearing down on the capital. Did he really mean to plant doubts in Thorne's mind at this late date, and all because Miss Heller had laughed at an inappropriate moment? How ludicrous. How impossible. But if he stayed silent, what then?

The sinking in James's gut revealed the hopelessness of his situation, but he couldn't ignore his instincts. For Thorne's sake, he must say what needed to be said, even if it meant destroying their friendship.

But not here and not now.

Following Miss Heller's excellent example, he pasted his most social smile upon his face and rejoined the conversation.

CHAPTER TWO

London, 1882

Bother, blast, and bugger!

Not a ladylike thought, but then Francesca Thorne was anything but ladylike. *All* her ideas and beliefs, all her feelings and reactions, were inappropriate or just plain wrong. Or so her husband had spent the past ten years telling her.

Yet, on today of all days, surely the odd bit of mental profanity was justified.

The parlor of Aunt Helena's house on Berkeley Square hadn't altered noticeably since the day long ago when Edward Thorne had gotten down on one knee and promised to love her for eternity if she would only consent to be his wife. They'd been bathed in sunlight then. Now, she waited for him in gloom, the heavy drapes drawn shut to protect the expensive silk of the upholstery. How fitting that they discuss the dissolution of their marriage and the collapse of all their hopes in the dull light of a gas lamp.

Leaning over, she straightened her skirts. It wouldn't do to appear rumpled. If only her cursed hands wouldn't shake so. Yes, this little meeting would almost certainly prove the pinnacle of all the ugly confrontations they'd endured at one another's hands over the years, but she must never let him guess how easily he upset her. Just as she mustn't *ask* for a divorce—she must demand. If she appeared weak, even for an instant, if she came to him like a petitioner, he would crush her, and that she would never permit. If ten years of marriage, ten years of putting up with an endless parade of strumpets, hadn't broken her, this paltry skirmish wouldn't either.

She drew deep, calming breaths, in and out, in and out again, and turned her thoughts another way—to Aunt Helena and Uncle Arthur.

When she'd inquired into their whereabouts, the butler had been carefully vague in response. Truth was, she wasn't welcome in this house. If Francesca's estranged husband, always Aunt Helena's darling, hadn't thought this room a more discreet venue for a meeting than a solicitor's office in The City, Francesca wouldn't have made it past the threshold. But since she'd been—and still was—adamant that she'd never willingly set foot inside any of her spouse's residences ever again, her aunt and uncle had made an exception. For today only.

Yet, as the drawing room door opened at last, she failed to stifle the foolish leap of hope that they'd changed their minds about receiving her personally. That was why she craned forward in her seat—as if she might spy them hiding there. As if Aunt Helena might dash forward and embrace her like she used to when Francesca was young.

But no. Her not-so-dearly-beloved husband came in alone, and hope plummeted like Icarus after he flew too near the sun. They would never forgive her, not unless she took Edward back. The pain of their estrangement cut deeper because they still received *him* after all he'd done. Just the sight of him—still handsome, like a knight stepped from the pages of an Arthurian legend—sickened her. Lancelot reborn. If Lancelot were a conscienceless cad.

"You look like Botticelli's *Fortitude*," he remarked. Like her, he often thought in literary allusions or, as in this case, artistic ones. It was one of the things that had tricked them into thinking they'd suit. "You have your throne," he said, gesturing at the chair she'd chosen. "All you need is armor."

In a way, he was right. She hadn't done a thing today without careful consideration, whether choosing which dress to wear or selecting a straight-backed chair. She wanted to sit tall so as to appear resolute and unyielding. If he thought she looked like the Botticelli panel, it was a happy result.

"Thank you," she said. "I always excelled at *tableau vivant*."

"I remember."

As far as she recalled, Botticelli had never painted *Dissipation*. If he had, it might have resembled her husband. Dark circles ringed his still beautiful blue eyes, and his flushed cheeks suggested he'd imbibed too much wine the previous evening. With Edward, last night often stretched far into the next day.

They exchanged pleasantries, both instinctively observing the niceties. It reminded her of breakfasts during their early years or those rare, brief visits he'd made after he'd left her. Two years together. Eight years apart. So many meals ruined by cold courtesy.

Their conversation today would be different.

She began by asking after her aunt and uncle.

He confirmed what she already knew. They were not at home. "You can't seriously have expected anything else," he said, not unkindly. "They are willing to meet with you whenever you say."

"Yes, if I do what's expected of me."

He gazed at her but said nothing.

She knew this trick well. Whenever they disagreed, he allowed the silence to lengthen until she felt compelled to speak. In times past, she might have filled the pause with capitulation or appeasement. Well, she would not do so this time.

She studied the gilding on one of the Queen Anne chairs—golden, but only on the surface, much like their marriage. The thought depressed her.

As several silent minutes passed, she occupied herself with thoughts of Uncle Arthur. How he'd thundered at her when he came to see her at the Cavendish Hotel a few days after she'd arrived in London. He'd called her a few names even Edward hadn't tried yet. He would not see her again, he'd vowed, until she started behaving like a proper wife. Since then, she'd had the temerity to purchase a house of her own—a powerful declaration attesting to the permanence of the path she'd chosen. In response, Arthur had sent what she knew to be the last letter he would ever write to her, severing what remained of their connection forever.

But thoughts of Helena caused Francesca the greatest pain.

"I didn't choose my marriage," her aunt had said. "But I endured it for the sake of the people who love me—for my husband's sake and, yes, even for your sake, to spare you the unpleasantness. It will hurt me very deeply if you refuse to do as much for us."

Francesca, who had freely chosen Edward, felt the rebuke like a wound that festered and never healed.

"You didn't used to mind doing what's expected." Edward's voice, quiet with reproach, brought her back to the here and now. The words hung in the air and quashed any triumph she might feel at resisting his tactics. "Are their expectations really so onerous? You don't want to live with me. We'll live apart then. They can tolerate that. Surely you can content yourself for your family's sake. A divorce gains you nothing and causes them, causes all of us, a great deal of unpleasantness."

That word again. Guilt tugged at Francesca. Guilt and its frequent companion since all this started, irritation. Why, oh why did everything have to be so bloody pleasant all the time? Why was propriety more important to her family than the fact that Edward was a philandering rogue? No point asking Edward; he never questioned the status quo. Screeching at him wouldn't help either, no matter how much she might long to give full voice to her feelings. He'd give her that small contemptuous smile she'd seen so often during their marriage and she wouldn't change his mind one jot.

She tried her damnedest to emulate his polite tone. "Can you honestly say you don't want children? An heir? Because you can't get them from me." If only she could make him see how much better off he'd be without her. The scandal would hardly touch him. He could start again and marry someone who wouldn't disappoint him. Someone who'd let him sleep with whomever he wanted, and welcome him home afterward with a smile and a peck on the cheek.

"Perhaps what we want isn't the most important consideration." He spoke in the careful, measured tones of a man clinging valiantly to patience. "Why can't you understand?"

At that, her temper slipped its feeble restraints. "I understand, Edward. But I wonder where your sense of duty was while you slept your way through half the opera dancers in London. Did you honestly expect me to wait patiently in the country for the rest of my life while you peopled the city with bastards?" Her voice had risen so that now the question rang in the silence.

For once, his contemptuous smile wasn't forthcoming. She'd succeeded in angering him past that point. "Yes," he snapped, and then, his voice rising to match hers, "God knows why. God knows I should've long ceased expecting anything from you. Do you think you're the only wife who's had to bear such things? Is that any reason to subject me, to subject yourself and our families to this . . . this farce?" He raked all ten fingers through his hair, until great clumps of it stood on end. "You seem determined to expose us all to contempt."

She'd hoped to shame him with her accusations, but instead *she* felt ashamed for bearing things so long. Inwardly she counted, one, two, three, determined to be rational by the time she got to ten. "It's an ugly mess, but—"

"But you still refuse to see reason," he snarled. "You don't wish to reconcile? Well, I don't wish to support a wife who is not a wife. As of next quarter, your allowance will be stopped."

Laughter bubbled up from somewhere deep within her. Of course, he didn't want to go on paying her bills. Why should he? *Oh, well played, Edward.* If she didn't want to throttle him so much, she might have spoken the praise aloud. "You look pleased with yourself," she said instead. How calm and quiet she sounded; she rather admired herself for it.

"You really didn't see it coming?" He spoke like a little boy who'd just hidden a toad in the governess's bed.

"Of course I did, but I thought you'd have the decency to wait until *after* the trial."

They sat in silence for a moment as she considered the situation. She had very little money of her own. By the time she'd paid the lawyers . . .

"So, if we divorce," she said, "I have precisely nothing because everything I once owned is now yours. Is that an accurate assessment?"

"Not quite nothing, no. You still have the inheritance from your mother. The way it was left to you, I can't touch it. So you aren't a complete pauper." The insufferable smile was back. "If you find your income insufficient, you could always come back to me."

"I don't think so, Edward." She smiled and summoned the spirit of the long-ago debutante who'd remained serene throughout innumerable stilted social calls. "Cut me off then. You'll probably be giving me the grounds I need, a little desertion to go with all your adultery."

He stretched inelegantly, his shoulder and arm bones cracking. "I don't think so, my love. That won't work. I'm not a lawyer of course, but as you've left the marital home at your own instigation, I don't think you'll get me on desertion. It's debatable at the very least. Divorce is very expensive. You'd have to make economies. You won't like that."

How obscenely pleased he looked. Worse than that, he was probably right.

"Sweetheart," she said, pouring every ounce of scorn she felt into the mockery of an endearment, "I understand your feelings, but if you want to save your pennies, surely it's in your best interest to let me divorce you."

Smug look vanishing at last, he leaned forward in his chair. "Try it, and I'll file a countersuit and name Trafford as your lover."

She felt the color drain from her face. For the second time, he had her reeling. Did he even believe what he was saying? In the eight years since he'd left, he must have had upward of fifty affairs. Yet he still found time and energy to form this disgusting blackmail plot.

"You didn't think I knew, did you?" he asked, smiling softly.

He *did* believe it, then. "You've been listening to gossip," she said.

"Not gossip. Just our servants performing their duty in my absence."

"Why are you doing this?" She'd asked him this so many times during their life together, and she couldn't stop herself asking one more time.

"I don't want to support a wife who whores herself to half the demimonde. Let Trafford support you. He's still about, isn't he, or am I behind the times?"

She shot to her feet. "Did you . . ." A deep breath. "Did you just call me a whore? How dare you! Let me explain something to you, Edward. You deserted me in the country. You betrayed me many times and with many women. You broke your marriage vows repeatedly. When I left, it was a formality. This divorce is *another* formality. Our marriage was over a long time ago."

She strode to the door and turned back toward him once she'd reached it. She had no idea what she was going to do when she left this room, but she was going to get the last word if it killed her. "This may shock you, but even if I were guilty as charged, I still would not consider myself an adulteress."

He stared at her, shaking his head. "I don't know you at all, do I? There is no meeting between our two minds. We don't even speak the same language."

As she fumbled with the doorknob, he came closer. The clean citrus scent of his cologne enveloped her. The familiar smell evoked the touch and taste of him, suddenly vivid years after she'd consigned them to the most dark and distant recess of her mind.

"Do you ever wonder how we got here?" he asked.

Their eyes met as the latch finally gave with a loud click. She raised her chin, looking him in the eyes as she replied. "We got here one mistake at a time."

James Standish leaned his cheek against the soft, leather scroll wing of his chair, and stretched his legs toward the smoking-room fire. He cherished his quiet evenings in this soothing, tobacco-scented haven. In the parlor or the drawing room, concessions to feminine comfort abounded. One couldn't move for fear of tripping over an ottoman or careening into a potted palm. With a lady present, one had to be sociable and at least *attempt* intelligent conversation, but the smoking room, the billiard room, and the gentleman's study endured as reassuring, masculine refuges where a fellow didn't have to speak at all if he didn't care to.

This evening, the customary peace proved elusive. Thorne was of a mind to talk. Usually a peaceful companion, he'd just come from an interview with his estranged wife. To understate the case dramatically, their discussion hadn't gone well.

"She was like a stranger," Thorne was saying. "I wouldn't have believed it if I hadn't seen it for myself. I couldn't reason with her."

Thorne had been talking this way for ten minutes, and it wasn't the first time he'd launched into a prolonged monologue on Fran's faults. Clearly, he needed a sympathetic ear, and James fully intended to provide one, but a gentleman shouldn't criticize a lady, especially his wife, to a third party.

"Women are a plague, Standish. Never get married," Thorne said, and paused to take a swig of brandy.

Unlike Thorne, James had never believed in the goddess of the hearth or, her infernal sister, the fallen woman. To him, young or old, fat or thin, genteel or earthy, women were just women. He liked talking to them, looking at them, and, if mutual attraction struck, sleeping with them. He couldn't decide if Thorne disliked all women or just his wife.

"Indeed, I have no plans to marry," James answered. "If I ever had, listening to you spew vitriol on the subject would soon put paid to them. You're ruining this cognac."

But Thorne kept on spewing until everything he said became noise. James tried to listen at first, but he felt like a cad just *hearing* some of the things his friend said about Fran. Eventually, he allowed his gaze to wander to Thorne's hands; he had a curious habit of waving them about as he ranted. They swooped and jabbed, filling the air with invisible punctuation.

"Standish?" Thorne said. "Are you even listening?"

Caught out, James straightened in his chair. Perhaps he could skew the conversation in a slightly different direction. "What do the families say?" he asked.

"Hers feel as mine do. They are all, quite rightly, against the divorce. She won't get any help from that quarter." Thorne sounded like a general determined to rout a renegade force. His tone formed a stark contrast with his appearance, which with his fair hair flopping into his eyes, resembled an injured sheepdog. "They all think she's being extremely perverse."

Poor old Fran.

The Thornes and, on Fran's side, the aunt and uncle, Mr. and Mrs. Lytton, had closed ranks, and neither family lacked influence.

No one would receive her without their support. If he understood Thorne's tirade, her finances were their next point of attack. Most unsporting. James couldn't help feeling sorry for her. He'd known from the start the two were a mismatch, but when he'd tried to warn Thorne a week or so before the wedding, they'd nearly come to blows.

As James had predicted, Thorne hadn't known what to do with a girl who threw back her head when she laughed, let alone one who had reportedly declared, in a fit of temper six months into their marriage, that she'd read what she "*bloody well liked.*"

As for the consequences if she persisted in this divorce madness . . .

They didn't love each other, so he didn't think the break would hurt her in that way. Thorne had left her eight years ago, so she'd had *most* of her pain then. But there were other, more material considerations. James shuddered when he considered what economies she might be forced to make.

Thorne would be fine—he had deep pockets—but Fran had already been spotted looking for a house in Bloomsbury, when everyone fashionable lived in Mayfair. In her place, he'd come to heel like a shot. He knew what it was to depend on another person's largesse and how much power a benefactor could wield over one's life. But he liked his creature comforts too much to sacrifice them for the sake of winning an argument, and, when one got right down to it, wasn't that what Fran was doing? She and Thorne didn't live together anyway, so why not leave things as they were? What would she really gain if she persevered?

"Actually, there's a reason for my boring you with all this." Leather creaked as Thorne shifted in his seat. "Ordinarily, I wouldn't ask it of you, but the more voices we add to the chorus the better."

James felt a portentous twinge at his temples. He placed his drink on the table and pushed it away. What was the point? He wouldn't enjoy it in these conditions. Something was coming, and he didn't think it would be good. "Before you say anything—"

"I was hoping you might convey a message." Thorne blurted the words out before James could marshal his thoughts.

"You *do* know how much I detest people speaking over me, don't you?"

Thorne's lips twitched with amusement, but he didn't apologize.

James might've reacted to his friend's request with more compassion if he thought Thorne cared for his wife instead of society's whispers. But Thorne had made his feelings—or lack of feelings—explicit over the years. Though the desire to avoid a scandal was a motivation James understood and even applauded, it didn't stir his feelings the way genuine mourning for a lost love would. Having said that, he didn't *enjoy* seeing his friend besieged by gossip, either. He opened his mouth to say so, but Thorne cut him off.

"I want you to make her an offer."

An offer? This was worse than James had feared. From what he'd heard, Fran was already drowning in opposition, while Thorne had everyone, even her family, on his side. Was it fair to add yet another soldier to the army?

Thorne waited, his expression hopeful.

"Don't you think—" James cleared his throat. "Don't you think this is rather a lot to ask?"

"I realize that. I just think my offer will sound better coming from a friend than a lawyer."

James doubted it. From what he'd heard, the messenger usually ended up with an arrow in his back. If only Thorne didn't possess such beseeching eyes.

Since a blunt refusal—*any* refusal—seemed out of the question, evasion struck James as the next best course. "But I hardly know her."

"Nonsense," Thorne said, "you visited us in Hertfordshire dozens of times. You call her Fran, for heaven's sake."

"Yes, to annoy her." And she'd smiled and promptly begun calling him Jemmy. Despite her husband's low opinion of her, she really was a terrific sport. "I haven't seen her since you decamped to London. Past foolishness aside, and considering the eight-year gap, it's hardly an intimate connection. What about the Lyttons? Surely one of them would be a more appropriate choice. Didn't Fran and the aunt-with-the-phenomenal-bosom used to be great friends?"

"The Lyttons are done with her. The only way they'll even see her is if she gives up this idea of divorcing altogether. You'd be doing her a service." Thorne stared down at the vague flowery shapes and curlicues patterning the carpet. "I know she wants to reconcile with them, and I imagine she could use a friend. She doesn't have many left. You're certainly the only one I'd trust."

Ah, an appeal to sentiment. James wished he were immune. Even recognizing it for what it was—a not-so-subtle manipulation—he felt its tug. With his head down and speaking in that rational tone, Thorne actually sounded concerned for Fran's well-being. *And* he'd invoked the sacred trust that existed between gentlemen and certainly between two friends of such long-standing. It made James long for the days when he would never have questioned Thorne's honor.

A stray recollection of those times prompted him to ask, "Do you remember that time at Oxford when they caught me trying to smuggle that pig into the junior proctor's bed?"

Thorne laughed. "Good God, I'd almost forgotten. You nearly got yourself sent down. I had to ask my father to intervene with the vice-chancellor. You never told me why you refused to go to Mrs. Price."

"One never knows how Aunt Miriam will react. She's a great advocate of high spirits in young men."

"Ah, I see. On the other hand, she might've cut you off."

"Well, quite."

Sometimes James didn't like the person Thorne had become, but whenever he began to think their friendship might have run its course, he grew nostalgic. He still remembered the young man who'd been his companion at school, the same man who'd married Fran.

Perhaps Thorne's thoughts ran along the same lines, because his expression clouded. "You tried to help me once before, remember? You told me she wasn't the right girl." He laughed without mirth, as if to say, "*What an understatement* that *turned out to be!*"

"I wish I'd listened," Thorne went on. "You couldn't help me then—my own stupid fault, I know—but you can help me now."

That was quite the speech. James closed his eyes, but it was no good. Thorne's plea had already stolen past his weak defenses. How could he pass up a chance to compensate his friend for the mistakes of the past? He couldn't, so he might as well surrender to the inevitable.

"What sort of offer exactly?" he asked.

Thorne leaned back and rested his glass on his lap, both hands loosely clasped about its circumference. "Look, I'm not unreasonable. I know it can't have been much fun for Francesca. I mean, stuck in the country with only my mother and sister for company." The words came in short bursts, as though his ability to sympathize with his wife had grown rusty from disuse. "It's not what either of us expected when we married. I confess I haven't lived like a monk since I came to London, and you know how gossip flies. It must embarrass her to hear people talk, but a divorce will only make things worse. If she's willing to come back, I'm willing to offer certain incentives."

Thorne smiled in the manner of one who knows he's about to say something profoundly witty. "To be precise, I'm willing to offer five thousand pounds per annum to be paid in quarterly installments. She'll be able to maintain her own establishment, if that's what she wishes, and in grand style. She ought to be happy. Any sane woman would be."

Amen to that, James thought as he sat back, momentarily stunned. Five thousand pounds per annum was an astounding sum, more than enough to keep a lady in fine food and furbelows. Suddenly he didn't feel quite so sorry for her.

Thorne traced the rim of his glass with one fingertip. "The thing is, seeing me doesn't bring out her rational side, such as it is. So, if you'll make the offer, I would be eternally grateful." He lifted his brandy and drank. He'd made his case, and now he relaxed and waited for the verdict.

The prospect of broaching so delicate and private a subject with Fran made James queasy. He'd exaggerated only slightly when he said he hardly knew her. Yet he didn't like hearing people gossip about her the way they had been lately. Jezebel, Delilah, Salome—James couldn't think of a single biblical hussy to whom she *hadn't* been compared. Maybe Thorne was right and he'd be doing her a kindness.

"Do you really believe it would sound better coming from me?" he asked. If it was true and he'd really help *both* Thornes by his interference, he'd rest easier.

"Oh my dear old thing, of course it would." Thorne grinned, obviously thrilled by James's crumbling resistance. "You'll do it then?"

Thanks to years of social training, James managed a smile in return. "Happy to help."

Having got what he wanted, Thorne lapsed into blessed silence.

James didn't return to his cognac. Peace eluded him now more than ever, and despite Thorne's assurances, his conscience pricked him every time he thought of what he'd agreed to do.

CHAPTER THREE

The fashionable hour approached as James rode through the triumphal arch on Hyde Park Corner. Already, Rotten Row was dotted with fashionably garbed ladies and gentlemen on their mounts. He found himself at loose ends this afternoon. Fran had answered his hastily scrawled request for an interview with a short note informing him that she'd recently purchased a house and would be pleased to receive him there once she'd organized the place to her liking. Then she'd proposed a Wednesday several days hence for their appointment.

He'd read these words with a sinking feeling since he'd hoped to get the delivery of Thorne's message out of the way by the end of the day. It was often the way. One got oneself all worked up about unpleasant duties only to find them deferred.

Riding always raised his spirits, especially on a beautiful afternoon like this. The rays of the sun still shone on the arch's elegant, fluted columns. The gradual lengthening of the days came as a relief after what had begun to feel like an interminable winter.

He had not progressed beyond where trees separated the Row from the South Carriage Drive when he spotted Aunt Miriam in her Victoria, the top down to better enjoy the gentle breeze barely rustling the leaves. He reined in some distance away and watched her order her coachman to stop. Leaning over the black-lacquered side of the conveyance, she exchanged greetings with a young couple in a phaeton. As always, she dispensed her favors regally, singling out only a select few for conversation.

Majestic she might be, but the only royal personage she resembled was the late Queen Charlotte, of whom someone had once unkindly said "the bloom was going off her ugliness." With Miriam's small eyes, bold nose, and pronounced frown lines, the same might just as easily be said of her, but those eyes missed nothing. She knew at a glance whose hat was made over or whose fringe was false. Tomorrow, when society came to call, as they assuredly would, she'd have ample stores of information to trade. She inspired fear rather than affection in everyone, except James.

Her eyes lit with pleasure as she spotted him guiding his gray toward her, but something white floated into his path. A piece of paper? He shaded his eyes against the sun. No, it was a handkerchief. A trifling scrap of fabric borne aloft by the breeze. It danced in the air before gliding straight for him, colliding weightless with his chest, its linen and lace resting on the herringbone wool of his gray morning coat. He stared at it for the briefest of instants before plucking it up.

"I'm terribly sorry." The female speaker's voice was low and melodious.

He turned toward the sound and saw her seated in a cabriolet with a dour-looking lady's maid. Although he'd seen a lot of beautiful women in his time, this one shone them down. She had a luminous complexion, like a Bouguereau painting made flesh. She reached out her hand, her blue eyes wide and appealing.

He returned her property with a flourish, always delighted to flirt with a striking woman, and was pleased to see her cheeks turn a becoming pink.

"Thank you."

"It's no trouble at all, Miss . . ."

"Sylvia." Her blush intensified. "Miss Randle, I mean."

Not married. Freshly out, if he were any judge. In the market for a husband, then. Not someone whose acquaintance he should cultivate if he wished to remain in his blessedly single state.

"A pleasure." He tipped his hat, and she moved on.

As beautiful as she'd been, he might have forgotten her the next moment if not for Aunt Miriam. "Come here, you rascal." Her Victoria took the place of Miss Randle's cabriolet. She beamed up at him, her wide smile giving her a roguish appearance. "You're continually charming the ladies. Don't you know you ought to be charming me? But you've always been incorrigible." She craned her neck in the direction Miss Randle had taken. "What a lovely little thing. I was quite dazzled by her. How gallant you were to come to her aid."

"Do you know her? I've never seen her before."

"Of course I know her. I know everybody, my boy." She cocked her head to one side, like a thoughtful parakeet. "Miss Sylvia Randle. Such an elegant young lady, and well-bred too. I had a perfect view of the entire interlude, and it all looked very romantic."

Miriam's mind wasn't generally of a sentimental turn; it was one of the things he enjoyed best about her. The remark boded ill for his continued bachelorhood.

"Now, don't look like that," she said, fixing him with a glare. "We must domesticate you. You haven't come to see me all week."

"I visited six days ago, Aunt." Though she complained no matter how often he called.

"Did you?" Her eyes took on a glazed appearance as she counted. "Well, that's near enough as makes no difference. Now, I don't mind you going off on your adventures, provided you pop in at regular intervals and regale me with all the amusing details."

It had been a long time between adventures. He liked to travel, but one had to come home eventually. He craved something different—a more permanent change, but not the one to which his aunt referred. These little hints about matrimony grew more blatant each time they met.

Her glare had deepened into a veritable scowl, but he knew exactly how to handle her in this mood. He scowled back, imitating her expression as closely as possible.

A corner of her lips twitched up in a wobbly smile. "What a bounder," she said, swatting at him.

He bowed. "But a lovable one, I hope."

In perfect accord once more, they continued together up the Row.

"What a handsome gentleman, Miss."

Sylvia had already forgotten the handkerchief incident, so she glanced at Dorcas with surprise. "Was he?"

"Oh, yes," the maid said. "Tall, dark, and very handsome."

"I suppose so." Sylvia hadn't really noticed.

"I wonder who he is. He shouldn't have drawn attention to you like that." Dorcas frowned, no doubt worrying what Sylvia's mother would say when she found out. "Though I suppose you would have lost the handkerchief if he hadn't."

But Sylvia's thoughts had drifted to another gentleman entirely. One she'd seen here in the park only yesterday.

She'd been out with Mama, taking the air. Everything had been as usual: the same well-trodden path and the same pleasantries exchanged with the same old acquaintances. But Mama had suddenly stiffened in her seat. "Driver," she'd called. "Take us home at once."

"Mama, we've only just arrived."

A harrumph was the only response. Sylvia had followed the direction of Mama's gaze, and everything had changed.

She'd seen *him*.

The most beautiful man she'd ever beheld.

He'd been on horseback, fair hair gleaming like gold in the sunlight as he tipped his hat to a female acquaintance.

"Who is he?"

Mama's lips had thinned. "A gentleman with poor taste in companions."

The woman was not respectable, then. Sylvia had experienced a tiny thrill at the realization. Ordinarily, she would have carefully examined this person, the first woman of ill repute she'd ever seen. As it was, she couldn't take her eyes from the gentleman.

"Look away, dear," her mother had said, tugging at her hand.

"Must we really leave?"

"If we didn't, I'd be forced to acknowledge him. That's Edward Thorne. Despite his defects of character, he's received everywhere. We can hardly cut him, but I don't want my daughter exposed to such wickedness . . ."

There had been more, but Sylvia didn't remember the rest of her mother's tirade. Edward Thorne had leaned forward in his saddle, holding something in his hand. A flower. A white rose. She'd watched, mesmerized, as he placed the bloom in the lady's hair.

Fancy filled in the details. How it would've felt, if Sylvia had been that woman, as his warm hand grazed her cheek. How he would have held her gaze, lips curved in a knowing smile, as he tucked the fragrant rose into her curls. Even now, she shivered imagining his fingers in her hair.

In the hours since, she hadn't stopped thinking about him. He was the first man to make her feel anything besides boredom. Unfortunately, because Mama considered him "fast," she would never even meet him.

That was why she'd come here, hoping for another glimpse of him. She should've known better. Naturally, a man like Edward Thorne didn't spend every afternoon gadding about the park. He'd have more exciting ways to occupy his time, which meant she'd wasted hers.

"Miss?" Dorcas's brow creased with concern. "Is everything all right?"

Sylvia shook her head and sighed. "I have a headache, that's all."

Dorcas clucked sympathetically and instructed the driver to take them home.

The appointed Wednesday came, and James grumbled his way to once-fashionable Bloomsbury. The faded grandeur of the terraced townhouses depressed him. One could hardly move here for bourgeois businessmen and the dreaded People Who Wrote. Fran—he really must stop using that frightful nickname—*Francesca* ought to move southwest. She belonged in Mayfair with the fashionable set. She'd grown up there, and he didn't like to see her sinking in the world's estimation. At least the street she'd chosen seemed quiet and respectable.

He instructed his driver to wait in the next road and approached her tall gray-brick on foot, running his cane along the metal fence, and dragging his feet slightly on his way up the stone steps to the door.

He'd spent a fair amount of time with Francesca back when she and Thorne still threw house parties. Their fledgling friendship had grown from a shared appreciation of the absurd. Their adoption of silly nicknames for each other had created a false sense of intimacy, perhaps. A pity today's errand didn't lend itself to levity. He had no idea how to proceed in its absence.

A maid, middle-aged and dignified, showed him to the first-floor parlor and left him with a somewhat terse "Wait here, sir." She didn't even offer him a seat.

He debated whether to remain standing as a matter of principle but subsided into the nearest chair when he began to feel foolish. If he didn't take care, he'd end up as hidebound as Aunt Miriam.

With nothing to do but wait, he considered his surroundings and decided he approved. The red and gold wallpaper looked as if it had been hung decades ago, judging by its uneven paleness, but the once-rich colors had mellowed. He'd stayed in rooms with walls like these in Italy, and the association was a pleasant one. The dwindling sunshine streamed in through tall multi-paned windows, gilding the room with light. He allowed himself to sink back in his chair, as he might if he were alone in his own home, and listen to the restful ticking of the clock on the mantel.

"I'm so sorry to have kept you waiting," Francesca said from the doorway.

He fought the impulse to bolt upright and rose slowly. "Not at all. I arrived only a few minutes ago."

She stood just inside the room, a small figure clad in a russet tea gown. He wouldn't have expected her, of all people, to favor artistic dress. In fact, he remembered her as a woman who liked frills and ribbons. Simplicity suited her better. Of course, eight years had wrought a multitude of changes if her current conduct was any indication.

From the look of her cheeks and nose, both rosy, she had only recently come in from outdoors. Perhaps she'd forgotten their appointment.

She led the way toward two chairs positioned on either side of the fire and sank gracefully onto a red damask armchair. "Won't you sit down?" she asked, gesturing to the other.

He eyed the brown tapestry of the larger, more comfortable-looking seat. "They don't match," he said. It was, perhaps, a rude remark, but they'd never stood on ceremony.

"So they don't. I'm afraid nothing in this house does. Most of the rooms are yet to be furnished. It's all something of a miscellany, isn't it?"

"I like it," he said as he sat. And he meant it. He felt comfortable here in this room, if not in her company. He couldn't be fully at ease until he'd told her why he was there.

"I was walking in the garden." A sort of happy wistfulness filled her voice. "It doesn't get enough sun, but I don't care. This is the first house that's ever truly been mine."

He hadn't expected her to talk about her circumstances unprompted, even in this oblique way. He prided himself on his ability to talk a great deal without saying anything of import, a skill she really ought to cultivate. The intimate details of one's personal life ought to remain . . . personal. Given that he'd come here today specifically to pry into her affairs, he should encourage her to talk, but it felt wrong. As if he'd be taking advantage of her openness.

"Will you ring the bell?" she asked.

"Of course." What gentleman worthy of the name let a lady ring her own bell?

"The cord's just above the mantel."

The brusque maid from earlier entered almost as soon as he rang. She must have been poised outside. The tea tray clattered as she set it down. When she'd withdrawn again, Francesca shrugged. "You must forgive Barker. She mistrusts anyone intimately connected with Edward. She's very loyal."

"Loyal servants are hard to come by." It seemed a nice, safe remark—something polite to cling to before he threw himself into choppier conversational waters.

"So they say," she said, pouring steaming tea into plain china cups. "Do you still take it with lemon?" At his nod, she added just the right amount and passed the cup across. "Well, Jemmy, it's been almost a century."

His old nickname. He felt eight years fall away as if she'd last called him Jemmy an hour ago. He hadn't expected her to remember.

That she did made what he'd come to say even more difficult, so he allowed himself to be distracted. "You used to wait until I called you Fran first."

"No one but you ever called me that." Her gaze swept down to assess his attire from necktie to narrow-toed shoes. "You look exactly the same. Just as fashionable as ever. Tell me, are those clothes from Paris?"

How easy it was to slip back into their old, teasing way of talking. Now, he affected a world-weary drawl. "Sorry to disappoint you, Fran, but I grew tired of Paris. These are from Savile Row."

He returned her scrutiny. In theory, aesthetic dress was very practical, leaving a woman more room to breathe. In practice, he could see the soft curve of her natural waistline and her breasts straining against the modest, ruffle-free neckline.

Christ, he didn't want to think about Fran's body. Thorne wouldn't appreciate James's ogling, and quite right too.

"I'm thankful you raise the subject of appearances," he said, "because I may now say, with perfect gentility, that you don't look anything like your old self. I think there must be a mere fifty pins in your hair instead of your usual five hundred."

Her cheeks turned even rosier than fresh air had made them. "I prefer to do things with less fuss when I'm in my own home."

She gave the last words no special emphasis, and yet they recalled him to his purpose in coming. Perhaps she sensed his ease evaporate because she looked away, staring into the fire. The crackling of the flames seemed louder in the sudden silence.

"It must be difficult for you." He didn't know what else to say. He usually avoided matters of a serious or personal nature and took great care never to attempt both at once. Today's meeting was highly irregular.

Apparently, Fran didn't share his discomfort. She took the poker from its stand next to her chair and prodded at the coals. "I struggled at first, but it's silly to feel miserable about it. If my own family refuses to meet me, I can hardly expect more from my acquaintances. I chose my path and I accept the consequences." The fire stirred to life, and she set the poker back in its place.

If she didn't mince words, why should he? "Do you really intend to pursue a divorce?"

"Of course."

He'd expected anger or at least irritation; she ought to scold him for impertinence and have him thrown onto the street. He cursed himself for coming, for involving himself in this messy, emotional business.

"Forgive me." He set his tea aside and leaned forward. "You say yourself you're treated badly as a result. If you go back, if you make it clear there will be no divorce, all this talk will die down. Your family will rally round even if you stay in your own establishment. With them behind you, all will be forgiven."

She smiled sadly. "All will be forgiven, will it? I'm not so sure it will."

Did she mean the rumors circulating about her? He hoped not because he had no intention of tackling that particular issue. "If your family backs you—"

"No, you misunderstand." She shook her head with a determined air.

He'd forgotten her earnest way of communicating. How she met one's eyes, forthright and direct to a fault, and gave herself up to the conversation. He'd always liked that—her abandon.

"Perhaps society might be persuaded to accept me, though I doubt it, but I am by no means sure I could be persuaded to accept society."

James had heard this sort of thing before, and always from someone at risk of ostracism. He put it down to sour grapes. "I don't understand," he lied.

"That's what Edward always says."

She didn't mean it as an insult, yet irritation pricked James, nonetheless. A voice from somewhere deep inside him cried out *I'm nothing like him.*

"I knew I'd be cast out when I decided to leave," she went on. "I don't like it. I don't think it right. But I would rather pay that price than go back."

How could she simply toss the rulebook aside and the rule makers with it? He liked to bend the rules from time to time. Who didn't? But he'd mastered the art of doing so without great loss to himself or his comfort, while Fran . . . she stood to lose everything.

"Is it . . ." He closed his eyes, momentarily at a loss. How awkward. "May I ask . . . is it because you intend to remarry?" Even though it meant trespassing beyond his remit, even as he berated himself for giving in to vulgar curiosity, he leaned in to hear what she would say.

"You must be thinking of Mr. Trafford." She spoke without even a trace of embarrassment.

Ah, so she knew what they were saying about her. The rumors might even be true. How odd that he hadn't considered the possibility before. But why not? Her casual mention of her purported lover's name shocked even James.

He met her frank gaze without wavering. "I didn't mean to refer to any particular person."

"I'm sorry to be blunt," she said, ignoring his second lie. "But I know what everyone says. Edward told me. It strikes me as strange that he should be the one to break the news. When I came home, I asked Barker about it. She said she'd known people were talking but didn't want to upset me." Francesca shrugged. "So you see, if everyone's gossiping about me, I can't very well ignore it, can I?"

She could and she should, but as the question was obviously rhetorical, he kept quiet.

Her green eyes searched his face, though he couldn't imagine what she hoped to see. "Do you believe what they're saying about me?"

A true gentleman could never answer that question honestly.

To his relief, she forestalled him with an impatient sigh. "It doesn't matter anyway."

He'd pushed far enough. Yet his promise to Thorne cast a long shadow. "You must know no one wants you to be unhappy. Thorne admits—" He needed to be careful, or he'd sabotage Thorne's case. "He admits he hasn't always behaved as well as he might toward you."

She smiled as though she knew very well he'd almost confirmed her worst suspicions about her husband. "Is that what he told you? That he hasn't always behaved well?"

"I think he understands more than you imagine, but he finds it difficult to comprehend your insistence on a divorce that won't benefit anyone. If, as you imply, you have no plans to remarry, what is it you hope to gain from all this?"

"My freedom."

The two words rang in the stillness of the room. He knew he would never forget the look on her face as she'd said them, her eyes brimful of zeal and unshed tears.

James didn't believe in freedom. She might as well say she wanted a genie to appear and grant her three wishes or the ability to spin straw into gold. It wouldn't sound more improbable to his ears. Everyone, even the privileged elite, had a role to play and a script to follow. Yet her voice stirred something in him, a yearning for a different sort of life.

What rot. He had everything he could ever want. If he experienced moments of dissatisfaction, he didn't permit himself to wallow in them. He accepted life for what it was. He didn't see the point of trying to find meaning in it. She wanted freedom? Well, she was already as free as anyone he knew. "Don't you think you're free now?"

"But it's a lie." She leaned toward him with the strange eagerness of an evangelist. "It was never a real marriage."

"I don't understand. Do you mean there's some impediment?"

"No." She frowned and shook her head as though she thought him deliberately obtuse. "I just mean a marriage is more than a legal contract. It's so much more, or at least it should be. I don't know how to explain it." She cast around as if the answer might be hidden somewhere in the room. "The way Edward behaved—"

"But if his behavior altered?"

The question took them both by surprise. He certainly hadn't meant to ask it and didn't want to hear any details, not to mention the fact that Thorne had never once uttered the word "reconciliation."

She clutched at the arm of her chair. "What do you mean?"

"If he treated you with more kindness, would you go back to him?"

"He never offered such a thing."

"But would you?" He had no idea why he kept pressing. He just knew he needed an answer.

"No." She sounded almost panicked. "Yes. I don't know. He isn't offering that, is he?"

"No." His eyes never left hers. "I'm sorry, I only wish to understand."

"But he *is* offering something. And he sent you to make the offer."

It was time to say it. He'd come too far for concealment. "He wants to be generous. He's willing to offer you a great deal to remain as his wife."

"I see." The two lone syllables sounded oddly clipped.

He felt like Brutus right after he buried the dagger in Caesar's back, but he named the figure anyway.

Her face went blank. "And that's per quarter?"

"Yes."

Abruptly, she rose and moved to the window. Standing in the fading light with her head bowed, she didn't look like a woman who'd been offered a fortune; her shoulders slumped like somebody who'd lost one.

He studied the toe of his shoe—the shine of the right looked a little duller than the left—reached for his tea, surely cold by now, and realized his hand was shaking. A coal shifted in the grate. The seconds hand on the clock moved slowly, *tick, tick, tick,* as inevitable as death.

"Tell him no." She spoke without turning.

Even after all she'd said and all he'd seen, he scarcely believed it. "But it's enough to make you independent."

"On the contrary. As things stand, I may feel robbed, but what's left is mine beyond dispute."

"But it's a fortune." He heard the awe in his own voice and couldn't decide if he was impressed by her lack of avarice or stunned by her foolishness.

"I want you to do something for me." She still stared out at the street, but now she held her shoulders straight and her head high.

"I will if I can."

When she turned, her eyes shone with emotion. "Don't come here again if you're going to carry messages from Edward. He has enough confederates." The words and her steely tone pricked him.

She showed him her back again, her spine straight, a clear dismissal.

And he deserved it, too.

It took him only an instant to decide how to act. He couldn't leave things like this.

He went to her, stopping less than a foot away. She didn't move, but she must have sensed him or heard him. He touched her shoulder and felt it leap under the gentle pressure of his hand. "I'm sorry, Fran."

He would have said more, but she confounded both of them by bursting into loud sobs.

* * *

Francesca couldn't see James properly through the blur of tears. Still, she could imagine how aghast he must look. He kept touching her shoulder. Strange, jerky, irritating pats, as if he'd never dealt with a crying woman before.

"Please don't," he said. "If you don't stop, I'll have to put my arms around you and that would never do. That granite-faced maid of yours will throw me out on my ear. Perhaps I should leave, but I don't want to make things worse by storming off. I'd *have* to storm, you understand, and there's always a chance a storm might be mistaken for a flounce. I couldn't have that, now could I? What if it got back to my club that I'd been observed flouncing about Bloomsbury?"

She'd never heard a man babble before. A laugh built in her chest until she thought it must burst out, but more sobs came instead. He kept up a steady stream of nonsense, while she simply listened, allowing his words to drown out her thoughts. Strange solace, but it calmed her.

"God, Fran, I never meant this to happen." The awkward patting tapered off. Sighing, he slid an arm about her shoulders, pulling her around and against him. "There. My arms are around you. Prophesy fulfilled," he murmured, his free hand moving in soothing circles on her back.

She ought to resist the intimate press of his body, pull away, and pretend to feel insulted, but she couldn't muster the necessary outrage. He meant nothing by it except kindness, and she'd never been good at behaving as she ought. Drained of tears, she rested limp-boned and empty in his arms. Then she closed her eyes and concentrated on the gentle rise and fall of his breath and the scent of clean linen over warm skin.

"There now," he said, and stepped away.

With him went the illusion of safety. He might very well repeat the events of this afternoon to Edward, but it was too late now to regret her loss of control. She swiped at her wet cheeks, sniffling inelegantly.

"Here," he said, putting a clean handkerchief into her hand. "Take care of it. It's very fashionable."

She tried to smile, but it came out wobbly. "A fashionable handkerchief? I've never heard of such a thing." But she accepted the small white square and unfolded it. Four neat creases divided the linen into precise quarters. So much care taken over something insignificant.

"That's because you're a country bumpkin. Feeling better?"

"Yes. Thank you. I'm mortified, naturally."

"I wish you wouldn't be."

"I—" She had to stop and take a deep, calming breath. If she didn't get him back to teasing, she'd soon be in tears again. Serious subjects weren't in his usual line, or at least they hadn't been eight years ago. "You know as well as I do," she said, adopting a mock sophisticated air. "It's very bad form to cry in public."

"It's just me, Fran." His voice sounded far too sympathetic.

No more hiding. She made herself look at him.

He had kind eyes. Why hadn't she ever noticed that before?

"You know, Jemmy, before today, I don't think I've ever heard you say anything that wasn't completely trivial."

His eyebrows shot up, and he laughed a little. "How clever you are to notice."

Gingerly, she stepped past him and sat in her favorite chair by the fire. She didn't need to invite him to take the seat opposite. He sat, picked up his cup and saucer, and sipped, only to grimace as soon as the cold tea touched his lips. Even that he did gracefully. How did people like him contrive to look so perfect at all times? It wasn't only his expensive Savile Row tailoring. Not a single strand of his dark hair was out of place. She felt a powerful desire to ruffle it. How that would baffle him.

She dabbed her nose with the handkerchief. "I'll have this laundered before I return it."

"Keep it. What will you do now?"

She didn't pretend to misunderstand. "I don't know. Go on as I am. Make economies." She had to laugh at his pained wince. "I'm sure it won't be that bad."

"If you say so."

She rang the bell, then stretched her feet toward the fire. Heat curled round her, and she felt the return of something like peace. Nothing so very terrible had happened. Edward had sent an emissary to pester and bribe her. What did it really matter in the grand scheme of things?

"Do you suppose it will rain tomorrow?" she asked.

"I see no sign of it."

"I hope your aunt is well."

"Yes, quite well." Then, peering at her, he added, "Is it my imagination or are we suddenly conversing by rote?"

Now that was more like the James she remembered. "I think it might be for the best. I should have begun that way instead of blundering in as if eight years were nothing."

"Ah, but then you wouldn't be you."

True enough. Yet, shouldn't she have learned the perils by now? "Sorry if I made you uncomfortable."

A strange look crossed his face, nine parts puzzled and one part irritation. "I dare say I'll survive."

She gave a solemn nod. "Glad to hear it."

"Actually—"

The door opened and Barker came in. "You rang, ma'am."

"Oh. Yes, Barker. Mr. Standish is ready to leave." He'd already risen, so she stood too and offered her hand. "I'm glad you called, despite what prompted your visit."

He smiled, polite mask firmly in place. "I'm sure we'll see each other soon."

When he'd gone, she sat back down.

So, Edward was throwing money at his problems again. He must learn she couldn't be bought, just as she was learning it. Wealth and respectability were powerful lures, but more tempting had been the possibility of reconciliation with Aunt Helena and Uncle Arthur. They were her only remaining family and, despite everything, she missed them. But, after a moment of weakness in which she'd considered relenting, she'd passed this latest test of her resolve.

How strange to think only moments ago James Standish had stood in this room with his arms around her.

She didn't believe his assurance that they'd meet again soon. Perhaps she might see him at the theater or out walking in one of the parks. They'd nod and maybe even exchange a few polite words. But this afternoon's brief intimacy would be forgotten. There was no reason it need ever be repeated.

CHAPTER FOUR

On the first night of the Royal Italian Opera, neither James nor his Aunt Miriam accorded Rossini's *Il Barbiere di Siviglia* much attention. He stared toward the stage without seeing, his mind idling.

As for Miriam, she peered through mother-of-pearl opera glasses. She'd finished examining the crowd below and now directed more surreptitious attention to the tiers of boxes. "Mrs. Kirkpatrick looks particularly pleased with herself this evening," she said. "Must be something to do with those diamonds she's wearing."

At any other time, he might have found her remark about Thorne's mistress amusing, but tonight dissatisfaction dogged him. The feeling had first stolen into him at Fran's. She'd broken with convention and now she had to pay the price; he shouldn't envy her escape, and yet this restlessness lingered.

Escorting Miriam to opening night was one of his few obligations. Even if it hadn't been, attending the opera was simply something one did, like joining a gentlemen's club or taking brandy and a cigar after dinner. Yet he found himself entertaining strange, whimsical fancies. He wanted to empty out all the stalls and boxes. In fact, why not clear the stage and orchestra pit too? He'd like to sit in silence and gaze upon a vista of empty seats. He'd climb down to the arena, lie flat on his back, and stare up at the vast dome of the ceiling.

Oh, for goodness' sake! You're bored, that's all.

Wherever one went, the place was sure to brim with jaded gentlemen, their eyes glazed over with ennui just as his must be. As for the older men, some looked a lot like Arthur Lytton, Francesca's elderly uncle, gray and impassive in the dignity that only years and rank bestowed. Others had red faces, paunchy and bluff with age and decadence, the product of wasted youths much like James's. Sometimes he feared a dotage distinguished by nothing but gout and habitual drunkenness.

He shook his head, trying to dispel the gloomy thoughts.

"Cushion-shaped stones," Miriam said. "Heaven knows how many carats. Still, she's fleshy enough to carry them off. Must seem like a banquet to a starving man after that little morsel he married."

It took him a moment to recall Mrs. Kirkpatrick and her diamonds. He raised his opera glasses and looked at the box where Thorne and his mistress sat. Virginia Kirkpatrick's generous curves and fiery red hair always put him in mind of Amazons or Queen Boadicea. He almost forgot to take note of the necklace. The row of brilliants glimmered against her pale skin. Suspended just above the crease between her breasts, there hung a huge central drop.

Good Lord, Thorne had more money than sense.

"Still," Miriam said, swiveling her gaze toward the far side of the house, "Mrs. Thorne makes up for any shortness of stature with showy presentation."

He followed Miriam's line of sight to one of the far boxes and spotted Fran seated next to a tall, fair-haired lady. Now that she lived in London, he'd expected to see her again, but he hadn't thought it would happen so soon.

As far as he could tell from this distance, she seemed untroubled by Thorne's presence or by his paramour seated beside him, those ruinously expensive diamonds flashing in the gaslight. Fran gazed at the stage with every appearance of attention. How disappointed their fellow theatergoers must be. In the absence of any offstage drama, they'd have to content themselves with the onstage antics of Rosina, Figaro, and Count Almaviva.

"That red is quite flamboyant," Miriam said, brows knit. "A woman contemplating divorce shouldn't make herself conspicuous."

"What color would be more to your taste?" he asked. If he hadn't, he might have been tempted to offer his opinion with regard to his aunt's attire. She'd dressed in a particularly vibrant shade of yellow that made him think of bile.

"Lilac, perhaps. No one would notice her in lilac. She'd simply fade from view."

No one would ever compare Fran to an Amazon. When he'd held her in his arms, she'd fit neatly under his chin, and her uncorseted flesh had felt soft and warm. He'd tried not to think about the unexpected intimacy of embracing a woman with whom he'd been acquainted for so long. Now, for the first time, he understood why so many sticklers condemned rational dress. Without the fortification a corset provided, she could have worn a nightgown and her body wouldn't have felt any different.

Tonight, she'd cast aestheticism aside for less practical attire, taming and restraining her unruly curves. The ruby-red silk, though vivid and unashamed like its wearer, revealed no more than was proper. He saw a hint of upper arm bracketed by short sleeves and long white gloves, and the gentle swell of her décolletage concealed behind the black feathers of her fan. She didn't go out of her way to display herself, but she disdained to hide.

"Perhaps she doesn't wish to fade from view," he said.

"That's precisely my point. I remember her when she was plain Miss Heller. Sweet little thing. Wouldn't say boo to a goose. But, when I think of the shame she's causing the Lyttons . . ." She gave a theatrical shudder. "No family feeling at all."

To Miriam, family, or at least lineage, was sacrosanct. She had a long gallery filled with works of art depicting august cousins and illustrious ancestors. Fran's faded red and gold walls boasted not a single picture. He'd wager the Lytton house abounded with family portraits, but she might never look upon them again, much less own one. "I'm sure they'd prefer she appeared in sackcloth and ashes," he said. "Or, better yet, that she'd stayed buried alive in the country."

"As indeed she should," said Miriam, undaunted. "What would become of society if every wife with a philandering husband made such a spectacle of herself? Her family is quite right to take a stand. And if the rumors about her and Trafford are true . . ." She let the sentence taper off suggestively. "With those tales flying about, she could wear the sackcloth until it rubbed her raw and not a soul would pity her."

"Why, I wonder?" He spoke quietly to mask a sudden and quite unreasonable surge of anger. "If Thorne doesn't want her, why shouldn't she take a lover?"

He didn't quite believe what he'd just said. Did he really think a woman justified in taking a lover if her husband abandoned her? How very bohemian of him.

Miriam didn't appear shocked in the least. "Whether or not she has a lover is irrelevant," she said with the air of a seasoned pragmatist. "It's the indiscretion that's objectionable. A married woman can do as she pleases as long as she observes the strictest secrecy. If I were to take a lover, you can be sure no one else would ever hear of it."

If Miriam said anything more of her lover, theoretical though he might be, James would never recover. To his relief, she narrowed her shrewd little eyes and said instead, "Don't tell me you feel sorry for her. If you do, you're a fool. She didn't lose her reputation. She threw it away like rubbish."

He remained silent for several moments longer. Though he didn't disagree with anything she'd said, he didn't share her sense of outrage. "You're right," he said. "Say what one likes about Mrs. Thorne, she chose her fate with both eyes open. Instead of enduring more years of marriage to an absent and unfaithful husband, she chose to sacrifice her position and her friends. Presumably, she thought it the lesser of two evils."

"She must be mad. It's a case of moral insanity. It has to be."

Moral insanity? The thought hadn't occurred to him. True, turning down five thousand pounds per annum for the sake of an ideal smacked of lunacy. Yet, to his way of thinking, it seemed less wicked than his aunt's laissez-faire attitude to marital fidelity.

"Oh, I don't think so," he said. "Her behavior may be hopelessly vulgar by society's standards, but at least she isn't a coward or a hypocrite like the rest of us." Yet another thing he hadn't meant to say.

Miriam pursed her lips but otherwise gave no sign she perceived an insult. "When you marry, I advise you to choose more wisely than your friend Thorne. Don't choose a furtive little thing who can't look you in the eye, and don't choose a bold piece who's no better than she should be. The chit you met in Hyde Park might suit you."

He smoothed nonexistent creases from his white gloves. "Which chit?"

"Miss Randle of course. Very elegant figure. I saw her riding in the park with her father today. She has an excellent seat."

He had no idea who she meant. For several seconds his mind stayed blank, until at last he remembered.

"Ah yes, Miss Randle. She of the renegade handkerchief."

"She's a beauty and so stylish." Spoken in the tones of a hostess persuading him to take one more slice of cake.

With any luck, he didn't look as ill as he felt. "I'm sure she'll make an excellent wife for some lucky fellow."

"But you're too busy enjoying yourself? Gracious, James. You're thirty-six and I'm not going to live forever. I should like to see you settled and settled well. Girls of that caliber are few and far between. You should consider her at the very least." She must've noticed his pained expression because she gave a huff of laughter. "Gentlemen are always so reluctant to relinquish their freedom. I can't imagine why. Your friend Thorne has an excellent time."

He looked and saw Thorne trailing Mrs. Kirkpatrick's closed fan along the curve of her bosom. Yes, an excellent time.

"But not with his wife, ma'am." He glanced in Fran's direction, but she still stared impassively at the stage. Perhaps she hadn't noticed what her husband was up to.

This situation wasn't his concern. He knew it, yet he stood anyway. "Aunt Miriam, it occurs to me I need to have a word with my friend. I know it isn't quite the thing to leave you here, but—"

"But I am to be deserted by my escort for a time? I quite understand. The young like to be together." Her eyes twinkled up at him as he backed out of the box.

Francesca had come to Covent Garden to say her goodbyes. She wanted to watch the performance, soak up the theatrical atmosphere, and take enough of it away when she left to last the rest of her life, if need be. After tonight, there would be no more opera box, no Italian opera at all, unless she went as someone's guest. She simply couldn't justify the expense if she intended to live within her income.

So far, concentrating had proved harder than she'd expected. Though she'd prepared herself for the likelihood of Edward's presence, she'd forgotten all about his little friend.

"He's actually touching her in full view of all these people," Caroline said, clearly scandalized. Though a loyal friend, tact had never been her strong suit. Shock always made her blunt. Francesca could never decide if she found it refreshing or unfortunate.

Caroline took Francesca's hand and squeezed gently. "How can you be so calm?"

"With a great deal of difficulty." She gazed up at the huge chandelier. Its crystal shone and sparkled, illuminating the gilded moldings of the ceiling until they seemed to glow with their own inner light. "It might help if you'd stop narrating their every move."

Caroline grimaced. "Sorry."

"Let's just try to enjoy the performance."

The tenor appeared to be both drunk and in disguise, but why? The entire first act was a blur. She couldn't concentrate with Edward and that creature so near; perhaps one more peek. She adjusted the angle of her opera glasses. "I think you'll find the fan is doing the actual touching," she said after observing them for a few seconds.

Blast Edward, anyway. For someone who claimed to abhor scandal, he was doing his best to create one. Funny how propriety mattered only when it saved *him* embarrassment.

"Look somewhere else," Caroline advised.

"Quite right. I ought to appear serene and indifferent, which will be very difficult if we keep talking about them."

Caroline gazed in the direction of the proscenium arch, as if absorbed by the performance. "What do you suppose he sees in her?" she asked out of the corner of her mouth.

"I think that's perfectly obvious. I mean, look at her."

Mrs. Kirkpatrick was resplendent in a dark blue gown with a plunging neckline. Tall, handsome, and alluring, she wore jewels garish enough to make a Mughal emperor blush.

Caroline took Francesca's hand and squeezed. "She's probably a shrew."

"Oh God, I hope so." No one had any business being *that* beautiful unless they had character defects to balance things out.

Onstage, the tenor and bass attempted to out-sing one another. Were they meant to be arguing? She'd lost her grip on *Il Barbiere* entirely.

"Who's he?" Caroline asked.

For a moment, Francesca supposed her friend equally confused by the onstage capers, but a quick glance at the Thorne box explained otherwise. A familiar figure eased into the vacant space next to Edward.

"That's James Standish," she said, and tried to quell an unreasonable surge of pique. He and Edward had known each other since childhood. She was nothing to either of them by comparison and, therefore, had no reason to feel betrayed.

"Is it indeed?" Caroline sounded distinctly impressed. "Well, he cuts a very fine figure."

Francesca couldn't stop her lips from pursing. "He takes very great care that he should."

"How disapproving you sound," Caroline said as she lowered her glasses, allowing them to rest on her rich silk skirt. "I can't think why. There's nothing wrong with an attractive man."

"I'm not sure how your husband would feel if he heard you."

Caroline laughed. "Philip's used to me. I love him dearly, but I can still appreciate a thing of beauty when I see one. I take it you're well acquainted with this Mr. Standish?"

Well enough to weep in his arms. "A little," she admitted. "He is not the sort of gentleman with whom it's easy to form an intimacy."

"Do you mean he's merely decorative?"

"No. It isn't that exactly."

"Don't tell me he prefers the company of other gentlemen?"

"Not as far as I'm aware." She searched for the right words. "He's simply not a very serious person. He cares too much about decorum and the cut of his coat. He never talks about anything of any substance. Although . . ." She thought of their recent encounter. How he'd looked at her. The genuine concern in his eyes. "People can sometimes surprise one."

Caroline stared at her. "What a deliciously intriguing response."

During the long walk to Thorne's box, James couldn't stop picturing Fran as she'd looked standing at the window, her shoulders slumped, after he'd made Thorne's offer. She'd seemed so calm and poised until then. What if this evening's apparent sangfroid was a similar dignity-preserving front? She'd chosen a difficult path and society's lions stalked it. He wouldn't blame her if the strain began to tell.

Thorne didn't notice him immediately, too preoccupied making a scene with Mrs. Kirkpatrick. Whatever Fran might have done during the long, lonely years of her marriage, she didn't deserve to be made a laughingstock in front of the entire fashionable world.

James took the seat next to Thorne's and spoke low in his ear. "I'd like a word with you."

"Can't it wait? The first act's almost over." His head turned, for an instant only, in his wife's direction.

If James hadn't been waiting for it, he might not have appreciated the significance of that tiny movement. It confirmed his suspicion. This unseemly display was a calculated attack aimed at Fran. "I'd like to talk to you now. Alone."

Thorne heaved a theatrical sigh, kissed Mrs. Kirkpatrick's hand, and whispered his excuses. James led the way out of the box and along the crimson-carpeted passageway. He didn't stop until they'd reached the first-floor landing gallery and the double doors leading into the crush room.

"Well?" Once they were inside, Thorne sat down, resting his head against the back of his chair. In ten or twenty minutes the early birds would start to drift in. For now, they were the only occupants. "I assume you spoke to the estimable Mrs. Thorne. What's the verdict?"

"She still wants a divorce." James stated it as baldly as he could. He was in no mood to cushion the blow.

Thorne's face cleared of all expression. His air of confidence vanished. "Are you sure?"

"Of course I am."

Neither of them moved. Thorne seemed at a complete loss, his entire world overturned. "I'm sorry," he said at long last. "It's only because I felt so certain. If I made the offer myself, I expected she'd turn it down at first out of spite. I thought, by using an intermediary, we'd avoid the usual hysterics." He slumped farther down in his seat, defeated. "Sit down, sit down," he snapped. "You make my neck ache."

James considered delivering the rebuke he'd set out to give, but Thorne's spirits had crashed so dramatically he hadn't the heart for it. At the very least, he'd allow him time to come to terms with what had happened.

"You did tell her the amount, didn't you? She didn't misunderstand you?"

James took the chair opposite. "She was very firm in her refusal."

"And you're sure there's no room for negotiation? What if you spoke to her again?"

He'd have to be dragged kicking and screaming. For one thing, he liked her company too well to risk offending her a second time. For another, what if she cried again? One more scene like the last didn't bear thinking of. No, if he saw Fran, it would be on his own terms, not Thorne's.

"She was firm on that subject too," James said. "I am not to act the part of advocate." He'd opted for diplomatic phrasing, but hopefully Thorne took his point.

"Damn it, that was an extremely generous offer. Do you think she's holding out for more money? What were her precise words?"

It took James less than a second to discount such a possibility. She'd been sincere. He was sure of it. The zeal in her eyes . . . "That she'd rather have her freedom."

"The little fool. What a lot of sentimental claptrap. You must have had a hard time not to burst out laughing."

Another twinge of annoyance. He experienced those more and more in Thorne's company. "I don't suppose it occurred to you that your . . . assaults on Mrs. Kirkpatrick's person might work against you?"

"I don't see why they should," Thorne said. "What does she care if I bring my mistress to the opera? She's not exactly blameless herself."

The twinge became a wave. "Perhaps not," he said through clenched teeth. "But what's the point of sending me in to reason with her if you humiliate her by carrying on in this fashion? Tonight's work will hardly encourage her to see things your way. You might have waited until the outcome was certain before you antagonized her. Besides which, I thought you cared about public opinion. Taking your mistress to the opera is one thing, but parading her in front of your wife . . ."

Thorne had the sense to look chastened. "I take your point."

James applied pressure to the bridge of his nose with his thumb and forefinger. Only then did he realize his neck ached and his temples throbbed, the onset of what promised to be a spectacular headache.

Thorne peered at him. "What's the matter with you?"

"I merely resent being caught in the middle of this." He'd spoken more loudly than he intended, so he took a deep breath and went on more calmly. "I'm trying to be loyal, but I won't bully Fran for you. This has been very difficult for her and, whatever her faults may be, you must admit she has her reasons for pursuing this course."

Thorne stared at him in obvious surprise. "I hadn't realized you held such an unconventional view of things."

"Nor had I."

"I don't believe this." Thorne's voice shook with suppressed laughter. "You drink tea with her once and suddenly you're her knight errant. I hope the courts aren't as easily won over."

Won over? Is that what had happened? "Don't be ridiculous. I think this is the first time anyone's accused me of anything as insipid as chivalry."

"*She* brings it out in people." Thorne invested a world of scorn into that tiny pronoun. "Just remember, she isn't what she first appears. Now I really must get back to Virginia. If I'm not there at intermission, she'll be knee-deep in my rivals," he said, and glanced at his pocket watch. "Buck up, Lancelot. Straddle the fence all you like but, if you should topple over to her side, do let me know. It will give me something to tell my lawyers." He winked and walked out of the crush room laughing.

Lord, what a bitch of an evening.

James settled back in his chair and closed his eyes. Even the muted light of the gas lamps seemed too bright.

He ought to go back to Miriam. As her escort, he shouldn't leave her alone, but a few more seconds' rest wouldn't make that much difference.

He laughed softly. Some knight in shining armor he was.

Ten minutes before intermission, Francesca entered the crush room and found James asleep in his chair.

He looked different in repose, gentle and unguarded. Faint laugh lines marked the corner of each eye and, underneath, light shadows. What had put them there? Not worry, surely. Too many late nights, perhaps? His lips, so often curled sardonically, looked different too—softer, capable of compassion as well as teasing.

Ah, she'd seen his compassion. The remembrance made her want to smooth the hair from his brow.

The stray impulse took her by surprise. He didn't need her tenderness. He was an English gentleman of means. Problems melted away before the bright rays of his wealth and breeding. She'd long lost her tendency to romanticize men of his type, or so she'd thought. Yet here she was again.

His breaths grew shallower. Soon he would open his eyes and they'd exchange awkward greetings. His duty to Edward discharged, he'd have nothing left to say, and, anyway, how did one behave toward a man who'd seen one fall apart? If only she'd waited for the end of the act, Caroline would be here now and this whole encounter with James could've been avoided. But even though Edward had stopped pawing Mrs. Kirkpatrick, Francesca had wanted to escape. Fleeing from trouble—a worrying tendency she needed to check.

Just when she'd decided to back away slowly, James opened one eye. He smiled up at her and shut it again before she had a chance to speak. Since he made no effort to hide a broad grin, she knew he wasn't still sleepy. What did he mean by it?

"Jemmy, are you perchance a little the worse for drink?" she asked, escape plan forgotten.

"Certainly not, you rude girl," he said, though his eyes remained closed.

Laughter welled up in her chest, but she held it in check. "Then perhaps you're feeling unwell?"

"I'm never unwell." How he managed to convey urbane insouciance while sprawled in a chair she'd never know. "This is the crush room, is it not?"

"Of course it is."

"Well, there you are, then. I slipped in early to avoid the crush."

How provoking he was when not comforting crying women. She waited, but he didn't speak. "You were sleeping," she informed him.

"Nonsense, I was resting my eyes."

"That's what all the old men say."

At last, both eyes snapped open. "Has anyone ever told you that you have a forked tongue?"

She refused to laugh. "No one ever used those precise words, no."

The final distant strains of music died, signaling the beginning of intermission. He stood and checked his attire, presumably for wrinkles. But his white tie remained immaculate, unblemished by even a speck of lint.

"Fran," he said on a sigh. "It's been a rotten evening."

He spoke as if it were nothing and yet . . . "Jemmy, is something the matter?"

She expected him to deny it. Instead, he looked at her. His teasing smile dimmed until he resembled the stranger who'd held her while she cried. He had silver-gray eyes. With his coloring, she'd expected brown.

The double doors opened and Caroline stepped through with a swish of yellow silk. Whatever he'd been on the verge of confiding, he wouldn't say it now. She didn't know whether to feel disappointed or relieved.

He spoke quickly. "Are you busy tomorrow morning? If you aren't, come riding."

"Oh, she loathes riding," Caroline said, reaching them. "I can never convince her to accompany me."

"Mrs. Ashton, may I present Mr. Standish?" Francesca said. "Mr. Standish, this ill-bred creature is Mrs. Ashton."

"How do you do?" Caroline said, suddenly remembering her manners.

He bowed. As more people began drifting in, his eyes met Francesca's. "Tomorrow morning, then?"

She shook her head. "I have an appointment with my solicitor."

"Then I'll call afterward. Five o'clock." And, with a muttered apology about his aunt, he was gone.

Caroline peered at her, eyes narrowed. "How very high-handed of him."

"Why do you look at me like that?"

"I'm just curious. You see, when he asked you to go riding, *which you hate,* you didn't provide the usual litany of excuses."

"He didn't give me a chance." True enough, but she'd also felt flustered by the invitation. If she refused, when would she see him again? Possibly never. Yet James was the last person she wanted witnessing her clumsiness in the saddle. No doubt he rode like he'd been born on horseback. No, it didn't bear thinking of. She *had* to decline.

Caroline lowered her voice. "He's divine."

Even if he were, even if God himself sent him wrapped in ribbons and gold paper, Francesca still wouldn't go riding tomorrow.

"I'll send him my regrets," she said.

"Will you indeed?" Caroline smiled like a lazy feline playing with a mouse. "If only I were the wagering sort."

CHAPTER FIVE

"*How* much?" Francesca winced at the sound of her own voice, loud and strident, bouncing around the four walls of the solicitor's office. Just like a servant dickering about the price of fish on market day, except she wanted to buy freedom, not dinner.

Of course she knew divorcing Edward wouldn't be easy, but she hadn't given enough serious consideration to the expense. In fact, she'd never concerned herself with money at all. She hadn't needed to. Now she understood the point her former husband had tried to make when he'd stopped her funds. Her expenditures dwarfed her income. She didn't have five hundred pounds capital, and giving up opera wouldn't suffice to change that.

The solicitor, Mr. Hieronymus Flint, exhibited no surprise at her outburst. In fact, she had yet to detect any sign of human emotion at all. He remained the epitome of professionalism. "Five hundred pounds," he repeated. "Possibly a great deal more by the time the divorce is final."

He sat on the opposite side of an enormous desk strewn with papers. Otherwise, the room was tidy and well appointed, its only drawback a lack of natural light. "If your husband doesn't choose to offer a defense, the cost will be a fraction of that sum, but from what you tell me, such a turn of events seems unlikely."

"But, if the court finds in my favor, Mr. Thorne will be liable for my fees?"

"If you win, yes." He didn't need to expound upon his thoughts. They both understood victory was uncertain.

Mr. Flint reached for his spectacles and peered at his case notes. "If you are to succeed, we must prove your husband guilty of aggravated adultery."

"Aggravated?" How ignorant she was. But that was why she'd come here today—to educate herself.

"Adultery alone is insufficient grounds. We must also prove cruelty, bigamy, desertion or . . ." He hesitated. "If I may speak plainly, sodomy or incest." The old lawyer spoke of scandal so decorously that she had to admire him. She'd heard the weather discussed with greater animation.

She recalled reading something in the paper years ago about a campaign to make divorce regulations fairer. She hadn't really paid attention, but she remembered one thing. "Am I right in thinking that, if he files a countersuit, he need only prove adultery?"

"That is correct."

He waited, perhaps giving her time to throw a tantrum at the injustice of it all, but she didn't have time for sulks or fits of temper. The law was the law; she needed to find ways to navigate its twists and turns.

Edward was nothing if not conventional in his appetites, which left incest, sodomy, and bigamy out of the equation. "What constitutes cruelty?" she asked.

"In legal terms, physical abuse only. Did your husband ever strike you?"

"Never."

He scribbled something on the bottom of his notes.

Her stomach tightened. If he told her she didn't have grounds, she'd be trapped. "Mr. Thorne said I wouldn't be able to prove desertion because I chose to leave the marital home."

"That may not work in your favor." He stroked his graying sideburns. "But it's a complex matter. He's certainly liable for your living expenses until the case comes to trial. His withdrawal of financial support may actually constitute abandonment. If we can also prove he was absent from your side throughout much of your marriage, we might be able to argue desertion successfully."

She smothered the tiny spark of hope and focused on his prevarications. Those *mays* and *mights* weren't much on which to pin all one's prospects, though a great deal better than nothing. "Will I be required to testify?"

"Indeed, no. Neither you nor Mr. Thorne will be permitted to speak on your own behalf. Your case will be heard through witness testimony only. Couples in these cases are always presumed biased and, therefore, anything you said would be disregarded anyway. You need not even attend if you don't wish."

She began to agree with Charles Dickens—the law truly was an ass. Yet, though she'd mustered her courage and was prepared to testify, her heart felt lighter now that she understood such bravery wasn't required. "My maid is willing to testify. She's been with me since before my marriage. She can confirm Mr. Thorne lived permanently in London while I was left behind in Hertfordshire."

"Excellent. If you can think of a friend or a relative, someone from your own social sphere, who might verify her account, it would be even better." He set one sheet of paper aside and reached for another. "Now, as to the charge of adultery, do you have any evidence?"

"I have some letters." Love letters, really. The most incriminating of the bunch had been hidden in her jewelry box for almost nine years, ever since she'd first discovered Edward's affairs. Suspicion had driven her to break into his desk. What she'd found there confirmed her worst fears. When she'd confronted him, he hadn't even cared enough to take the letter back, a mistake that would hopefully prove his undoing.

"Letters? Good. I'll need to see them as soon as possible," said Mr. Flint. Then, after a slight pause, he cleared his throat.

Francesca somehow sensed that this was a portentous throat-clearing and his next words proved her right.

"Now I must ask you something of a most delicate nature," he said. "Is it possible Mr. Thorne is in possession of any evidence, anything that might be used against you?"

She tensed. No one else had dared to ask her this question. Not even Aunt Helena or Uncle Arthur. They, and everyone else, seemed to consider it too vulgar a subject to broach. "I don't think so," she said, softly.

"Think carefully. Remember, a reasonable suspicion of wrongdoing is all your husband needs. Is there anything in your past behavior, even though it may be perfectly innocent, which might have given him reason to doubt you?"

How she deplored that little weasel word "reasonable." Edward entertained all manner of suspicions as to her conduct. Whether or not they might be considered reasonable was another matter.

Mr. Flint watched her closely.

She chose her words with care. "Mr. Thorne may be privy to some ugly rumors regarding a Mr. Trafford."

She waited, allowing the old lawyer time to parse her words.

"Mrs. Thorne," he said. "In order to obtain a divorce a vinculo matrimonii, by which I mean a divorce allowing you to remarry, it will not be enough to prove your husband guilty. You must also prove yourself innocent."

She stared at Mr. Flint's lips until they blurred. For a woman, one silly slip meant ruin. Never mind the long years she'd stayed faithful. Never mind that Edward had spent those same years populating his bed with an assortment of ladies, barmaids, and opera dancers. It infuriated her, but it was the way of the world. She would not give in to anger or despair.

When she felt capable of it, she met Flint's eyes and smiled brightly. "Please, do go on."

"I'm speaking theoretically now, of course."

"Of course."

How easily she slipped into old habits. Her small display of emotion a moment ago hadn't been lost on Mr. Flint. Being a shrewd lawyer, he would see it as strongly suggestive of her guilt. He now believed her an adulteress and equivocated to spare her feelings. Francesca knew all this and, what's more, Mr. Flint almost certainly knew that she knew. The pretense of ignorance was simple good manners on both their parts; it wasn't designed to fool anyone.

"Theoretically, if you admit the charges, you can accuse Mr. Thorne of culpability in your adultery. If we can prove he neglected you during the marriage or he knew of your affair but turned a blind eye, you will be awarded a separation and he will be liable for your future living expenses." A pause. "You will not be able to remarry of course."

Accept a separation and continue taking Edward's money. That had been Aunt Helena's solution. James's too, come to think of it. "No," she said. "It must be a proper divorce, if such a thing is possible. I have no intention of remarrying. Heaven knows once ought to be enough for anybody, but I must have the freedom to make my own choices without interference from Edward Thorne or anyone else."

"It will not be easy to achieve."

"But can it be done?"

"I really cannot say for sure. Twenty-five years ago when I first began to practice, it would have taken an act of Parliament. As it is, much will depend on what evidence and witnesses we can procure. I'm sure I don't need to urge you to be extremely circumspect in your behavior in the interim."

By the time she emerged from the dim office into the glare of the afternoon, her mind reeled with information. She wanted nothing more than to go home and lie down. If only she'd done as she'd promised herself and canceled her appointment with James.

"Oh, this blasted feather!" Fran snapped.

From the lofty height of his own mount, James glanced to where she struggled with her own sorry beast. To be fair to the horse, Fran's choice of headwear was the real problem. The black plume atop her hat kept drooping into her eyes. Every time she attempted to blow it back up with a short, sharp puff, down it fell again.

In deference to her obvious foul temper, James had allowed the first six incidents to pass unremarked. "I thought feathers were supposed to be jaunty," he said now.

"Well, this one isn't."

She'd been cross since they'd set out. At first, he'd assumed she was angry because he'd bamboozled her into meeting him this afternoon. He still wasn't sure why he'd done it. He'd woken to see her standing over him in the crush room and felt absurdly pleased to see her face. He hadn't been ready to relinquish the feeling when Mrs. Ashton interrupted them.

Despite today's ill humor, she looked fetching in her dark green riding habit. It hugged every curve. What a pity she had such a deplorable seat. The business with the feather made her shuffle about in the saddle, which must be very distracting for her poor horse.

"I'd take the whole hat off and throw it away but, according to my lawyer, I can't afford a new one."

"You're always talking about money," he said as they passed through Apsley gate. "It's very ill-bred of you. Happily, I enjoy the occasional lapse into bad taste. Let's hear it, then. Why can't you afford a new hat?"

"Because divorce is expensive."

He reined in his horse and waited for her to come alongside. "Ah. So that's the reason for this black mood."

"My mood is black because, despite the necessary future outlay of a great deal of money, I cannot be certain of a happy outcome."

He leaned over and plucked the offending feather from her hat. "Much better. I think you should avoid plumes in future. You cannot manage them." A dubious piece of gallantry, but it won him a small smile.

They ambled along, side by side, in companionable silence.

"I don't think divorces are supposed to be easy," he said, after several minutes had passed. "If they were, I predict fully one third of English couples would want one, and that would never do. Again, and at the risk of making you very angry, why not just accept a legal separation?"

"For a whole host of reasons. Why should a woman whose husband repents his choice suffer? Why must she resign herself to a life of loneliness while he is free to start anew? It's unjust, and if saying such makes me unwomanly, so be it."

"You could never be unwomanly. Impractical perhaps, but then ideals are rarely practical."

He watched her out of the corner of his eye. She remained an uncertain rider but, with the feather gone, at least she'd ceased bouncing about in the saddle. They turned onto Rotten Row, along with several other riders, then picked up the pace slightly to avoid the ire of their fellows.

"I suppose the practical thing to do is take the money," she said.

"Perhaps."

"That's what you think I should do, isn't it?"

Did he? He didn't know anymore. He might be disappointed if she gave up now. Strength and determination like hers were rare. Rare and magnificent.

"Perhaps it's just what I would do if I were in your place," he said, and nodded to an acquaintance whose name he couldn't for the life of him remember. "I couldn't do what you did the other day. Turning Thorne down like that."

"Why?" She guided her mare closer. "It's just money."

"No, it isn't. It's an entire way of life. I don't mean being received and all that twaddle. I couldn't care less about any of those dreadful people who shun you. Most of them are boring and stuffy anyway. No, I like my expensive tailoring and my quiet, lazy life. I couldn't give it up. Not for anything."

His words appeared to make her thoughtful. "Well," she said, after a while, "it's a good job you'll never have to."

Though her chestnut mare did more or less as bid, he was pleased when Fran said she wanted to walk for a while. She didn't look in imminent danger of falling off, but neither was she entirely comfortable. He dismounted and steadied her as she slid from the horse's back.

"I've been such a fool," she said, lowering her voice. "I spent the afternoon looking at the household accounts, such as they are. My first time. I never once bothered before. Edward's mother always took care of that, and I let her because I'm stupid."

He opened his mouth to acquit her of stupidity, but she wasn't finished.

"I never realized, until I tried to live by myself, how completely dependent I was on Edward. He paid for the roof over my head and the clothes on my back, and I never gave a thought to where it all came from. I have an income of my own, but I've been frittering it away for years. It never occurred to me to save it. I used it as pin money, for heaven's sake." She stopped walking and turned toward him. "What about you? Do you fritter?"

Fran must know the rules of good form as well as he did and her question was a serious violation. "I do believe you're the most vulgar girl I've ever met," he told her, struggling manfully to keep a straight face. "It's bad enough you pollute my ears with all this talk of accounts books and pin money, but it's beyond impudent to pry into my finances in this fashion."

"Balderdash."

He gave a shout of laughter and then quickly stifled it. Hyde Park was hardly the place. "I've been known to fritter on occasion. The truth is I'm as dependent as you. All my money comes direct from Aunt Miriam." Fran's candor must be contagious; James wasn't usually prone to self-disclosure.

"Oh, I remember Aunt Miriam," she muttered, darkly.

"Everyone says her name in that tone, but she's really very sweet. Generous too. All expenses paid."

"And one day it will all be yours. Thank heaven for great expectations." She tossed him a wicked smile. Another one of those and he'd get light-headed. "So, the money she gives you, do you spend it all?"

"Most of it." This time, he didn't notice her complete disregard for social nuances until after he'd answered the question. He must be getting used to her.

"Ah, so you did save some. You see? Even you are less foolish than I."

Even him? He glimpsed her quickly concealed smile.

"Fran, thus far good manners have kept me silent, but now I find I must ask. What's your horse's name?"

Her brow wrinkled in confusion as he'd intended. She kept him perpetually off balance, and he was glad to get a little of his own back. He wouldn't mind seeing her smile again either.

"Strawberry," she said. "Why?"

"I knew it. Strawberry. That explains a great deal. You sit that beast almost as well as a drunken bedlamite, but what can one expect from a woman who gives her horse a cow's name?"

"I happen to like strawberries." She looked a picture of mock dignity. "What's yours called anyway?"

"Hades," he said, all innocence.

She laughed low and throaty—a wonderful sound.

"Have a care, Fran. You'll wound his feelings."

"I apologize. I was aiming for yours. While we're on the subject, he's a stallion, is he not?"

"If you need me to tell you that, there's no hope for you."

"Wouldn't a gelding be more tractable?"

He raised both eyebrows suggestively. "What a typically feminine attitude. What's poor Hades ever done to you?"

"It's quite all right. I understand perfectly. If riding a stallion helps you to feel manly, who am I to gainsay you?"

"You have a wonderful laugh. Although I think I detected a hint of a snort that time."

"You certainly did not." She turned quite pink, which made her look adorable. "Well, perhaps a small one."

They were grinning at each other like fools when, out of the corner of his eye, he caught sight of Miss Randle. Now there went a girl with an excellent seat. She handled her white gelding with confidence. And she was even prettier than he remembered. He must hand it to Aunt Miriam; she had an excellent eye.

"Look over there, will you?" he said, nodding over his shoulder.

"What am I looking at?"

"The fair-haired lady in blue."

Fran glanced discreetly. "I see her. Who is she?"

"I don't know. That is, her *name* is Sylvia Randle. I met her the last time I was here. Aunt Miriam wants me to marry her."

Her eyes widened. "She's very lovely. Why does Mrs. Price want you to marry her? Does she know Miss Randle well?"

All very good questions. Though this wasn't the first time Miriam had hinted about marriage, she'd never been quite so forceful.

His age must be to blame. "She informs me she's recently made the acquaintance of the lady's mother. Apparently, the family is eminently suitable."

"Eminently? How grand and important that sounds. And is this something you're seriously considering?"

"Aunt Miriam is considering it *for* me, which means eventually . . ."

"You'll have to consider it," she finished.

"Precisely." His problem in a nutshell. Family duty versus personal inclination. One did one's duty or one reaped the consequences like Fran.

As if by unspoken consent, they slowed again until they reached a complete halt. The horses cropped the grass, their heads together like an old married couple eating from the same plate. Fran stared off into the middle distance, lost in thought.

"You're uncharacteristically quiet all of a sudden."

"Would you really allow Mrs. Price to dictate your choice of a wife?"

"I have no other option if I want to inherit her money." Which he did. Hadn't he always known what the cost would be? No point trying to wriggle out of it now. "I wonder how one goes about courting a debutante, anyway."

"You must work it out for yourself."

Miss Randle was one of a small party of gangly youths and demure girls, all as fresh and green as she. She laughed at something one of the ladies said, a merry trilling as soothing as a wind chime on a summer's day—a world away from Fran's wonderful cackle.

"How old is she?" Fran asked.

"No idea. How old does she look to you?"

She considered with her head tilted to one side. "Eighteen perhaps. Too young at any rate."

He agreed. "It's criminal, really. By the end of the season, she'll be engaged to one chap or another. She's too young to know what she's about and perhaps that's the point."

"Perhaps it is. Oh dear. If only you didn't love money so much."

Fran's tone was light, but he saw through it. Clearly, she disapproved.

"It's not the money I love; it's the things it can buy. Comfort, the trappings of respectability."

"I don't think money brings respectability and, in your case, it looks like a burden. Admit it, if money were not the overriding desire of your life, you could make your own choices." She looked directly at him and her next words hit him like a slap. "I wonder what you'd do then."

Money is not my overriding desire.

But the protest of that small, inner voice failed to convince even him.

CHAPTER SIX

Generally, Francesca didn't mind when people teased her, but as she stood before a full-length mirror clad in only her chemise, corset, and drawers, she realized she had her limits. Caroline had been impossible since meeting James at the ball.

All afternoon, Francesca had fended off hints and innuendos, and she was damned if she'd keep doing it when Barker, her maid, had her stripped down to her underwear. Since Caroline still had all *her* clothes on, she had a rather unfair advantage. After all, it was very difficult to maintain one's dignity in one's undies. Time to fight back.

"Really, Caro," she began. "You mustn't say such things about Mr. Standish. He's practically engaged."

Until that moment, Caroline had been lounging on Francesca's bed. Now she bolted upright. "Engaged? What do you mean he's engaged? To whom?"

"There's no need to sound so aghast. And, in any case, I said *practically* engaged."

While Caroline gaped, Francesca twisted so she could watch her maid work in the mirror. Barker had just finished fastening the bustle support. The mesh added several inches to Francesca's posterior. Barker knelt to adjust the wire.

"Be honest, Barker. Does this make me look like a snail?"

The bustle arranged to her satisfaction, the maid struggled to her feet. "If all the other ladies look like snails, you'd best look like one too."

Francesca repressed a smile. "You know, that isn't quite the answer I was hoping for."

Caroline, partially recovered from her shock, scrambled to the foot of the bed. "Who's he marrying?"

"Hmm?" Francesca wrinkled her brow and hoped she looked confused rather than myopic. "Oh, you mean Mr. Standish," she said, as if her thoughts had been elsewhere. "I don't know. I never met her. I think her name is Sybil or Selina. Something like that, at any rate." She wished she really had forgotten, but the name Sylvia seemed indelibly imprinted on her mind. She was already sick of it.

"How long has it been going on?" Caroline asked, sounding just like a wronged wife.

Francesca hesitated. If Caroline supposed James in love with Miss Randle, perhaps they might finally drop the subject. "Not *very* long. He only met her a week or so ago, but he's giving her his serious consideration." There. She'd even managed not to lie.

"Lift your arms please, ma'am." Barker held out the sumptuous sapphire silk they'd chosen for this evening. Silver-blue embroidered vines covered the bodice and bustle and glinted in the light.

Francesca frowned at it despite its beauty. "I'm still not sure this is the right gown. What about the green watered silk?"

"They're both very elegant, ma'am."

Caroline rolled her eyes. "Never mind the dress. It's only dinner with a lot of boring writers. Aren't you upset?"

"Why ever should I be? Mr. Standish is only an acquaintance."

Better to ignore the boring writer's comment. As the bourgeois wife of a publisher, Caroline rarely found herself on aristocratic guest lists, but the Ashton name commanded respect outside those circles. Some middle-class hostesses were willing to overlook Francesca's problematic marital status because of her breeding. An equal number were not. Tonight's dinner was this week's sole engagement.

"You're forgetting I saw you together at the opera. I recognize suppressed attraction when I see it. Are you honestly telling me you felt nothing when he told you? Not even a twinge of jealousy?"

Barker slipped the dress on over Francesca's up-stretched arms, sparing her the necessity of answering right away.

She considered lying. After all, whatever her feelings for James might be, they were her own business. She preferred to be truthful, but when people pried, perhaps one could be forgiven for fudging the facts.

But where would such thinking lead?

"Yes, perhaps a twinge," she admitted. "If you must know, you were right about my going riding as well. I think I went because it was an opportunity to spend time with him, though I didn't realize it until afterward."

One of the most gratifying things about honesty was the way it confounded people. Caroline's eyes grew round. "So, you admit it?"

"I admit I'm exhibiting all the early signs of an infatuation, if that's what you mean. It's not just the twinge either. At the opera, I noticed his laugh lines and just now, when I was looking at myself in the mirror, I found myself wishing I were taller."

"I'm not sure I'm with you. About the wanting to be taller, I mean." Caroline's gaze swept Francesca from head to toe. "I will say, at this stage, further growth is unlikely."

"Mr. Standish is tall," Francesca said, and sighed. Next time, she'd just lie. To hell with scruples. Honesty could be thoroughly exhausting.

"Mr. Standish is tall." Caroline's sarcasm was, as always, palpable. "Oh. Yes, of course. That clarifies things. Thank you."

"Mr. Standish is tall, so I assume he prefers taller ladies," Francesca explained. "Although I suppose it doesn't necessarily follow. Not that it signifies, for heaven's sake. His preferences are irrelevant, or at least they should be."

Barker finished fastening the gown. "Is that all right for you, ma'am?"

Francesca studied her reflection. Yes, she looked very well. Elegant and fashionable. Not at all the sort of woman who needed to count pennies. "You're a treasure. You can dress my hair now." She sat down at the dressing table and closed her eyes while Barker removed the first hairpins.

Since coming to London, Barker had taken on duties more befitting a maid of all work, and without complaint, but she was the ideal lady's maid. She had no time for matters of the heart, never probed for information, and offered sympathy only in the direst of circumstances.

Caroline, on the other hand, would make an appalling lady's maid. "Are you going to tell him?"

Did Barker just tut? "Caroline, I think we're trying Barker's patience. And no wonder after all the nonsense we've subjected her to. She must have the patience of Job. As for this silliness about Mr. Standish, no, I'm not going to tell him. Why would I? As I said, it's just an infatuation. It'll pass soon enough. In the meantime, it's an inconvenience."

Caroline stretched out across the bed again. "How unromantic of you."

"Sorry to disappoint you. Edward is probably scrutinizing my every move in the hope of detecting what my lawyer, in his usual impenetrable fashion, calls an *actus reus*. I can't *afford* to be romantic."

"What rubbish. How can you be caught in a "guilty act" by Edward when he hasn't lived with you for years? What sort of husband is that?"

Francesca didn't roll her eyes, but she wanted to. "The legal sort."

"The most troublesome kind, ma'am." Barker gave her a small smile and took up a silver-backed brush. "One, two . . ." she counted the strokes under her breath.

"Oh, bother the legalities," Caroline said. "He threw away any right to call himself husband years ago. He's spent the last ten years telling you he doesn't want you."

"None of that makes a whit of difference in the eyes of the law, but thank you for your support. Let's hope the courts agree with you." Francesca twisted in her chair, disrupting the rhythm of Barker's brushing. "Now, will you do me a very great kindness?"

Caroline sat up and leaned forward. "Anything."

Just what she'd hoped to hear. "Please shut up about Mr. Standish."

Miss Randle's faultless soprano and the piano accompaniment filled the music room. "*Meine ruh ist hin, meine herz ist schwer.*" *My peace is gone, my heart is heavy.*

She looked like an angel in pale pink silk shot through with silver. The other guests sat in awed silence. She'd bewitched them. James tried to succumb, but so far he stood immune.

Which was dashed awkward really.

Aunt Miriam had gone to a lot of trouble to get him and the object of his supposed suit under one roof. She loved to plot and scheme, and so planning tonight's gathering must have afforded her plenty of amusement. Oh, he knew very well what she was up to. She possessed many fine qualities, but tact was not one of them.

Take poor Miss Browning. She was neither young nor pretty. He'd wager Miriam wouldn't have invited her otherwise. A pretty girl might distract James from Miss Randle. The extra gentlemen, Mr. Fellows and Mr. Henshaw, provided a spot of competition. After all, a fox hunt would be dull indeed if one were the only rider in on the chase.

Naturally, he'd found himself seated next to Miss Randle at dinner. She'd proved a pleasant enough companion. Like most marriageable ladies, she'd been taught the trick of inviting one to converse about oneself. What gentleman would fail to enjoy himself in such company? And now he discovered she possessed the voice of a siren, too.

"*Mein armer sinn ist mir zerstückt,*" she sang. *My poor mind is torn apart.*

Inwardly, he recited the conventional wisdom. Eighteen was just the right age for a woman to marry. Youthful wives kept their looks longer, were malleable, and had more years left to bear children.

He didn't envisage himself as a permanent bachelor. As a young man he'd felt differently, but lately he'd thought it might be pleasant to come home and find someone adoring and sweet waiting. Miss Randle's beauty promised to ripen with maturity, and her accomplishments spoke for themselves. He must marry sooner or later if he wanted to provide Miriam with heirs. Why not Miss Randle?

There are eighteen years between us.

Not a trivial disparity, even if one failed to take into account the fact that she was an innocent, untried girl, while he was in danger of becoming a jaded misanthrope. Was he really considering this girl as the future mother of his children? Never mind that he had no real desire to become a father.

"*Seiner rede zauberfluß, sein händedruck, und ach, sein kuß!*" *His mouth's magic flow, his handclasp, and ah, his kiss!* Miss Randle's voice soared, resonant with passion, as the song reached its pinnacle. She truly seemed like Gretchen singing ecstatically of her love for Faust. James listened with the same rapt attention as everyone else.

Afterward, the small gathering applauded with genuine enthusiasm.

While his rivals clapped, he crossed the room to the piano and offered his hand. Instead of leading her back to her mama, as was proper, he led her to a settee. To court or not to court, that was the question.

"You play and sing very well," he told her. An understatement.

"Thank you, Mr. Standish. I've always been partial to Schubert."

"No doubt Schubert would return the sentiment."

Another pretty blush. "I've been meaning to thank you again for your assistance in Hyde Park. I am forever losing my handkerchiefs."

"I saw you there again a few days ago. Do you enjoy riding?"

"Very much. There's something so liberating about it, don't you think?"

"I do." Just when they'd hit upon a subject of interest to both, he thought of Fran. He'd never seen anyone look so uncomfortable in the saddle. And that ridiculous feather . . .

"Mr. Standish?" Miss Randle sounded concerned. "Are you quite well?"

He didn't need a mirror to tell him he was grinning like a fool. He tried for something more neutral but feared he'd only succeeded in making himself smirk. He must be losing his mind. Why did these moods always come upon one at the most inopportune moments?

"Forgive me," he said. "You reminded me about a friend of mine. She doesn't care for riding. But I must compliment you. You ride almost as well as you sing."

She smiled as if to say she quite forgave his inattention. Immediately, his urge to grin subsided to a more manageable level. This girl certainly had a talent for putting everyone in her company at ease.

"I like to do things well. Mama says . . ." She hesitated. "She worries I overtax myself."

"Is she right?"

"I don't think any of the things I do are terribly taxing. Riding, playing the piano, embroidery. None of it—"

"Are you talking of embroidery, Sylvia?" Mrs. Randle joined them. A handsome woman, the mother. Older than him, but probably only by one or two years. "She embroiders quite beautifully, Mr. Standish."

Apparently, there was nothing at which Miss Randle didn't excel. Was it possible for a lady to suffer a surfeit of perfection?

"I suppose you are also a great reader?" He meant to tease, and thought he detected an answering smile starting on her lips.

"Oh, Sylvia loves to read, but we do not allow her to do so to excess. She is a very dedicated sort of girl, sir, but my husband and I believe too much mental stimulation can be bad for a young woman's health."

Aunt Miriam bore down on them. She always claimed her hearing had begun to fail, but he'd noticed it came and went depending on her wishes. "Oh, indeed," she cried. "Any mental activity, if carried too far, can be harmful to the female constitution."

Miriam never denied herself anything, mental activity included. The constant indulgence hadn't done much harm, if her robust health were any indication.

The mother sipped at her champagne. "You are quite right, Mrs. Price. We are very careful and, you know, Sylvia never takes cold."

Though the daughter evidently inherited her beauty from her mother, the same could not be said for her sense or her charm.

Perhaps he was imagining things, but Miss Randle's smile seemed strained. He warmed to her at once. "Do you paint?" he asked.

"Landscapes and still life, but I am not very good. I—"

Mrs. Randle spoke over her. "Come now, you paint beautifully."

That word again.

"My paintings are technically proficient, but they have no . . ." She searched for the right word.

"Soul?" he supplied.

"Oh, young people are always so theatrical," Aunt Miriam said. "It's why I enjoy their company. They feel everything so deeply. Just hearing them makes the years fall away."

Miss Randle ignored her. "That's it exactly," she said, her eyes earnest as they gazed into his. "They have no soul."

Oh, he liked this woman. She struck him as genteel but passionate. He could think of no rational reason why he shouldn't pursue her. Miriam would be thrilled, and no doubt she thought him safely on the path to matrimony.

As for whether he actually was, he only wished he knew.

CHAPTER SEVEN

Bloomsbury was an unlikely place to collide with an angel, but that's what happened to James the next morning.

What had possessed him when he'd arranged to call on Fran at ten instead of a more reasonable hour, the Lord only knew. He'd arrived home from Miriam's party feeling restless, panicked, and slightly tipsy. With no company and nothing to do, he'd gone temporarily mad and sent a footman to Fran's with a note. Now, stone cold sober and back in his right mind, he had to follow through.

Careening round the corner, he ran smack into her—the angel, not Fran—and sent her plummeting to the ground.

She yelped as her backside hit the pavement with a less than celestial thud. The packages and parcels she'd carried rained down on top of her, and her smart yellow hat fell over her eyes.

"I'm terribly sorry," he said. What an awful blunder. At any moment, he expected a chaperone to stride forward and take him to task.

None appeared. The angel—apparently unattended—adjusted her hat and peeked up, from under the narrow brim, with familiar blue eyes.

"Miss Randle! What a surprise to see you here of all places." Hopefully he seemed pleased, but a queer, queasy feeling—reminiscent of the time he'd spent with her last night—overtook him. He could be wrong, but he didn't think it was love.

"Mr. Standish!" she cried, sounding rather horrified. But she took his arm and allowed him to assist her to her feet.

"I hope you're not too bruised."

"Not at all. I wasn't looking."

"Neither was I."

"So, we're both to blame?"

He shook his head. "In these situations, the gentleman is always at fault."

"Oh. That's very handsome of you."

He knelt down and gathered the parcels, all brown paper rectangles of a similar size. She must have come from the little bookshop on the corner. "Please allow me to carry these for you."

"Oh, no! I couldn't."

"No need to sound so aghast." What on earth was the matter with her?

Naturally, her cheeks turned rose-petal pink. Debutantes of this caliber didn't turn beetroot red. A ruddy complexion wouldn't go with the pretty white dresses they wore.

"Mr. Standish, forgive me. The truth is I'm not supposed to be here. No one knows. Well, except for you of course."

The paper on one of the parcels had torn. "Aristotle," he read through the gap. "Good heavens. Tell me that's not the original Greek."

She laughed nervously. "Of course not."

"Perhaps this is a gift for your father or your brother." But then why sneak out? She went from petal pink to ashen. "Or perhaps you are simply a very intelligent lady who likes to read, and I should mind my own business."

She started walking, and he had no choice but to fall into step beside her. He could hardly permit her to walk home alone, despite the risk of the gossips spotting them.

"You must think me very strange," she said, so quietly he almost didn't hear.

"Not strange, but I confess I wonder why you go to these lengths to visit a bookshop."

"Do you read, Mr. Standish?"

"Yes, of course. Art books, travel guides, even novels."

"And how often are you permitted to read?"

"How often . . ." Ah. He saw her point.

She smiled. "My hour for reading is between three and four on days when I have no engagements. Even then, my parents would never allow me to read Aristotle. Too demanding for the delicate female brain."

Was *that* what had the Randles so worried? Too much mental stimulus could drive a woman mad, or so said the British Medical Association. Still, Miss Randle seemed sane enough, if a little overwrought. He'd hit the mark last night; she was an interesting girl.

"Your aunt gives such a pleasant party," she said. "I'm so glad she included us."

"Never mind the party. How are you going to sneak these books into the house without anyone noticing?"

She smiled again, but properly this time. A real smile, not the counterfeit he'd seen every other time they'd spoken. It lit her already beautiful face, infusing it with life and humor. "I bribe one of the footmen. He lets me in at the servant's entrance."

How easily she gave her trust. She made him feel about a hundred. "I knew a boy once," he told her. "He was . . . sweet, for want of a better word, and earnest, and intelligent. You remind me of him."

He didn't realize he'd stopped walking until she touched his arm. "What happened to the boy?"

"He married unwisely."

"And that changed him?"

Was it marrying Fran that had changed Thorne? James didn't think things could be so simple. "Unhappiness," he said. "Unhappiness changed him, but I'm not sure that's any excuse."

They'd reached the corner of her street. Just as well. He should never have raised such a subject with an unmarried lady, even one as unique as Miss Randle. She looked thoroughly confused.

"Will you be all right from here?" he asked.

"Oh. Of course."

"I'll wait until you're safely in." He returned her parcels and watched until she'd run down the steps to the basement entrance.

Francesca waited for James in the parlor, fidgeting with the glass buttons decorating the cuffs of her sleeves. He should arrive at any moment. This morning, while she'd sat in bed drinking her daily cup of hot chocolate, Barker had given her his note. And it was too much. First a call, then the ride in Hyde Park, and now this. What might Edward make of James visiting her at home for a second time?

Perhaps nothing. Though he didn't trust her, he surely knew James would never betray him. He might be the one man in the world she could safely befriend, but she wasn't certain. Caution was best. She wouldn't be a coward about it. She'd simply describe her situation to James. Not this silly attraction, but the bit about protecting her good name—ha!—or what was left of it. He would have to understand.

She heard the sharp rapping of the doorknocker and stood.

Moments later, Barker appeared, her face paper white. "Mr. Thorne's here, ma'am."

Francesca couldn't think, much less speak. Had Barker really said—

"No need to stand on ceremony, Barker." Edward swaggered in and straight to the small settee. "Your mistress is still my wife no matter where she lives."

He filled the room, the very house, with his presence, sucking up all the air and light.

You don't belong here, she wanted to shout. She hadn't even donned her defensive armor. Where was her snail-shell bustle with its elaborate drapery? Where was her straight-backed chair, her fortitude?

He nodded to Barker. "You may go."

How dare he give orders to the servants as if he were master here?

Barker waited uncertainly, her hand on the doorknob.

"It's all right, Barker. Do as Mr. Thorne says. Oh, and if anyone else calls, put them in the drawing room."

He raised his eyebrows, but in that moment Francesca didn't care. The last thing she needed was James barging in. Things were difficult enough.

"Come on, Mrs. Thorne," Edward said, once Barker had gone. "You can't spend the whole interview gaping like a fish."

A tide of heat swept her and she knew she'd gone red. She lifted her chin and stared down her nose at him, the interloper, sprawled there on her furniture. "Do sit down."

He made a great show of surveying the room from floor to ceiling, from end to end. "Bit shabby, isn't it?"

She smiled, pretending to a self-assurance she was far from feeling. "Should one of us ring for tea?"

"Don't you have anything stronger?"

"I'm saving that for when you've gone." No tea, then. She chose the seat nearest him and sat down. "Are we going to play games all day or are you going to tell me what you want?"

"You know what I want," he said. "What I've always wanted."

"Oh, but that's where you're wrong. Your desires are something I've never understood."

His expression turned wintry. "Enough, Francesca. You've made your point. You've embarrassed my family and yours with this foolishness, but now it's over, understand? God knows I don't want you under any of my roofs, so we'll find you a house somewhere else, somewhere more fashionable. I'll bear the cost, but let's have an end to your nonsense."

"That was quite a speech." She kept smiling even though his words had turned her from hot to ice cold. "But we've been here before. I gave you my response through my lawyer and in person. I gave it again to Mr. Standish just last week. One would think you'd comprehend me by now."

He stayed on the sofa, but he went a trifle stiff. "Francesca, I'm warning you—"

She stood. "Wherever did you get the impression I'm the sort of woman who gives in to threats?

He shook his head. "My God, I can hardly believe this is the woman I married. When we met, you seemed so damned innocent."

"Oh, I was. But now I'm what you made me." Only a grain of truth to that statement. Yes, Edward had partially influenced the person she'd become, but she'd never been innocent, at least not as he understood the word.

He flinched, sending a tiny thrill through her. "A lady should be—"

"I know, I know." She forced herself to laugh. "A lady should be an angel of mercy, the goddess of the hearth, a paragon of maidenly virtue untainted by lustful thoughts."

"That's not what I meant."

"Isn't it?" Old hurts rushed back to taunt her. "Then why did you . . . that first night. I trusted you with everything, and you—"

"Damn it, Francesca." He sat forward and, as he tended to when he got upset, raked his fingers through his hair until it stood up like the spikes on a hedgehog. "I was so young, practically a boy. I had no idea what I was doing."

"You were twenty-six, only four years younger than I am now."

"But I didn't know anything. You've been a wife and . . . I didn't know how to react when you . . . wives should be . . ."

"Less passionate? Is that what you mean? Is that what you wanted? Someone to lie still and stare at the ceiling?" She waited, but he didn't react. "Well, I wanted a friend and a lover. When you rejected me on our wedding night, you made me feel . . ." He'd broken her heart.

"Must we go through this again?" His question rang in the ensuing silence. He crouched over in his chair, cradling his head in his hands, as if last night's carousing had just caught up with him.

"No," she said quietly. "No. We discussed this enough during those first months, before we began smothering one another with courteousness." She sat down, smoothing her skirts. "But I'm going to ask you a question."

Head still down, he held out his hand palm up, as if to say *Be my guest.*

"I've always wondered, when did you first decide to . . . look elsewhere?"

"No," he said, his voice muffled. "Not that question."

"All right. Then at least tell me why." After the first time, their lovemaking, if one could call it that, had turned perfunctory, but not infrequent. "Why go to other women, when I would gladly—"

He sat up, the movement sudden, almost violent. "I didn't want that. You were my wife. There are things a wife can't . . . but I shouldn't have to tell you this."

"I see." She'd suspected as much, but now she knew for sure. "You couldn't ask me to do those things because wives are a breed apart and must be kept pure. Tell me, Edward, now that you've sampled a great many wives and widows, do you still believe that?"

He had that look, the one that told her he was about to deliver the coup de grâce. "Ah, but you see, by the time I found out how wrong I was, I already knew I didn't love you."

It shouldn't hurt after all this time. She didn't love him anymore either, and yet . . . she felt a pang. An echo of an old emotion.

Sometimes remembered agony was almost as difficult to bear as current pain.

"Was that when you decided to leave?"

"I answered your question," he said. "You don't get another."

"Then I don't think there's any reason for you to stay."

She rose to ring the bell, but he crossed the room quickly and blocked her way. "Not yet, Mrs. Thorne. You didn't let me finish my warning."

"Your threat, you mean." She wouldn't look at him, not when he stood this close. Even when he took hold of both her arms, she kept her eyes on the bell pull. He didn't hurt her. He'd never hurt her physically, but his hands on her served as a reminder of his superior size and strength.

"No threats," he whispered. "But I feel it's only fair to tell you that if you don't stop, things are going to get very unpleasant. I'm not going to lie down and take this any longer. Do you understand?"

Inclining her head, she spoke softly into his ear. "Do your worst."

He released her so suddenly that she had to steady herself on the mantel. "I'll see myself out."

Air and light rushed back as he made for the door.

CHAPTER EIGHT

"Your eyes are very bleary this morning," Francesca observed, as James flung himself into her dilapidated tapestry chair. "What *have* you been doing?"

He stifled a yawn. "Nothing disreputable, I assure you. It's merely that I woke so confoundedly early. And it's *still* early, obscenely so. The light's all wrong at this hour."

Perhaps he played a part, exaggerating his tiredness for her amusement, but how wonderful if he were truly this ill-tempered in the morning. If she unearthed a few bad habits, she might get over these silly feelings. "It's eleven o'clock," she pointed out in case his pocket watch had stopped.

He slouched back in his chair with a self-satisfied smile. "Precisely."

Not for the first time, she wondered what he'd do if she crossed the space between them and mussed his hair. No one who stayed abed so late had any business looking this presentable. He ought to have sheet marks on one cheek at the very least.

"You're very late, and I've yet to receive a word of apology." But she smiled as she said it to show she wasn't truly offended. After all, if he'd arrived on time, he might have run into Edward—a complication she didn't need. Even if Edward didn't misconstrue the situation, she didn't want James mixed up in the chaos. And she'd required every second of his lateness to regain her equilibrium. "So, what brings you here at such an ungodly hour?"

"I've come in search of distraction."

She wasn't sure she liked the sound of that. How was she supposed to distract him? "From what exactly?"

His eyes rolled ceiling-ward. "If I tell you, I'll have to think about it, which would defeat the purpose." But she continued to gaze steadily at him until he heaved a put-upon sigh. "If you must know, it's this business with Miss Randle. She was at a dinner my aunt gave last night and then I ran into her just now on the street."

Oh, *her* again. The pretty blonde with the excellent seat and powder-blue riding habit. How could James let his aunt dictate to him this way? He didn't seem particularly weak-minded, so avarice must be to blame. There. A glaring fault right in front of her. So why wasn't she more put off?

"Mrs. Price is pressing forward with her campaign, then?"

"It would seem so."

"And what of the lady? Is she not to your liking?"

"She ought to be. She's everything a man should want."

She heard Edward's voice reverberating from ten years distant. *You're everything a fellow wants in a wife.* He'd said those words, or something like them, more than once during their short courtship.

"Be careful, Jemmy. Marriage can be like a cage for a woman if her husband doesn't care for her, and perhaps it's just as true for the husband." But her disastrous marriage needn't dominate every conversation. A change of subject was in order. "As much as I enjoy listening to you extol the virtues of another lady, especially one who made you an hour late for our appointment, you did say you wanted distraction. As do I. Perhaps we ought to go out."

He grinned and folded his arms. "I knew you'd help. Where to?"

She had absolutely no idea, but she knew she didn't want to be alone with him. It felt . . . honestly, it felt dangerous. In more ways than one. "Mrs. Ashton is expecting us for luncheon." A lie and not even a clever one. Caroline might not even be home.

"Did you just say Mrs. Ashton is expecting us? How on earth can that be?"

"I sent her a note after I received yours this morning." What was the matter with her? Miraculously, he seemed to accept the flimsy deception. He waited while she went to fetch her outdoor things: gloves, a bonnet, and a white lace parasol of which she happened to be rather fond.

"Shall we go then?" He offered his arm, and she stared at the offending limb as though it were a snake.

Oh, don't be so absurd, Francesca.

Gingerly, she laid her hand upon his sleeve.

There. Nothing extraordinary about it. Just a sleeve with a perfectly normal, albeit pleasantly firm, arm.

Then she met his gaze. Terrible mistake. Beautiful gray eyes laughed down at her.

"I'm sorry I was so ill-bred as to praise another lady in your presence," he said. "I neglected to tell you before, but you look very fine."

As compliments went, it won no points for originality or poetry. Nonetheless, pleasure swept through her like a warm breeze. "You know, I begin to suspect you aren't as dreadful as you make yourself out to be."

"*Do* I make myself out to be dreadful?"

"You do, but I'd much rather that than the reverse."

His gaze dipped to her lips. A shiver of awareness shot right down to her toes. She understood what a look like that meant. All her muscles seemed to tense as his hand reached toward her face.

This couldn't happen.

She brought one arm up between them, fully intending to push him away if she must, but she'd forgotten she still had the parasol.

He dropped to his knees.

* * *

His balls were on fire.

He gasped out a volley of Anglo-Saxon curses.

"Oh! Oh, I'm so sorry!" High and panicky, Fran's voice pierced through the mist of pain. She flung her parasol away as if it had bitten her. It hit the floor, laying there, frothy with lace—a piece of feminine nonsense, yet a quite formidable weapon if one knew how to wield it.

"What the bloody hell were you thinking?" The words were his, but the madman's snarl that went with them couldn't be. A gentleman never lost his temper with a lady, no matter how grievous the offense.

Fran clamped shaking hands over bright red cheeks. "Oh God, I'm sorry. I thought . . . Oh, I'm so embarrassed."

The pain was all he could think about, but he rose from his undignified crouch and sat down heavily on the edge of a spindly chair. "Just give me a minute." He struggled to reorder his sluggish thoughts, something he could have done a lot faster if she'd only stop apologizing.

"I'm so sorry," she said yet again. Tears of remorse and, he supposed, humiliation welled in her eyes, but he couldn't muster much sympathy. "I panicked. You probably don't even find me attractive."

"Not at this precise instant, no. Most women would have slapped my face if they thought I was about to insult them with unwanted attention. You might try it next time."

"I didn't actually mean to hit you." A defensive edge had crept into her voice.

Ha! After assaulting him, *she* sounded cross. And why not? As a woman, she couldn't possibly fathom the pain searing his nether regions. Neither did she have any idea how she'd butchered his pride. She'd obviously thought him about to make some sort of advance, and her response put him firmly in his place.

The pain receded ever so slightly but, in its stead, arose an unpleasant throbbing, along with a strong conviction that he hadn't behaved well. One strove for a certain manly stoicism, even in the face of extreme agony.

Well, bugger that. It was too late now, anyway.

"I was going to straighten your hat," he said.

"I am truly sorry, but it *was* an accident."

Clenching his teeth, he began a slow count to ten. By the time he'd finished, he felt just about well enough to rise.

The worst of it was that the thought of kissing her had been very much at the forefront of his mind. He never would have done it, but he'd be a liar if he pretended he hadn't considered the possibility.

She's still Thorne's wife, you dolt.

And it didn't matter how fetching she looked in that bonnet, or how incredibly green her eyes looked swimming in unshed tears—tears she refused to cry. The mere threat of them stole the heat from his anger and forced him to master himself.

Say something polite. Make her feel better, you selfish arse.

He took a deep breath, looked at her, and smiled: a polite rictus of manic cheer. "Mrs. Thorne," he began, because somehow this seemed like a *Mrs. Thorne* moment. "If I offended you, then of course I'm sorry."

"You're sorry?" Her lips twitched and for a horrible second he thought her about to cry after all. "I imagine you're *very* sorry," she added, and this time he heard the suppressed laughter in her voice. "I only hope children are still a possibility. I quite understand if you wish to take out an injunction."

Only she could make him laugh when he was still dizzy with nausea. Well, he *had* visited in hopes of distraction, and Francesca had certainly obliged.

* * *

As they walked the short distance to the Ashton house on Bedford Square, Francesca was sure she talked too much—a bright, barely coherent stream of chatter designed to conceal her embarrassment. The mortifying business with the parasol had been bad enough, but to compound things she'd made it all too apparent she'd expected him to try to kiss her. How vain he must think her. That ugly scene with Edward paled into insignificance in the face of her complete and utter humiliation.

When they reached the grand townhouse on the north side of the Square, she began to pray: *Please Lord, let Caroline be at home. Otherwise, I'll have to tell James I made a mistake and he'll probably see through me, so if you wouldn't mind helping me just this once* . . . Of course, God wasn't generally a great admirer of lying, so best get inside before the lighting hit.

Just as she raised her hand to knock, the door swung open. Caroline stepped over the threshold, head down as she pulled on a pair of gloves. Oh dear.

"Here we are!" Francesca sang out. "On time, just as I promised."

Caroline stared in complete astonishment.

"I don't mind telling you, I'm absolutely famished," Francesca said, keeping her tone light, but trying to communicate desperation with her eyes. "I hope lunch will be ready soon." Why, oh why had she told James lunch? If this was simply an impromptu call, the imposition on the Ashtons wouldn't be so great.

Only a second passed before Caroline spoke, but it seemed an age. "Excellent. Come in." She flashed her best smile at James and turned to a footman who stood at attention in the hallway. "Thomas, please tell Mr. Ashton our guests have arrived and lunch will be ready in an hour. Remember to mention it to Cook as well." She put especial emphasis on the last part.

"I hope we aren't too early," James said, as they followed Caroline into the parlor.

"Not at all, Mr. Standish."

"It's just you look as though you're dressed to go out."

"Oh no, I was just going to take a breath of air."

"On the front step?"

Fortunately, a convenient housemaid appeared. "Ah, Agnes," Caroline said, as though she hadn't heard him. "Take Mr. Standish's hat, would you?"

While the girl divested James of his outdoor things, Caroline whispered to Francesca. "My cook is going to be in fits."

"I'm sorry," she mouthed. It was far from her finest hour, and she only hoped Caroline forgave her.

"So, Mr. Standish," Caroline took his arm. "Francesca tells me your horse has an absurdly fanciful name."

James admired the deft way Mrs. Ashton carried things off. That split second of hesitation on the doorstep, coupled with the walking dress she wore, were enough to convince him their appearance had come as a total surprise. But she rallied quickly, and if Fran hadn't looked so pale and worried, he might almost think he'd been imagining things.

Why? Why had Fran lied, and over something so trivial? Usually she told the truth even when a small lie would make life easier. Taken in isolation, this was a strange enough business, but it came hard upon the heels of the excruciating incident with the parasol. Something was the matter, and he found himself very curious to find out what it might be.

With the beleaguered household staff off improvising a suitable luncheon, Mrs. Ashton served tea. When Mr. Ashton, a plain-featured man of about forty-five, joined them, she went to him and took his hand, performing the introductions.

"Hello, all," Ashton said, by way of greeting. And James appreciated the way he didn't even blink on finding himself entertaining two interlopers; he greeted them as though they were not only welcome but eagerly anticipated guests.

After tea, everyone moved to the dining room. Despite what Aunt Miriam always said about the aspiring middle classes and their new money, the house looked no different from its Mayfair equivalents. He detected no hint of vulgarity or excess in the Ashtons' choice of decor. Just as garish taste was not the exclusive province of the lower classes, it appeared refinement wasn't restricted to members of the elite.

Despite the urgency with which it must have been prepared, the food looked appetizing. Though only cold cuts, everything was of the best quality.

While they ate, the ladies returned to the subject of equine nomenclature. After watching them tease James for several minutes, Ashton stepped in with a baffled frown. "You really must refrain from torturing our guest, Caro. I hope you haven't been too uncivil."

"Not at all," James said. "She and Mrs. Thorne have taken issue with the name I've chosen for my horse, that's all."

"Is that so? What's he called?"

James took another sip of the excellent Portuguese hock. "His name's Hades."

"And what's so laughable about that, may I ask? What *should* a man call his horse? I suppose you ladies would prefer Flossy or something equally inappropriate." He grimaced. "When we were children, my younger sister had a pony called Radish, poor creature."

"Mrs. Thorne's horse is called Strawberry," James said, shooting a quick smile Fran's way. The intimacy of teasing her this way—when the joke was one they'd shared before—spread warmth all through him. Not the sexual heat he felt with a new lover, but something altogether more vital. Something he couldn't put a name to.

Ashton's sandy brows drew together. "Strawberry? No, no. That will never do. Think of the poor brute's pride."

"Strawberry's pride is in excellent order, thank you, gentlemen." Fran affected an injured air. "She's quite happy with her name."

He and Ashton exchanged dark looks.

"Of course you may call your horse whatever you like, Francesca," Ashton said. "But no good will come of it."

It was pleasant to watch Fran with her friends. Even at the opera, he'd noted the ease and familiarity between the two women, but Ashton too fell in with their relaxed way of talking, trading jibes and making absurd jokes. James was glad she had like-minded people to keep her from getting lonely.

As the meal progressed he learned more about them, particularly Ashton, who owned a periodical: *The Gentleman's Artistic Review.* "Circulation is not what I'd hoped," he said. "And nor are the profits."

James could feel Francesca's eyes on him, her gaze steady. He'd told her more than once that he considered money talk vulgar, but surely she knew he'd never insult her friends by saying so now? He understood that men like him—the landed gentry and, even further up the social scale, the aristocrats in their crumbling stately homes—were an endangered breed. Their money had always come from the land and those who worked it. Heaven forefend they should soil their hands with trade. Those who refused to adapt to the modern industrial age were contemptuous of those who did, but it wouldn't do them any good when their great houses got sold off and demolished.

Ignoring Francesca's scrutiny, he concentrated on Ashton. "What's the trouble?"

"Funding, for one thing. I'm finding it damned tricky to turn a profit on my own. But it's not that simple. When I first read the journal, years and years before I ever thought of buying it, it was avant-garde, but now we're lagging behind and subscriptions are down."

"The public's taste in art is changing," Caroline said. "People don't want medieval subjects and all that spiritual claptrap. They want something more immediate."

"I like spiritual claptrap," Francesca said. "But you're right. The Aesthetics and the Impressionists are avant-garde now."

"But our staid fellow Englishmen disapprove of Impressionism," Ashton said. "They dismiss it as French lunacy."

James's cutlery clinked slightly as he set it down on his plate. Though he didn't know much about publishing, he knew a decent amount about art. "And what do they think of the new Aestheticism?"

"It's all the rage, which is enough to ensure censure from a certain sort. There's nothing one can do for those fools who deplore a thing simply because it's popular, but many of my contributors resist the notion of art for art's sake. They think paintings should represent reality or, if they must be narrative, some great and lofty moral theme."

"Surely something can be beautiful and noble at the same time?"

"Certainly it can. But the Aesthetics argue art need have no moral message at all as long as it's beautiful."

A footman stepped forward and cleared their things. Almost immediately, another appeared and began serving Bakewell Pudding. James liked sweet things, but he was more interested in the conversation. "If you truly wish to modernize, perhaps it's time to find some new contributors. Find someone who attended the Salon des Refusés and liked what he saw."

"What's the Salon des Refusés?" Francesca asked.

"It happened in Paris back in the sixties," he explained. "The Salon received too many submissions, and so the emperor decided to exhibit the rejects in an annex."

"And was it a success?"

"Yes and no. Everyone made fun of the paintings, even Mr. Whistler's." Idiots, the lot of them. How could anyone fail to appreciate Whistler's work? "But it got them talking and thinking."

Ashton laughed. "And that's easier said than done."

* * *

Francesca watched with interest. The two men continued their discussion throughout the meal and the obligatory drinks in the drawing room afterward. When she began to talk of leaving, Ashton even asked if she wouldn't mind waiting while he showed James a new article he'd received entitled "Art and the Tyranny of Nature." They left the room still talking volubly.

As soon as they'd gone, she leaned her cheek against the green-striped upholstery of the two-seater sofa on which she sat with Caroline, and closed her eyes. "I'm so sorry, Caro. I don't know what came over me. Mr. Standish called, and I knew I shouldn't spend too much time alone with him. I ought to have sent him off, but it seemed too rude, and I didn't truly want—"

Caroline squeezed her hand, halting the babble of words. "Don't be silly, darling. Fortunately for you, I didn't have anything important to do today. And anyway, I wouldn't have missed this for the world."

"But I interrupted Ashton's work."

"He had to eat sooner or later. It isn't good for him to stay cooped up all the time working such long hours. He'd waste away if I didn't occasionally send in provisions. And I think he enjoyed himself. He and your Mr. Standish seemed to hit it off."

Francesca almost agreed until she realized what Caroline had implied. "He isn't *my* Mr. Standish." Something she needed to keep telling herself. At times, she came perilously close to forgetting. As long as she remembered, she could stop her infatuation from turning into something more serious. "He's not mine."

"And it's a pity. You know, Philip always says one can tell a man's worth by the company he keeps. At first, I wondered if any friend of your husband's could possibly be worth your regard, but he's not at all what I expected. I like him very much."

"What were you expecting?"

"Honestly? An empty-headed dandy, I suppose, or a cold, imperious autocrat. I'm afraid it's what my admittedly limited experience with men of your class led me to expect."

Francesca hardly blamed her. She knew a few of those men herself, but James was different. Therein lay the danger. "I shouldn't be spending this much time with him. I meant to start avoiding him, but I weakened."

Caroline toyed with the tassel of one of the cushions. "Perhaps it's a good thing. Maybe you'll unearth some irritating opinions. He might be in favor of slavery or think women ought to be schooled in nothing but sewing and deportment."

Francesca doubted it. Only this morning, she'd thought something very similar, but what a naive fool she'd been. The more time she spent with James, the more she liked him. The more she liked him, the more she wanted him to kiss her.

CHAPTER NINE

After lunch, James convinced Fran to ride with him in his carriage to Hyde Park. It was a bad idea; he knew that from the start. Perhaps she sensed it too because she hardly said a word during most of the drive, gazing out the window at the passing streets. While she watched them, he watched her. Small details he'd never noticed before, like the turn of her throat, the little wisps escaping her hairpins, and when she bowed her head, the stark white line of her center parting—so precise, so neat and straight for such a chaotic person.

He wanted to reach across and take one of her small, still hands in his own. He'd carry it to his lips and—

"Thank you for coming today," she said.

He hoped his expression didn't give away the tenor of his thoughts.

"And thank you for being such pleasant company at lunch," she went on. "It was very wrong of me to accept their invitation without asking you first." She ducked her head as she spoke. He'd seen her do it a few times today. It must be one of her tells. He'd have to remember it in case they ever played cards.

"I enjoyed it. I liked your friends very much."

She smiled almost sadly. "They've been very good to me. There was a time when I might have shunned such an acquaintance. I might not have taken the time to get to know them. I would have judged them on social standing alone. Shame fills me whenever I think of it."

"You shouldn't reproach yourself. You're different now." Different from any woman he'd ever known. Funnier. More desirable. Perfectly imperfect.

She smiled but it didn't reach her eyes. "Yes, very different."

"We become what we're taught to become, don't you think? First, you learned from your parents, then your aunt and uncle, and now life has taught you something new." What had marriage to Thorne taught her? It was a question he'd never ask.

"I am surprised to hear you say so," she said. "I thought you would attribute yourself to good breeding."

He wanted to laugh. "I, an example of good breeding? I hardly think so." He'd met too many worthless aristocrats, not to mention gentlemen of leisure like himself, to put a great deal of store in pedigree. Men like Philip Ashton rose in the world by dint of their own diligence and tenacity, and James found he approved.

"How ridiculous it all is," she mused. "All those silly rituals and codes."

"You make us sound like the Freemasons." Though he kept his tone teasing, inside he felt hollow. Silly rituals and codes—was that all a gentleman was?

Her eyes blazed with evangelistic zeal, just as they had when she'd talked of freedom. "Don't you ever get tired of it? I mean all the mindless obedience to tradition."

He didn't look at her, sensing that she wanted a particular response. One he couldn't give. Yes, all those rules got tiresome at times, but they existed for a reason. "But where you see a prison," he explained, "I see structure and security."

The silence stretched out. He concentrated on the sway of the carriage as the horses ambled through the busy Mayfair streets.

How different they were. How unsuitable she was. Yet it was Fran, not Miss Randle, he wanted to kiss. The very attributes that should place her beyond the pale drew him like a lodestone. "Mrs. Price thinks you deliberately threw your good name away."

"I suppose I did." She smiled, but it seemed neither happy nor sad. He couldn't begin to guess what she felt. "It seems I'm the victim of my own choices."

"You don't seem unduly concerned."

"Why should I be? I chose this with my eyes open."

But she hadn't been blessed with many happy alternatives. "I know you're content with your new life now, but do you never consider the future? What if you have a child one day?" A child who would have to bear the consequences of her choices.

It was an abominably indelicate question but, true to form, she gave no outward sign she noticed. "I think if I were capable of bearing a child I would have done so by now, don't you?"

His stomach clenched. This was why the rules of polite conversation existed. To stop fools like him from blundering into sensitive territory. "I'm sorry."

"Thank you," she said, and to his surprise her voice didn't waver. "It was difficult at first, but it's been almost a decade since the doctors broke the news. Anyway, I don't intend to marry again. The fact that I'm barren is beside the point. Even if I *could* have children, I don't see why they should miss a world of which they were never a part. If I had a child, I'd want it surrounded by the very best people. I wouldn't care if they were from your class or the Ashtons'. It would make no difference."

He noticed she didn't say "our" class. She spoke as if she stood apart, and perhaps she did. He shook his head in wonder. "How long have you held these opinions?"

She thought for a moment and then laughed. "Since I was consigned to oblivion by my peers."

As he laughed with her, he realized he was happy. Happier than he ever remembered being. It didn't make sense. What was it about this one woman that moved him so? He'd met amazing women before but everything in him, every fiber of his being, shouted out *this one*. This *woman and no other*.

At last, the carriage drew to a halt. The darkening sky would deter many from venturing out this afternoon, but he welcomed the chance to escape to less confined quarters. When Fran saw the encroaching clouds, she opted to leave her parasol, *the* parasol, behind. By the time they reached the bridge over the Serpentine, the air had taken on a distinct chill. He removed his morning coat and draped it over her shoulders. Nodding her thanks, she pulled the front tighter across her chest.

The graceful hump of the bridge afforded them a splendid view of Kensington Palace. As she looked out across the water, she rubbed her cheek against the black broadcloth and silk lapels of his coat. She probably didn't know what she'd done. She certainly didn't realize he'd seen it.

"Earlier you called yourself a victim of your own choices," he said. "What sort of victim does that make me?"

She looked at him with her head tilted to one side, lips pressed together in sober consideration. The sight made him prickle with sexual longing.

"I already told you. You, my friend, are a victim of your own desires."

During their ride the other day, she'd said that if money were not the overriding desire of his life, he could make his own choices. He'd experienced a rush of emotion that was not quite anger. It came back to him now, but he still couldn't identify the feeling.

A sense of inevitability hung in the air.

He took a step toward her. "Money is not my overriding desire."

He understood himself at the same time she did.

Comprehension dawned in her eyes, yet she didn't back away. "Isn't it?"

A stray lock of hair, caught by the breeze, grazed her forehead. He tucked it beneath the brim of her hat. Not because it needed it. Just to touch her. He ached to kiss the skin in the hollow where her neck curved into her shoulder. Would she let him do that? He wanted so much, but meant to allow himself so little.

Testing her, he moved closer. But she stayed still, waiting for him, the air around her charged. Her body beckoned his, even with an inch of space between them. God, what was he doing? What were *they* doing? Where was her blasted parasol when they needed it?

He leaned in and gently, tentatively, he brushed her lips with his own. They hardly touched, but he felt the shock of it, the rousing of his body, a faint tingling everywhere just beneath his skin.

This close, she flooded his senses. She smelled of something floral. Perfume but fainter. Soap, perhaps. The soft plumpness of her lips cushioned his. Her wistful sigh was cool as her mouth opened to him. She tasted sweet, like wine. As small as she was, he had to lean down to kiss her, but it was easier than he'd imagined because she reached up to meet him.

Her perpetual composure vanished as he touched her tongue with his, and she came alive in his arms. He pressed against her until every part of him came alive, too. She belonged with him. She excited him, made him happy, full. This was as it should be. This was right.

This was *not* right.

She was, however technically, a married woman. Worse, she was Mrs. Edward Thorne. Like a drunken foul-mouthed interloper at a private party, the name invaded his mind and refused to depart. He couldn't ignore the loud clamor of his conscience.

He broke the kiss and stepped away so abruptly that she stumbled back. They stared at each other, their breaths fast and uneven. She looked beautiful and horrified all at once. Her hand shook as she pressed it to lips still rosy from his kiss.

"Fran, I'm sorry."

The light in her guttered and went out. She looked so stricken that he reached for her.

She blanched, her gaze fixing on his outstretched hand. Oh God, he'd ruined this. Ruined everything. How could he have forgotten what was at stake? Her freedom. All she'd ever wanted.

His heart seemed to shiver inside him as she spoke, voice trembling. "Let's go back."

If only that were possible.

Francesca hurried away from the bridge, James following close behind. A thousand imaginary eyes watched. It didn't matter that she saw only one other person, a gentleman walking a dog in the distance. Her face always displayed what she felt, and surely her guilt had wrought a permanent change. Anyone who looked at her now and for the rest of her life would know she'd lost her mind—and what little remained of the high ground—in the middle of Hyde Park. And at a time when she needed to behave like a paragon of virtue. If Edward ever found out . . .

If she hadn't feared making even more of a spectacle of herself, she would have run back to the coach. Even so, she reached it more quickly than she would have thought possible. The dim interior provided no sanctuary, however. Being alone with James in close confinement was worse than if they'd stayed on the bridge, except no one could see them. Yes, a married lady could venture out in public in the company of a gentleman not her husband, but even if no one had seen them kiss, it *had* happened, and awareness would thrum in the air around them. People would sense it.

She'd never had trouble meeting his eyes before, but as the vehicle lurched into motion, the best she managed was his nose.

"I don't know what to say." He spoke quietly, but after so long a silence, she jumped.

"It doesn't matter." A preposterous lie, but if they didn't talk about it, she could at least *try* to pretend it hadn't happened.

"It does," he said, expression grim. "It matters."

She wanted to cry, wanted to burst into noisy tears as she had on the day he first came. They gathered in the back of her throat, but she refused to let them out. She clenched her hands into fists and pressed them against her skirts. Her knuckles turned pale from the effort and she focused on the subtle progression from pink to stark white.

"Fran."

How had the silly nickname he'd given her when they were all but strangers turned into an endearment? She really had gone mad. His hand, so much larger and darker than hers, appeared and covered one of her fists. Gently but firmly, he uncurled her fingers.

"Well, this is just typical of me. Of all the misguided, inept—" Words failed her and she snatched her hand away.

"It was my fault."

How conventional of him, how like him, to try to take all the blame. "No, it wasn't, or at least not all of it." Though she hadn't planned that kiss, part of her had hoped it might happen. She'd known the right thing to do, but instead of taking the prudent course and telling him she wouldn't continue to spend time alone in his company, she'd courted disaster. Publicly, where anyone might see.

Stupid, stupid girl.

"No," he agreed. "Perhaps not all of it, but I wish you would stop berating yourself. It won't help." He bent forward, trying to place himself in her line of sight. "Today was probably one of the oddest days of my life, but . . . the thing is, it was one of the best, too."

That struck her as a thoroughly absurd thing to say. She had to look at him now, if only to ensure his sincerity. She saw serious gray eyes, the sort that invited trust. "One of the best? Today?"

"Is that so difficult to believe?" He took her hand back and must have thought it cold, because he started to chafe it. "I think we're becoming friends and that makes me happy. *You* make me happy." The admission clearly made him uncomfortable because he released her and leaned back in his seat. "I'm only sorry I've confused things because I can't control myself."

The lightness was back in his voice, and she responded automatically to his teasing tone. "Ha. You never seemed to have any trouble before today."

"Be that as it may, I don't want to lose our friendship. It's becoming too . . . necessary."

It was the same for her. Leaving Edward had shown her how few true friends she had. Her relationship with James, flimsy and precarious though it was, had somehow become precious. "We can forget about all this, can't we?" she asked.

He only smiled, but she'd take what she could get.

CHAPTER TEN

James knew he was dreaming because Fran was naked. Her dark hair spilled over her breasts. Her skin felt warm and soft, her hands firm as she took hold of him. He pushed her back on the bed until she laid spread out before him, completely vulnerable, totally exposed. When he covered her, she whispered wickedness in his ear and begged him to take her.

But something was wrong; he couldn't see properly. Though he rubbed his eyes with the backs of his hands to clear them, her features shimmered like heat on the desert. Freckles dotted her cheeks—he remembered them from before—but he couldn't tell if her skin was freckled anywhere else or make out the exact shape of her breasts and the color tipping them. Squinting, he tried to bring her into focus. When he reached out, she slipped away, dissolving into the gloom.

He ached with unfulfilled desire, but worse was the loneliness pressing in from all sides as if to crush him.

Someone—not Fran—put a hand on his shoulder and shook him. "Come on, sir, on your feet."

He wasn't alone after all. James opened his eyes, catching the exasperation in Stephens's expression a second before he schooled it into more subservient lines. If his valet had resorted to jostling his shoulder, he'd probably been trying to wake him for some time. He wasn't usually so forceful.

"Is there an emergency?" James said, his voice a slurred and sleepy mumble.

Stephens crossed to the window and opened the heavy drapes. "No, sir."

James sat up and swung his legs over the side of the bed—a feat of exertion of which he immediately repented—and winced into bright sunlight. "What time is it?"

"Almost noon, sir. You told me to wake you at nine."

"Then why didn't you?"

"I tried, sir, but you refused to rise and insisted I quit the room. You used very strong language, if I may take the liberty of saying so."

James groaned remembering some of his more colorful epithets. Dimly, he recalled throwing something as well. "Sorry about that, Stephens."

"It's quite all right, sir. Will you be requiring a bath?"

"Yes. Yes, thank you."

Stephens helped him into a silk robe and disappeared into the adjoining room.

James staggered over to the window and peered out. Another lovely June day. A pity he felt like death warmed up. He'd had a rotten night's sleep, hence his reluctance to surface from his pit. When he slept, erotic fancies plagued his dreams. When he woke, he suffered agonies of guilt. Why were human beings irresistibly drawn to forbidden fruit? Despite his remorse afterward, he looked forward to those dreams every night.

Since kissing Fran on the bridge three weeks ago, he'd censored his waking thoughts ruthlessly. Sometimes he even managed to convince himself that, as she said, it was a moment of madness, an aberration they could both forget, and that all he felt was friendship. But the truth surfaced in his dreams.

In the early hours of that first morning, he'd woken with a powerful erection. Still half asleep, he'd given in and used his hands, imagining all the while that it was her touching him.

Then the guilt had come.

"Your bath is ready, sir."

He hadn't registered the sound of running water issuing from the other room. Now Stephens stood in the doorway, a large white towel slung over one arm.

"Are you quite well, sir?"

Not really, no. "Thank you, yes. You can go now. I'll ring when I need you."

Alone again, he disrobed and went into the bathroom. He sank into the hot water and allowed the warmth to soak through to his bones.

Of course, as soon as he relaxed his guard, he remembered her kiss. Suppressed but always close to the surface, the thought bobbed up into the light. He closed his eyes and tried to wipe his mind clean.

Fantasizing about other men's wives was contemptible behavior. But fantasizing about Fran in particular was an act of out-and-out betrayal. He would not cuckold his friend, even in this small, secret way.

In the weeks since their day together, he'd tried avoiding her, sending flowers and several teasing notes to offset the neglect. She always responded in the same light, friendly tone, but never invited him to call. Sensible of her, yet he missed their talks, and longed for her company more than he'd thought possible.

A fresh bar of soap rested in a china dish just within reach. He used it to make a thick lather. All the time he scrubbed himself, his mind churned.

It wasn't much of a marriage. She wasn't *really* Thorne's wife, not anymore. It was all over. The small matter of their impending divorce would sweep away anything remaining. Thorne didn't even want her; he had Mrs. Kirkpatrick at his beck and call. Perhaps he'd understand.

James stopped scrubbing. Of all the infantile rubbish! He laughed out loud, the harsh sound echoing in the empty bathroom. What a fool he was at times. If there was anything less likely than Thorne clapping him on the back and offering his blessing, he couldn't think of it. How absurd.

He rinsed the last of the soap away and rang for Stephens.

James stood stiff as a post while the valet dressed him, fussing with the wings of his shirt for what seemed an excessive length of time. Once they'd finished, he'd walk to Curzon Street. If he and Thorne had a chance to talk like the old days, perhaps it would strengthen his resolve.

At the very least, it was worth a try.

At one time, the house on Curzon Street had felt like a second home to James. It always reminded him of summer holidays when he and Thorne, both home from Rugby, came and went from one another's houses continually. As a consequence of those long-ago days, he felt comfortable there and knew his way around.

"Still here, Beasley," he said, when the butler met him at the door. "You've been about longer than I have."

"A pleasure to see you again, Mr. Standish. Mr. Thorne just returned from luncheon at his club. He'll be down directly, if you care to wait."

"Thank you." James took the small liberty of showing himself into the family parlor, a more comfortable place to wait than the large front parlor usually reserved for guests.

He was already all the way inside by the time he noticed Mrs. Kirkpatrick sitting in a chair beneath a potted palm. Glancing up from her book, she noticed him at about the same time.

She rose abruptly. "Oh, it's you. This is a surprise." Coming from a notorious courtesan, it struck him as an awkward salutation.

"Forgive me, no one told me you were here or I would never have disturbed you." No one would've needed to tell him anything if he'd allowed Beasley to show him into the proper room. He should know better by now.

"Oh, not at all. I arrived only a few minutes ago. I came from in there." She waved her book in the direction of the door nearest her, which he knew led into the library.

"Well, again, I apologize."

"Not at all," she repeated. Recovering her poise, she pulled the bell rope that dangled to one side of the mantelpiece. "I think tea is in order."

He hadn't expected to find himself tête-à-tête with Thorne's mistress, but he had to admit to feeling curious about her. What must old Mrs. Thorne think of her son setting up his mistress in the family's main London residence? Perhaps she didn't know. Come to think of it, did Fran?

Once he'd taken a seat, they began with the usual inanities, inquiring after one another's health, commenting on the excellence of the weather and finishing with a short debate on the chances of rain in the next few days. During these preliminaries two housemaids arrived, one laden with a tea tray and the other carrying a platter of sandwiches and such. He waited while his hostess directed their arrangement, dismissed the servants, and commenced pouring.

Having exhausted the weather as a topic, he cast about for another. "I was just thinking about when I used to come here as a boy."

"I forget you've known Mr. Thorne so long."

"Things were very different when Mr. Thorne the elder lived here."

"He never talks about his father. What was he like?" She seemed genuinely interested. And why not? Thorne kept her, but it didn't necessarily follow that all their dealings must be mercenary. He saw no reason why a true attachment might not exist between them.

Even so, he worried what Thorne would think of their discussion. Too late now.

"He was a gentleman, decent and very steady." Aunt Miriam used to call him "that dull dog," but James had secretly adored him. He'd been kind, patient, and interested to hear what his son's young friend had to say.

Mrs. Kirkpatrick proffered the platter of sandwiches. "They were not very alike then?"

He coughed discreetly as the sip of tea he'd been about to swallow threatened to choke him. "There are very few men like the elder Mr. Thorne."

The younger Mr. Thorne chose that moment to stride in. He made straight for the food, bypassing the dainty sandwiches and proceeding directly to the cream cakes. Luncheon at his club hadn't satisfied, it would seem. "Hullo, you two. What an interesting picture. Been plotting, have you?"

"Not at all, my dear." She stood and straightened her skirts. "In fact, now you're here and Mr. Standish is no longer bereft of company, I intend to go out."

"Shopping on Bond Street again?"

Her lips thinned in a tight smile. "You know me so well."

She swept out, eyes flashing, her exit so abrupt James hadn't the chance to bid her farewell. He wasn't sure exactly what he'd walked in on, but it reminded him of his aunt and late uncle's long-ago marital spats.

"She's magnificent when she's in a temper," Thorne said. He picked up a sandwich and eyed it with distaste. "Fancy a game of billiards?"

Actually, James did.

The billiards room served as one of the few places in the Curzon Street house, the others being the smoking room and the study, to have escaped Thorne's mother's improvements. Instead of the cluttered floral paper that proliferated elsewhere, the walls were painted a calming olive green. The only embellishments consisted of a few framed prints hung in neat rows, all depicting gentlemen on horseback or playing cricket or other manly pursuits. A massive, green baize–covered billiards table dominated the space. James breathed in the familiar scent of old cigar smoke and a more pungent odor—the beeswax polish responsible for the high shine of the oak paneling.

They agreed on a short bout for five hundred points. While Thorne set up the game, James selected a cue from the rack on the wall. "Remember how desperate we used to be to get in here? Your father never allowed it. He didn't approve of young boys playing billiards."

"There were a lot of things of which my father didn't approve."

Thorne took aim and sent an ivory cue ball careering down the table. It rebounded, gradually slowing until it came to a stop in baulk.

"But you remember him fondly?" James asked, then took his shot.

"Of course."

Thorne's ball, only distinguishable from James's by a single black dot, had stopped nearer the cushion, which meant Thorne could choose whether to go first or second. He stepped out of the way.

James positioned his cue and aimed for the red object ball. With a satisfying crack, he sent it shooting down the table. He lined up another shot, and then another, always taking care not to pot Thorne's red.

"I'm only sorry he died so soon." Thorne leaned against the mantel as he jotted down the scores. "I could use his advice. Our father-son chats didn't prepare me for my current situation."

James missed his shot completely and yielded his place. He watched as Thorne's cue ball cannoned off one red and into another.

"It's no good asking myself what Father would do in this situation. The truth is he never would have let it come to this. When I think how disappointed in me he'd be—" Thorne hit the cue ball far too hard and potted James's red. With only one left on the table, he spent the next few minutes making low-scoring hits, until he finally missed altogether.

James took his turn, using the need to concentrate as an excuse to remain silent. Old Mr. Thorne *would* disapprove of his son's conduct, but it seemed churlish to say so.

Thorne obliged him in his wish for quiet, waiting until his own turn before continuing the conversation. "An estranged wife off doing God knows what with God knows who." For a while, the only sound was the staccato clack of each collision as he scored several times in quick succession. "Not to mention a mistress who's a notorious whore. All of that's definitely worth a caning or at the very least a stern lecture."

The white shot into the air and ricocheted off a framed picture of two men fishing. Thorne cursed.

Normally, James would take the opportunity to crow over an opponent who made a shot that bad, but he doubted Thorne would react well in his current mood. "Mrs. Kirkpatrick seems lovely," he said instead. "Today was the first time I've had occasion to talk with her." He took his time positioning his cue. So far, he'd played with greater consistency than his opponent, but Thorne was master of the flashier shots.

"Lovely?" Thorne mused. "I don't know about that. Honest, perhaps. Certainly voracious."

The ideal woman, then. James had never understood Thorne's contradictory attitude toward women. "Do you ever . . . forgive me, but do you ever miss Francesca?"

Thorne looked blank, and then roared with laughter. "Of course not. How could I? The woman's a monster."

James fouled the shot, pocketing his own ball without hitting anything.

Thorne let out a long whistle. "Steady on!"

"A monster?" James leaned on his cue, in part to stop himself brandishing it like a quarterstaff. "Don't you think that's a bit strong?"

"Well, what would you call it when a woman of her station plays the harlot?" Thorne's ball hit James's, then the side, and finally ricocheted until it hit the red again. "One expects that sort of vulgarity from someone like Virginia. She was an actress when I met her, and before that I'm sure she kept a very clean tavern."

James had stood meekly by while he heard Fran called a monster and a harlot, but "vulgar" was an insult too far. He held on tight to his cue, fighting a sudden urge to break it over Thorne's thick head. Only the knowledge that he'd applied that very word to her himself stayed his hand. He ought to brain himself. Perhaps she was a tad vulgar on occasion, but her stubborn idealism, even when it proved monumentally inconvenient for anyone who came in contact with her, was less crass than Thorne installing his mistress in their marital home.

"If your assessment of Mrs. Kirkpatrick's past life is accurate, then surely she is to be congratulated for rising so far," James said when he trusted himself to speak.

Better to steer the conversation toward calmer waters. After all, he'd hoped to establish common ground with Thorne so that he could *avoid* further entanglement with Fran. At this rate, he'd end by declaring himself her champion.

"She hasn't risen so far," Thorne said, scoring point after point. "She still makes her living lying on her back."

James's turn. He took aim.

"Bloody hell, Standish, I thought you had your eye on Francesca. Perhaps it was Virginia all along."

James froze. Fortunately, he'd already hunched over to take his shot. He kept his head down and made a show of concentrating, just about managing to hit the cue ball. But with an aim so haphazard it sailed past both object balls, rebounding off one of the cushions. "What *are* you talking about?"

"You've been spending quite a bit of time with my dearly beloved spouse, that's all."

"Yes, I have, and at your request. Did you or did you not tell me your wife was in need of a friend?" He potted a red, scoring ten points.

"I never asked you to take her to the park."

Under cover of lining up his next shot, James tried to think. Hyde Park was a public place. Anyone might have seen him kiss Fran. He'd been a bloody fool.

"I commend your patience," Thorne said. "She was always a lamentable horsewoman."

Thank God. He meant the ride on Rotten Row, not the walk to the bridge.

"That she is," James agreed. "But I don't mind if it means being seen out and about with an attractive married woman."

Thorne's eyebrows went up, but he didn't say anything.

James decided to press forward. "As it happens, I'm fixed on another lady entirely." His cue ball glided uselessly past the red. He stood back from the table. They both stood just a few points shy of five hundred.

"Oh?" Thorne stepped forward. "Who?"

"Miss Sylvia Randle."

"Don't know her."

"She just made her debut."

Thorne gave another long whistle. "Well, well. James Standish and a respectable lady. This is a surprise. I thought lonely widows were your usual line. Can that be wedding bells I hear?"

"If my aunt has her way."

"Dear old Aunt Miriam. Be careful, though. Remember what Cervantes said. Marriage is a noose."

Funny, Fran says the same thing. “Ah, but it’s a noose you may soon escape.”

It seemed the worst danger had passed. Thorne showed no sign of calling him out. “Tricky business, divorce,” he said, as he prepared a cannon shot. “There’s more to it than I thought. In order to win my case, I’m forced to amass evidence of Francesca’s sins and open them up for public scrutiny. If I succeed in hanging on to my wife, her reputation will have become even more unsavory than it is now.”

If Thorne said much more, James would find himself in the unenviable position of having to betray someone. If he passed on what he heard to Fran, Thorne would never forgive him. On the other hand, if he kept something this important from her, she’d never be free the way she wanted, and she might lose that zealous light from her eyes. Then he’d never forgive himself.

He could hardly say that to Thorne, so he said the next best thing. “Are you going to take that shot or am I to stand here all day twiddling my cue?”

“Your reluctance to take sides is duly noted.” Thorne’s cue ball kissed one red and cannoned into another. “I sympathize, but you do realize you won’t be able to keep it up forever. Things are bound to get nasty. There’ll come a day when a line will be drawn and you’ll have to choose whether to cross.”

“I hope you’re wrong,” James said, and perhaps that was admission enough that his allegiance had shifted. A month ago, he would have answered differently. A man had a right to expect absolute fidelity from his wife, didn’t he? Marital disputes should be kept private, shouldn’t they? Somehow the world had turned somersaults underneath his feet and he hadn’t noticed.

“You hope I’m wrong, but you know I’m not.” Thorne smiled and potted the red. The game was his.

CHAPTER ELEVEN

Economy be damned, one simply couldn't appear at one's first ball in months wearing last year's gown.

Consequently, Francesca left her final fitting at the couturiers the happy owner of a new dress, her pleasure only slightly diluted by guilt. She intended to finish the ensemble with items she already owned. Her lace fan would do very well, and she had a cloak and shoes she thought would suit. Even so, she could ill afford the expense.

She hardly knew James's aunt, so the invitation had come as a complete surprise. She had a shrewd idea she'd been included because of the scandal attached to her name, but as she no longer received invitations from the respectable old guard, and as the flow of invitations of *any* sort had slowed to a pathetic trickle, she felt bound to go where she was asked. It wouldn't do her any good to sit at home every night alone.

Besides, she might see James.

Amid a mob of respectable guests, she'd allow herself the luxury of his company. The silly notes he'd sent kept her spirits up, but she didn't dare invite him to call, not after Hyde Park. At the ball, they wouldn't dance. They might not even speak. A look, perhaps the touch of his hand atop her glove, was all she dared risk.

The business of the dress settled, she wandered along the busy street, enjoying the warmth of the sun on her back. With no particular plan in mind, she lingered outside a milliner's in whose window display she saw a mass of ribbon twisted together to form a rainbow. She had no intention of buying anything, but she could still imagine what she might choose if she had the money to waste. As she debated the merits of the Venetian red ribbon versus the cherry, she noticed a familiar someone reflected in the glass. She turned at once, her heart beating a little faster.

"Hello, Francesca." Tommy Trafford stepped forward and shook her by the hand. He greeted everyone with the same enthusiastic affability, but today she felt he might lift her off her feet as he pumped her arm up and down.

"Hello, Tommy." Pleased as she was to see him again after almost a year, she had no wish to find herself the subject of gossip at everybody's afternoon calls. Perhaps he didn't know their past relationship was the subject of such fevered speculation.

"How are you?" he asked. "You look well."

She reclaimed her hand with what she hoped was a reassuring smile. "I am. It's good to see you."

Beyond him she saw a gentleman. He glanced away when he caught her looking, or maybe she'd turned deranged and he'd never truly been looking at them in the first place. Either way, the small incident made her feel even more conspicuous.

She nodded in the direction of the Royal Arcade. "Shall we walk?"

Tommy offered his arm.

"I'm glad we bumped into one another," she said after they'd only gone a yard or two. "I've wanted to talk to you for a while now, but it's difficult. I kept hoping I could keep you out of it."

"The rumors are true, then? You're really seeking a divorce?"

This wasn't the sort of conversation one should conduct navigating a crowd—or indeed doing anything—on a public thoroughfare. But if they met at her home, people would call it an assignation. And if she spoke through her lawyer, she might as well announce Tommy her co-respondent and save Edward the bother. She didn't know the right way to go about this, if there was such a thing, so she led him to a bench on the far side of the street.

"Yes, it's true," she said when they'd both sat down. "I intend to get a divorce."

He looked past her toward Piccadilly, as though he might sprint off at any moment. He wouldn't of course. Tommy wasn't the sort to leave a lady in the lurch.

"I think it only fair to tell you, Edward threatened to name you as my lover."

He shook his head, his earlier ebullience crushed. "I see. I suppose it's understandable."

And he'd looked so pleased to see her, too, but then he couldn't have expected tidings such as these.

"What will you do?"

She told him what she'd been telling everyone. "I'm sorry, but I can't give up the divorce. I won't."

The silence lengthened. A bee droned nearby. And, more distant, she heard the steady clopping of horse hooves, the rattle of carriage wheels, and the muted rumble of a multitude of conversations. Yet still Tommy said nothing.

If Edward identified him, his name would appear in the papers. People would gossip and talk. Though she hated to cause him even that much pain, as a single gentleman, the long-term damage to his standing would be limited. The fuss would die down and his life would go on much as before.

"I understand," he said and covered her hand, which lay on the seat between them, with his own. "I'm still your friend and I always will be."

She wouldn't pull away despite the risk. It seemed too cruel after what he'd just said. "Thank you. Please know I will always be grateful."

She wanted to say more, but for the second time she felt eyes on her. The sense of someone watching was so strong her skin tingled. She looked up expecting to see the unknown man from earlier.

James stood on the opposite side of the street, his face grim as a thundercloud. She'd never seen him without a smile. She'd never seen him anything other than glad to see her. Now his lips pressed together to form a thin line. His brow hung low over cold, empty eyes.

So this was what anger looked like on James Standish.

She stood as he crossed the street toward her.

"*Mrs.* Thorne," he said, his voice so devoid of warmth she barely recognized it.

"*Mr.* Standish." She couldn't help mimicking his tone, and his expression darkened even further, something she wouldn't have dreamed possible. Her cheeks turned hot even though she had no reason to blush. "May I present Mr. Trafford?"

He transferred the full force of his glare to poor Tommy. "I don't think so."

When James turned his back, the last fraying thread of her temper snapped. "Just a moment, Mr. Standish."

He stopped and went rigid, as though he'd hit a glass wall. Turning again, he fixed her with a withering look, no doubt about to deliver a blazing set-down. But she wasn't of a humor to listen.

With deliberate rudeness, she switched her attention back to Tommy. "Mr. Trafford, forgive me but I have one or two important matters to discuss with Mr. Standish."

Tommy, bless his heart, searched her face. "Are you quite sure?"

"You mustn't worry. I'm safe with Mr. Standish even if he *is* behaving like an absolute blockhead."

James stiffened.

Tommy looked nervously from her to James and back again, so she tried to reassure him with a smile. Apparently satisfied, he nodded. "It was a pleasure seeing you again," he told her and bowed.

James watched him go, arms folded across his chest. "What a touching scene."

She covered the ground between them until they stood mere inches apart. "Do you have any idea how obnoxious you're being? That was mortifying." In the middle of Bond Street, she dared not raise her voice, but she only just restrained herself from jabbing at him with an accusing finger.

"My regrets, ma'am," he said through clenched teeth. He parodied apology, but they both understood what he meant. He regretted only that she'd lost his respect through her apparent licentiousness. She dreaded to think what he'd say if they were alone. "Now, if you will forgive me, I find myself with a yearning for less *promiscuous* company."

She'd never heard the word "promiscuous" used *that* way before. She seized his arm, no longer caring how it might look to anyone passing by. "Now listen to me, you half-wit. What I ought to do now is storm off in high dudgeon. I'm sure it would feel liberating right up until the point when it started feeling terrible. But I'm not going to do it. Do you know why? It's because one of us has to maintain a cool head and, judging by your conduct so far, that responsibility is mine. You don't deserve to be told this after your performance but I'm going to say it anyway."

She pushed a stray lock of hair out of her eyes. "I met Mr. Trafford completely by chance just now. There is nothing between us except friendship. As to what may or may not have occurred between myself and Tommy in the past, it's none of your business, just as your intimate relations are none of *my* business. While we're on the subject, I'd be willing to wager you've more than one illicit union buried in the shallow grave of *your* past, so you can stop being such an old woman."

He looked like he wanted to speak, but she couldn't stop now. Even if Edward appeared, notebook in hand, and started to write down every word she said. "I'd also like to remind you that just a few short weeks ago, you told me we were friends. What's more, I believed you. Now I want you to think, Jemmy. Think really hard about everything you know about me, about the sort of woman I am." She peered at him. "Are you thinking?"

He opened his mouth, but she shook her head. "You've said quite enough for one morning. Just nod."

He nodded.

"Good. Now tell me, am I telling the truth?"

She waited. Instead of speaking, he sat down on the bench with the exhausted, traumatized air of someone who'd been taken unawares by footpads. She couldn't tell what he thought, but at least he'd stopped trying to escape. So much for the hoped-for immediate and resounding "yes." He just sat there looking at his feet.

She'd just begun to think of how this must look, about Edward and the need for circumspection, when James raised his head. "We need to talk."

It would have to do. "Yes, but not here."

A man and woman engaged in a blatant disagreement in the middle of Bond Street wouldn't fail to attract notice. Such a quarrel advertised an improper degree of familiarity, if not necessarily affection. It wasn't yet noon and she'd already publicly fraternized with two men not her blood relations.

"Where is your carriage?" he asked.

"I had to give it up." Admitting it shouldn't be painful. He knew her situation and that keeping a carriage was expensive. She'd shown uncharacteristic common sense when she'd decided to get rid of hers, but sometimes she worried if anything would be left once she'd stripped away all the trappings of class. "I came here in a cab," she added, defiant.

"We might take a stroll along Bruton Street to Berkeley Square."

When he failed to comment about the cab, the last of the heat died out of her anger. "Why there?" she asked. "It isn't exactly quiet."

He shook his head. "Because it's the right place."

Taking Fran to Berkeley Square was a stupid thing to do. Though much quieter than Bond Street, plenty of people milled about. The leafy plane trees provided shade, but only a modicum of privacy. They walked along one of the short paths that led to the center. In the very middle, surrounded by benches, stood a marble drinking fountain, on top of which posed a statue of a partially nude yet strangely shy-seeming nymph. They made for the nearest seat and sat on opposite ends.

"Why here?" she asked.

He followed the direction of her gaze toward the house where her aunt and uncle still lived. The associations must be painful. He'd been self-indulgent bringing her here, but this was where it had all started. More than a decade ago, he'd sat on one of these very benches and waited for Thorne, waited to meet the very suitable, very dull girl his friend planned to marry.

"I felt nostalgic," he said. "It seems to happen frequently these days." He didn't know how to proceed. He'd behaved like an idiot. After all his fine words about friendship, he'd acted like a jealous lover. Perhaps worse, he'd placed the very worst construction on what he'd seen without allowing her the chance to explain. As a mere friend, he probably didn't even merit an explanation. "I know I ought to apologize. And I will . . . but not yet."

"Are you still angry?"

Again, he envisioned her small white hand in Trafford's great paw. "I think I must be."

"But why? I explained. If you don't believe me, I see no point in my being here."

"It isn't that I don't believe you." He hesitated. Even his most intimate conversations took place in a cloud of obfuscation, until he barely understood himself. She lived her life outside the proprieties. She would never comprehend him unless he said plainly what was in his mind. "I don't know if I'm brave enough."

She frowned. Apparently, she still didn't understand.

He took a deep breath and tried again. "Your uncle's house is where it started, where we met. To be quite honest, at the time I barely noticed you. You've grown on me, I suppose."

"Like a fungus?" she suggested with the glimmerings of a smile.

For a man who prided himself on a certain facility with the English language, he was making a complete hash of this. It had to be the least romantic declaration any man ever made. "You were quiet," he explained. "And so badly dressed."

She started to laugh, then clapped a hand over her mouth to stifle it. "I'll have you know Aunt Helena was in charge of my wardrobe in those days. Anyway, I remember that day. You were rotten. So obviously bored until you noticed Helena's bosom, and even then—"

"Thank you, yes. I remember." Not one of his finer moments.

"And so you didn't like anything about me?"

Just her eyes. Leaf green and so very serious. "Until you laughed."

"I couldn't help it. One would think you'd never seen breasts before. And Helena hadn't a clue."

"Your eyes lit up," he went on. "And that's when I saw how beautiful you . . ." Not a good idea. "What I'm trying to say is that my initial disinclination has turned into a decided inclination. I like you. I feel an affection for you. A fondness."

He watched her face, usually so easy to read. For once, she gave nothing away. "And not because we're friends?"

"No," he admitted. "Not because of that. That's not what I mean."

It wasn't a small bench and she seemed very far away. He wanted to hold her hand. Unlike Trafford, he'd never had that honor. He'd helped her into carriages, and once he'd tried to chafe some warmth into her, but those weren't the same thing at all. "I want what happened between us on the Serpentine Bridge to happen again. I want more to happen."

"Oh." A single flat syllable, as indecipherable as her expression.

"I know—that is, we both know it can't happen. You aren't free and Thorne is my friend. He'd never forgive me."

For some reason, that earned him a smile.

"What are you thinking?" Usually, she'd have told him by now.

"I'm glad you're loyal to your friend, that's all."

"Do you see now why I behaved the way I did when I saw you with Trafford?"

"It was nothing."

He closed his eyes. "I know." If Trafford had been her lover once, it must be over now. She'd never entertain two men at once. "I'm sorry."

"Thank you for believing me," she said. "And thank you for being honest with me." Her arm twitched, and he thought she might reach across and take his hand. When she didn't, he tried to feel glad.

"Thank *you* for forgiving me. I behaved like an ass."

She dismissed his apology with a wave of her hand, her fury of twenty minutes ago forgotten. None of that mattered now. "What are we going to do?"

"When I saw you holding his hand, it was as though my field of vision shrank until all I could see was that one small spot where you touched. Any possibility of rational thought went up in smoke. My feelings are stronger than I realized."

She waited. No trace of her smile remained.

He *hated* this. "I think perhaps I shouldn't see you for a while."

"I'm invited to your aunt's ball." The sudden tremor in her voice made him feel like a monster.

"That doesn't matter. There'll be hundreds of people. It's being alone with you I can't bear."

She stood, her face pale. "I have to go. Don't," she added when he started to rise, too. "Please."

He reached for her, but she never saw. His hand fell useless to his side as he watched her walk away.

CHAPTER TWELVE

One had to admire Aunt Miriam's flair. She'd brought the ballroom, shrouded in dust sheets since Uncle Price's death almost twenty years ago, to vibrant life.

James had arrived early to help her receive. As they stood near the grand entrance, the lively strains of a mazurka filled the air. Three enormous Bohemian crystal chandeliers, newly fitted gas lamps ablaze, glimmered with reflected light. No doubt prompted by her love of intrigue, Miriam had ordered trellises erected to form secluded nooks in dim corners. Garlands of gardenias fresh from the hothouse weaved their way in and out of lattice work, festooning walls and even chair backs. The great French doors at the far end of the room stood open and lanterns, placed at intervals along the garden path, glowed with invitation.

James had smiled when he'd first seen the beckoning path. His aunt baited her traps with subtlety. But he didn't care if she got down on her knees and begged; he still wouldn't escort Miss Randle outside to take the air. Neither would he court one woman while in the grip of such strong feelings for another.

"Ah, Mr. and Mrs. Lytton," Miriam said. "It's been an age. We're so glad you came."

For a fraction of a second, James indulged himself in the forlorn hope that she spoke to a different Mr. and Mrs. Lytton, but no. Fran's uncle and aunt returned her greeting. Miriam's eyes twinkled with mischief, and with a sinking heart he realized he ought to have requested a copy of the guest list. More than that, he should have asked himself why. Why throw a ball now, after all these years?

Fran longed to see her relatives again, but not like this.

He schooled his features into a smile of polite welcome and stepped forward to welcome Lytton. "It's a pleasure to see you again, sir." They hadn't met since all this divorce business began. The elderly gentleman—he must be nearing eighty—appeared frail. Even with the help of an ornate gold-handled cane, his progress toward the nearest seat looked laborious. Mrs. Lytton, undeniably middle-aged now, still retained most of her beauty. She smiled civilly and followed her husband.

James hadn't seen Fran in over a week. Honor dictated he stay away. What a shame he hadn't considered his principles sooner. If he'd reined in his thoughts, if he'd controlled himself in Hyde Park, if he hadn't behaved like an imbecile when he'd seen her with Trafford, if he'd kept his mouth shut afterward, their tenuous friendship might not have fallen apart. So many ifs. He hated himself for each and every one, because tonight she was going to need a friend.

Thorne arrived about twenty minutes later, while James and his aunt still stood by the main doors welcoming people.

Miriam greeted him first. "Edward, my goodness, how handsome you've become. It's marvelous to see you." She didn't scruple to address him familiarly. She'd known him since he wore short trousers. She even allowed him to take her gloved hand in his.

"Ravishing as ever, Mrs. Price," Thorne said.

While they flirted, James spotted Mrs. Kirkpatrick standing just inside the door. Surely Miriam hadn't invited her? This must be Thorne's idea of a joke. The courtesan looked lovely as always, her auburn curls piled high and studded with diamonds. She wore her necklace again with its enormous stones. Impossible not to follow the line of the pendant to her impressive cleavage, so advantageously displayed by yet another plunging neckline.

Concentrate, you dolt.

As a rule, Thorne attended all the usual London events. Fran would expect to see him here, but the mistress?

"Ah, Standish. You remember Virginia?" Thorne drew her forward.

James hoped he concealed his dismay. "Yes, of course. It's a pleasure to see you again, Mrs. Kirkpatrick."

To his infinite surprise, Miriam beamed at her unexpected guest. "Welcome, my dear. I was so thrilled when I received your acceptance."

Not so unexpected then.

Thorne winked at him, clearly trying not to laugh.

"Thank you for inviting me, ma'am," Mrs. Kirkpatrick said, behaving with better grace than the rest of them had shown thus far.

"We're much obliged, ma'am." Laughing in earnest now, Thorne led his mistress into the first set.

It was past time for Miriam to mingle with her guests. Clearly, she'd been waiting for Mrs. Kirkpatrick. James ought to have anticipated something like this. He knew how she enjoyed throwing gladiators into the arena. Now she could step back and enjoy the carnage. As much as he longed to confront her, years of experience had taught him to keep his council and bide his time. He'd try to be on hand to greet Fran, but in the meantime, he needed a glass of champagne or he wouldn't make it through the evening with his sanity intact.

He offered Miriam his arm.

"That young scamp," she said as she took it. "He's isn't embarrassed in the least. He paraded that strumpet in here as bold as you please. I must say I admire the way he carries things off. This is even better than I bargained."

* * *

Edward Thorne took a large gulp of Mrs. Price's excellent champagne. He stood amid the glister, wishing himself in one of the low taverns he frequented in London's less rarefied districts. Once, centuries ago, he would have cared about the splendor of the ballroom. A budding Aesthetic, he'd believed in beauty. Now, he didn't see the point. Whenever he chanced to remember what a romantic he'd been as a youth, he felt only a vague sense of embarrassment.

"Thorne."

Ah, he knew that voice. As it happened, he was in just the right humor for a chat with an old friend. "It was kind of Mrs. Price to include the Lyttons, wasn't it?"

Standish didn't even crack a smile. "Kind? I think we both know kindness had nothing to do with it. How will they react when they see Francesca?"

Personally, he couldn't wait to find out. If his wife would only do the right thing and give in gracefully, her family would welcome her back into the fold. Tonight's scrape was one of her own making. "I don't suppose they'll like it."

"It's almost as bad as you turning up with Mrs. Kirkpatrick." No mistaking the reproof in Standish's tone. Had he always been such a moralizer?

"I couldn't disappoint Mrs. Price. She so enjoys a good joke."

"A joke, is it?" Standish fairly bristled with indignation. "This one seems unusually cruel."

A spark of guilt struggled for life, but Edward smothered it. Standish sympathized with Francesca because he wanted to sleep with her. Perhaps he'd done so already. "Concerned about my wife's feelings, are you?"

His old friend's lip curled with something very like disgust. "One of us needs to be."

Edward had to smile at that. *To hell with you and your morals, you steaming hypocrite. Take my wife to bed, then. I'll eviscerate the pair of you in court.*

Beyond the archway where they stood, the younger set took to the floor, neatly matched, whirling past in a giddy waltz. Bovine ingénues and their credulous mates, all of them heedless, like animals lined up for slaughter—the slaughter of innocence.

"You know, you might consider Mrs. Kirkpatrick's feelings in all this. I suppose you're too busy using her to taunt your wife."

He heard Standish's words, but his attention had wandered. Two women, one much older than the other, stood in the grand entrance. He couldn't stop looking at the younger lady. Her creamy white skin and plump lips reminded him of a painting of Eurydice he'd once seen. Sparkling gold lace draped the skirt of her champagne-colored gown. *She* sparkled too, a glittering golden lady.

"Thorne, are you listening?"

"No. Who's that just arriving?"

Standish looked. "Sylvia Randle and her mother."

"That's Sylvia Randle?" This goddess was the lady about whom Standish had spoken in such lukewarm terms? He'd always had execrable taste in women. What an appalling waste. If Edward had met her first . . .

But it wouldn't have mattered. A long list of insurmountable obstacles stood between him and thc newest object of his desire, her connection to Standish the very last item. A not-quite-divorced man with an unsavory reputation had no business lusting after an innocent. He'd fallen far in recent years, but even he wouldn't debauch an unmarried girl.

"Congratulations," he said, but he didn't mean it.

* * *

"Now be sure you don't fill in your whole dance card at once. You never know who might arrive late. It's best to leave a set or two empty, just in case."

As they wove their way through the crowd toward two vacant chairs, Sylvia listened to her Mama recite an overwhelming catalogue of instructions. Like Flaubert—not that Mama would have even heard of him—she believed that God resided in the details.

"Do remember to smile, dear. Gentlemen prefer ladies of cheerful temperament. And try not to talk overmuch. Gentlemen appreciate a serene companion. Oh, but don't be dull either. One must strike the perfect balance between dullness and liveliness."

Miraculously, the seats were still vacant by the time they reached them. Mama's gentle squeeze on Sylvia's arm meant "wait," and so Sylvia stood still, like a statue unveiled. The inscription on the plinth would read HEIRESS FOR SALE.

"Remember not to favor any one gentleman too plainly," Mama whispered as they sat down. "We wouldn't want people to talk, would we?"

A ring of male acquaintances surrounded them, each man eager to persuade Sylvia to write his name on her card next to a waltz or a schottische.

"Do not dance with Mr. Hepplethwaite, dearest. He is overly fond of champagne and will likely trip over your train. Tell him you are already engaged to dance or, if you are free, say you do not know the steps. Oh, my love, Mr. Standish is smiling at you. Smile. Remember to smile."

But she didn't feel like smiling. Her head ached and she longed for quiet.

"How singular Mrs. Price is in her choice of guests." Her mother stared rudely at the gentleman with Mr. Standish.

Sylvia had been feeling so out of sorts that she'd barely noticed her surroundings but, at her mother's words, she glanced up, and there *he* was. The man from the park—Edward Thorne—staring back at her with peculiar intensity. No man had ever looked at her that way. With such soulful, serious eyes.

"Who is he?" she asked.

"He's Mr. Thorne, but I don't suppose that means a great deal to you. Suffice to say, for him, no smile is required."

Actually, Sylvia had spent the last few weeks learning all she could about him. It never ceased to amaze her what people would say in her presence when they presumed her otherwise occupied. She found a facade of innocent inattention worked best if her curiosity on a subject needed satisfying. When she'd stare out a window or sit quietly in a corner with her embroidery, people behaved as though she were blind, deaf, and dumb.

She'd heard all about Edward Thorne, and she'd read about him in the day-old newspapers she smuggled into her room. The caricatures never did anyone any justice, but Mr. Thorne's beauty still shocked her. How could someone as shining, as golden as he, possess such a wicked heart? What a pity. And, an even greater pity, Mama would never permit her to talk with him, the first genuine rake she'd ever seen.

"James, come and say hello to Sylvia. You too, Mr. Thorne," Mrs. Price said as she swooped in from goodness knows where. Mama clutched Sylvia's hand, her customary composure undone by the sight of Mr. Thorne, in step with Mr. Standish, coming straight toward them. She wouldn't dare risk offending Mrs. Price by refusing the introduction.

"Mrs. Randle, Miss Randle." Mr. Standish bowed. "It's lovely to see you again."

They rose and returned his greeting.

"Mrs. Randle, Miss Randle," Mrs. Price said. "May I present Mr. Edward Thorne, a very dear friend of the family? Mr. Thorne, this is Mrs. Randle and her beautiful daughter."

Mama's lips went so thin they threatened to vanish altogether. Mrs. Price smiled, as though she hadn't done an extraordinary thing when she'd introduced a cad to a debutante, and vanished into the crowd.

As for Mr. Thorne, his behavior came as something of a disappointment. He bowed and murmured the usual platitudes, but otherwise stayed silent. He might at least say something shocking to brighten up her evening. At least his looks bore up under closer scrutiny. His eyes shone the deepest blue she'd ever seen. She knew, because he never moved them from her face. With his fair hair flopping over his forehead in apparent disarray, he resembled her idea of a poet or perhaps an artist starving in a garret somewhere. Naturally she hadn't any personal experience with either.

Mr. Standish never stared, and she'd always liked that reserve; he didn't pester her the way other men did. "I hope you're able to reserve me a set, Miss Randle," he said, as if he didn't mind very much either way.

She put him down for one of the waltzes. If she had to dance holding on to the same person for an entire set, she'd rather it was with Mr. Standish. She doubted he'd hold her too tightly as some of the men did, and as a graceful person he seemed unlikely to tread on her toes.

Once the gentlemen had withdrawn to wherever gentlemen went when they weren't making themselves agreeable to ladies, Mama sank into her chair with a muffled groan. "How could Mrs. Price do such a thing? I begin to think she does it for sheer devilry."

Sylvia thought so too. "At least no real harm has been done."

"But you must not dance with Mr. Thorne, Sylvia. If he should have the bad taste to ask you, promise me you will refuse."

"I promise." She spoke without thinking. If she dwelt too deeply on the many musts and must nots, she might start to scream.

It made no difference anyway because he wouldn't ask.

* * *

James did his duty as de facto host. He danced with ladies bereft of partners, entertained gentlemen who didn't care for dancing or card play, and generally kept himself occupied. As he stood listening to a bored retired colonel extol the merits of a life spent in the service of Queen and country, Fran walked in and paused, framed in the massive, ornately carved doorway. He wanted to rush straight to her, but he couldn't abandon his companion. Instead, he watched her over the colonel's shoulder, all the time waiting for the man to pause for breath so James might excuse himself.

A hostess wasn't obliged to meet every guest at the door. Miriam either didn't see Fran or deliberately chose not to cross the room to greet her. In such a situation, the rules of etiquette demanded that the guest seek out the hostess.

He found Fran easy to track as she crossed the room. She had little in common with the debutantes, youthful and shimmering in their pale silks, and she stood out from the soberly clad matrons. He understood her so well now that he knew the wry smile she'd have worn as she'd chosen the scarlet damask and blood red satin of her gown. She'd probably apply the word *demure* to the cream lace underskirt revealed by the drapery, but it made him—and probably every other man in the room—think of frilly underthings and sin. He found it impossible to concentrate on anything else.

"Here, old chap." He handed his champagne to the colonel, cutting short an impassioned speech about the importance of military funding. "You must be parched. I think I see Mrs. Price trying to get my attention. You stay here and have a good, long swig."

He sauntered forward, trying to appear casual when he felt anything but. As soon as Fran finished speaking with Miriam, he'd warn her about the Lyttons. Dancing couples spun across the floor. Guests in various states of intoxication talked and laughed, candles flickered, crystal glasses glimmered in the light, and the musicians played with zest. If the ball was a glittering whirl, Fran was the stillness at its center.

From several feet away, he watched the two women exchange what looked like the requisite civilities, but he didn't trust Miriam. He weaved closer and leaned against a column with his back to them.

"Not at all, my dear," Miriam was saying, her voice overloud, as if she wanted to draw an audience. "I do so like to have young people about me. I find it quickens the blood, and you lead such an interesting life, Mrs. Thorne."

He didn't catch Fran's response, probably because she spoke at a more natural volume, but she must have issued some sort of denial because Miriam said, "Oh, come now. Don't be so modest. We all wish we might kick over the traces now and then, but very few of us really do it. We're all secretly green with envy. Have a wonderful evening, my dear."

A clear dismissal. So much for a warm welcome.

He moved from his hiding place just in time to watch Fran turn.

He started forward but it was too late. She'd already gone still and pale. He followed her line of sight to the Lyttons. Cold gaze fixed on his niece, Mr. Lytton rose from his chair, his cane wobbling. Together, he and his wife turned their backs. Pain flashed across Fran's face.

James took another involuntary step forward, but she fled without even seeing him.

"Poor Mrs. Thorne." Aunt Miriam stood at his elbow. "But what did she expect? I doubt we'll see her again this evening."

James pressed forward on his toes with the urge to get to Fran, but she certainly wouldn't thank him for causing a scene. If he pushed through this mob to chase after her, that's exactly what he'd accomplish.

Miriam smiled. "How terrible for the Lyttons. They're such good people."

He felt something ugly and violent stir within him. When he answered, his voice shook with it. "Your definition of goodness must differ somewhat from mine."

She pounced like a rat-catcher's terrier. "Surely you don't think they ought to support her?"

"I think they should show some loyalty or, failing that, perhaps an ounce of familial feeling." *You arrogant, meddling harridan*, he wanted to add.

Her sharp little eyes narrowed. "Some things are unforgivable. Mrs. Thorne's notoriety will increase a hundredfold if she continues with this divorce nonsense. Her inevitable fall will taint everyone she knows. She's no better than Mrs. Kirkpatrick. The Lyttons are quite right to distance themselves."

"Which, in my opinion, says a great deal about the worth of their regard. Mrs. Thorne will still have the respect of those who truly know and love her."

"What an eccentric you're becoming, James. Even you, with your new permissive attitude, cannot seriously compare her to a true lady like Sylvia Randle."

That moment tipped the scales. He knew he was finished courting her good opinion at the expense of his integrity, at the expense of his soul. It appeared he'd finally found something that mattered more than his inheritance. No one would ever malign Francesca Thorne in his presence again without experiencing the full force of his displeasure.

"Mrs. Thorne is every bit as great a lady as Miss Randle. I'm sorry you saw fit to invite her here this evening when your only intention was to enjoy her discomfort." If they hadn't been surrounded by guests primed for a scandal, he'd have said a great deal more. Her fingers clutched feebly at his sleeve, but he shook them off. "Now, if you'll excuse me, I need a drink."

CHAPTER THIRTEEN

I will not cry. Francesca stared at her reflection and repeated the words over and over again, a mantra to ward off despair: *I will not cry. I will not cry. I will not cry.*

She sat at one of many elegant dressing tables in the spacious ladies withdrawing room, alone except for a servant who hovered in readiness to re-pin hair or perform quick repairs to torn hems and loose seams. It didn't signify whether she was alone or surrounded by people. Either way, she mustn't cry.

Her face showed no sign of what had transpired in the ballroom. She looked a trifle pale, but no visible mark or outward tremor revealed her inner pain. She could get through the rest of the evening. She wouldn't run away and cower in her bed. If she could find anyone brazen enough to ask her to dance, she'd stay all bloody night.

"Oh." Mrs. Kirkpatrick, of all people, had appeared in the doorway. When she saw Francesca, she stopped and dithered, obviously unable to decide whether to advance or retreat. "Excuse me," she said eventually. "I'll go."

Francesca sighed. "Don't trouble yourself."

The courtesan looked even more beautiful up close—tall and voluptuous, imperfect and vivid, with masses of red hair piled high on her head, an overly large mouth, a bosom that defied gravity, and those blasted diamonds to set it all off. God knows how such a creature came by an invitation to a respectable gathering. Perhaps Mrs. Price's penchant for sensationalism encompassed all fallen women, not just divorcées.

Mrs. Kirkpatrick turned to go, hesitated again, and then came fully into the room. "Mrs. Thorne, are you quite well?"

Francesca wanted to laugh, but held it in check, frightened it might come out a mad cackle. This was the last woman she'd have chosen to walk in on her and ask that question—last except perhaps for Mrs. Price. But her concern appeared genuine, and that seemed the funniest thing of all.

"Yes, quite well." After that, Francesca meant to stop talking—this was Edward's mistress, after all—but somehow she found herself continuing. "Things have changed a great deal for me of late. I'm still getting used to it."

Encouraged by this brief elaboration, Mrs. Kirkpatrick took a step closer. "Is it . . . is it about Mr. and Mrs. Lytton?"

A woman didn't reach Mrs. Kirkpatrick's position within the demimonde without learning one or two social mores. She must recognize the impertinence of her question. Francesca ought to cut her dead, but then she'd invited such brazenness when she expounded on her state of mind. "You saw that? Wait, of course you did. How silly of me. I suppose everybody saw. You'd think I'd be used to my own notoriety by now."

Mrs. Kirkpatrick smiled. It was rather a kind smile. "One doesn't grow used to such a thing. At least I never have."

How odd. It looked like they were about to have a personal conversation. Francesca reached up to unpin a curl. Her hair didn't need redoing, but she wanted something to occupy her hands and eyes so she wouldn't have to look at her companion. "How long have you been . . . how long has it been?"

The courtesan stepped forward and held out her hand for the pin. "Almost twelve years. I was fifteen when I lost my character. I worked in a tavern. I didn't know how some of the other girls made extra money, but one day a gentleman took a liking to me and the rest, as they say, is history." While she spoke, she went to work repairing the curl. "There. That's better," she said, smoothing the strands. Their eyes met in the mirror. "Not that I'm comparing us, you understand. There's a world of difference between our two situations."

"Not in Mrs. Price's eyes, it seems. Not in the eyes of that horde out there, and not in the eyes of my family."

Mrs. Kirkpatrick shrugged. The subtle rise and fall of her shoulders conveyed complete disregard for all those fine gentlemen and their ladies. Francesca felt braver just witnessing it.

"As for Mrs. Price," Mrs. Kirkpatrick went on, "she's played us both a rotten trick. I didn't want to come. Mr. Thorne persuaded me. I think my being here is his idea of a fine joke. I think Mr. Standish is displeased with him."

Francesca shouldn't be surprised that James and this woman were acquainted. As Thorne's friend, he must have been in company with them both often. "Why should he be displeased? It won't ruin the ball. Mrs. Price thrives on controversy." Unless . . . unless, he'd been worried about Francesca's feelings. He must know how difficult she'd find being in company with both her husband *and* his mistress.

"Yes, but I think he thought *I* might mind."

"Oh." She hated how plaintive the small word sounded. She ought to feel glad he considered Mrs. Kirkpatrick's feelings. Instead, her heart ached with something akin to jealousy.

"I've only met him on a handful of occasions, but he seems to be a very good sort of man."

"Yes," Francesca said. "Yes, I think he is." Until she saw Mrs. Kirkpatrick's eyebrows go up, she didn't realize how wistful she sounded.

"Are you . . . friends?"

How to answer such a question? She considered it unwise, not to mention indelicate, to talk of intimate matters with strangers. In this case, it struck her as particularly foolhardy. Despite the odd connection she felt between herself and Mrs. Kirkpatrick, the woman was still Edward's mistress. Francesca might be reckless, but not *that* reckless. "Mr. Standish is considering marriage to a respectable lady."

"Miss Randle? Yes, so Mr. Thorne told me."

"She's very beautiful, very young, and very eligible."

Mrs. Kirkpatrick snorted. "Why is it gentlemen insist on marrying these quiet mice when what they really desire is an equal? Since I've been keeping such exalted"—she laced the word with heavy irony—"company, I've seen numerous gentlemen marry one of these pallid children only to turn around and set up a more fiery-tempered woman on the side. Why not forgo the chits altogether and marry a woman of substance instead?"

An excellent question, and social spheres and economic factors aside, Fran had her theories. "Perhaps they fear being unable to hold such a woman's attention."

"You mean they fear for the legitimacy of their future heirs? How foolish. I've watched countless simpering virgins tire of their husbands and turn into voracious grasping sluts. When will gentlemen learn that virginity and ignorance do not necessarily coincide with good character?"

"Or that experience and intellectual curiosity don't necessarily equate to a bad one?" Francesca was starting to like her husband's mistress.

Mrs. Kirkpatrick rolled her eyes. "It's a pity so many men fail to recognize a good woman when they find one."

Something in her tone made Francesca wonder if Edward and his mistress had fallen out. A perfect time to say something cruel and cutting to her rival. "If that is so, then such gentlemen have no one but themselves to blame," she said instead.

Mrs. Kirkpatrick sank onto the nearest stool. "I did not think you would be kind. Nothing Mr. Thorne told me led me to expect it."

Francesca couldn't suppress a bitter smile. If Edward had ever thought her kind, he'd long since forgotten. "I have no reason to be *un*kind. Mr. Thorne hasn't been my husband in truth for many years."

"When I imagined our meeting, I confess I didn't envision anything like this."

"Nor I," Francesca agreed. In her more realistic imaginings, she always cut Mrs. Kirkpatrick with icy contempt. In her more fanciful ones, she'd pictured a great deal of hair-pulling and a diamond necklace broken beyond repair. "No, nor I," she repeated. "But I am very glad to have met you, and I'm pleased Mrs. Price invited us both, however mischievous her intentions."

With one more glance at her reflection, she was ready to go back to the ballroom and face everyone. Strange that this encounter had given her the extra strength.

It wasn't permissible to shake one's Mama or Sylvia would have done so. The woman wouldn't stop talking.

"I thought Mr. Biddle appeared very pleased with your company," she said. "It's a pity he's not handsome, but there, we cannot expect one gentleman to possess every virtue. At least he's rich."

Sylvia suspected her mother of overindulging in the champagne, but she made herself smile, though the dull throb of her latest headache had intensified until she felt as though someone stabbed her temples with red-hot needles. Dancing provided all too brief a respite, and every time she finished a set, her mother continued from wherever she'd left off.

"I will say, dearest, I think you might dance with more liveliness. I know showy stepping is frowned upon, but at times I thought you looked as lackluster as a sleepwalker. I know I'm criticizing you a great deal and I don't like doing it, but the season passes so quickly. It would be such a coup if we secured your future sooner rather than later and really . . ."

It went on and on.

Mama hadn't always been so overbearing. The season had transformed her into a nagging, ambitious stranger.

Sylvia glanced at her dance card to see whose name appeared next on the list, and her spirits plummeted. Mama had insisted she leave the next space vacant for any interesting late arrivals. None had come, and now she would have to endure an entire half hour of this incessant lecturing.

She stood, the movement so abrupt that her mother stopped midsentence, her mouth gaping open. "I'm sorry, Mama, but I have a headache. I think I need to go out to the terrace for some air."

"Of course, my dear, if you must. I'll go with you."

"No!" She hadn't meant to exclaim with such violence, so she modulated her tone as she continued. "That is, please do not trouble yourself. I know how you feel the cold and anyway we'd lose our seats. I won't be long."

Mama looked to the open terrace doors at the far end of the room. Outside, the lamps glowed with beckoning warmth. "Well, if you're sure, but don't stray beyond the steps."

It didn't do for a young lady to cross the floor alone, but she might skitter crab-like about the edges. As Sylvia edged around the perimeter of the ballroom, this rule seemed even more nonsensical than usual.

With relief, she stepped out into the cool night air. She hadn't realized quite how hot and stuffy the ballroom had become. She closed her eyes and breathed in deeply.

"Drink?" a voice said.

She snapped open her eyes and saw Edward Thorne beside her, holding two glasses of champagne. He offered one to her.

She stared at it stupidly before accepting. "Thank you."

"Bad night?"

She took a sip of the sparkling wine so she'd have time to consider her answer. She didn't know him and the question was an impertinent one, despite the timely glass of champagne. His blue eyes, clear and guileless, looked directly into hers, and the appropriate reproach stuck in her throat. She was, after all, simply longing to talk with him. "Yes, a bad night. Actually, a bad everything."

He leaned against the stone balustrade. "What's the trouble?"

"Honestly?" She paused until he nodded for her to continue. "It's only that I'm heartily sick of myself." It had to be the most candid answer she'd ever given to anyone. Another reason not to stray beyond the terrace—everyone behaved differently in the dark.

"That's very strange." He peered at her as if scrutinizing a butterfly pinned beneath a magnifying glass. "You seem charming, beautiful, elegant, accomplished."

His response disappointed her to such a degree that she couldn't stop herself sighing aloud. She'd expected more from a man with a reputation as wicked as his.

"What? Don't you like compliments?"

"Not when they're as unoriginal as those. I also suspect they're insincere." What was it about this man that made her say whatever entered her head?

He grinned, and her heart began to beat a little faster.

"Now, I'll admit to unoriginal, but what makes you suppose me insincere?"

"You don't know me, Mr. Thorne. You don't know what my accomplishments are or whether I'm charming."

"Then you at least allow that you are beautiful and elegant?"

She blushed, her conceit exposed. "Elegant, perhaps. Beauty is a matter of opinion."

He arched his eyebrows. "Is it indeed?"

She had no answer and, feeling no compulsion to think of one, gazed up at the stars instead. The headache had gone. Their discussion had distracted her so effectively that she hadn't even noticed it lifting.

When she glanced again at Mr. Thorne, she caught him staring.

"Are you ready to go in?" he said, averting his gaze. "Shall I escort you to your mother?"

"No." She couldn't face her. Not yet. She peered over the balustrade at the garden below and the path lit by multicolored lanterns. Stone steps led down to it, the very steps beyond which her mother had instructed her not to pass. "What I would really like is a walk in the gardens." A tiny thrill shivered through her as she'd made the suggestion. Until this moment, her defiance had extended only to book smuggling.

His mouth quirked up at the corners as he offered his arm. "Shall we?"

She reached out, then let her hand fall back to her side. "Where does the path lead?"

"No idea," he said with a smile. "Do you want to find out?"

She placed her champagne next to his empty glass on the stone, and, once her fingers had settled uncertainly on the sleeve of his black tailcoat, he led her toward the brightly lit path.

"You told me you feel sick of yourself. What would you like to change about yourself or your life?" He uttered the question so quietly she almost couldn't make it out.

"Change is neither possible nor desirable for a true lady," she told him. "One adheres to tradition. One doesn't deviate for fear of being thought unwomanly. Didn't anyone ever tell you?" If her father could hear her now, he'd scold her and send her to her room.

"Not exactly," Mr. Thorne said, and she heard laughter in his voice. "You don't seem in imminent danger of losing your femininity."

"Ah, but as we've already discussed, you don't know me, Mr. Thorne. I'm not very good at being a proper lady. Not at all."

The muscles in his arm tightened under her hand, but he said nothing.

"As it happens, I've been dreaming of the same things for most of my life. If I could have anything I wanted, I'd live on my own."

"On your own? No husband or family?"

She raised her chin. "Just me."

"Why?" He sounded genuinely puzzled.

"If it were just me, I might order things to my own liking. I'd furnish my room to suit my taste without referring to anyone else's. I'd read whatever I liked and for as long as I liked. I'd paint what I liked. No more landscapes. No more vases of flowers."

"Oh?" He laughed again, a low, soft chuckle. He must think them such trivial desires. "And what would you paint instead?"

"People, I think. You, perhaps." Now she thought about it, he'd make a wonderful subject. She wouldn't paint a simple portrait. What a pointless waste that would be. With his fine appearance and slightly dissipated demeanor, he reminded her of Cabanel's *Fallen Angel*. She would paint him nude. The thought made her cheeks burn.

He cleared his throat. An awkward silence descended, as if he'd divined her thoughts.

The path led them to a small, sunken rose garden with a massive marble fountain at its center. She inhaled the heady scent and plucked one of the nearest blooms, stroking one velvety petal with her fingertip. "What about you, Mr. Thorne? What would you change?"

"If I could have anything?" He smiled crookedly as he repeated her earlier words. "I would never have married."

Oh, this was much better. This was how rakes were supposed to talk—with no regard for the innocence and naiveté of their audience. "I suppose I ought to be shocked," she said.

"Are you?"

She shook her head. This was a night of strange confidences.

Another couple admired the roses on the opposite side of the flowerbed. Otherwise, they were alone. Even so, she lowered her voice. "Is marriage such a trial?"

"It is for me. I confess I've no idea how to treat a wife. Mine had so many needs, all of them contradictory."

She could well believe it. By all accounts, the wife was a scandal. The newspapers implied all manner of lewd goings-on. But Mrs. Thorne had a house of her own, so perhaps the wages of sin were real estate and not death after all.

"We should go back now," he said, no dashing smile or mocking laugh. Talking about his wife seemed to have soured his mood just when Sylvia's was improving.

"Oh, no," she said. "Mightn't we walk a bit further?" Without meaning to, she'd adopted a playful tone. His eyes glittered in the lamplight, and she knew she'd regained his attention.

"The lamps end here."

"But it's a full moon. We'll have plenty of light."

When she started walking, her escort had no choice but to follow. He couldn't leave her stranded.

"Not that way." He took her hand and led her away from the path like the wolf in "Little Red Cap." And why not? She'd practically begged this particular wolf to devour her. His touch burned through her long white glove. She'd never held a man's hand before and the simple intimacy was exhilarating.

They left the rose garden behind. He didn't speak, perhaps because he was angry. His quick strides and shallow breaths certainly suggested as much. He didn't stop until they reached the edge of the trees. "We should go back now," he said.

"I don't see why." But she did see. Oh, she did. She might know nothing about the world, but she knew his look in the ballroom had promised seduction. If Mama had her way, she'd be married off by the end of the year to someone dull and rich. This might be her only chance to experience what the poets wrote about. Not love. Passion. And with the only man she'd ever wanted.

"Because no one else is here," he said with a cruel bite to his voice. "It isn't wise for you to be out here alone with me."

She didn't know how she dared, but she moved closer. "Are you so terrible?"

"Miss Randle, I think you understand me much better than you pretend."

She didn't have a word for the look on his face, but it set her heart pounding. She took another step and flattened her hand on the front of his waistcoat. The warmth of his skin reached her even through all his layers of fabric.

"Miss Randle," he said, grabbing her wrist. "Stop looking at me like you want to be kissed."

He kept using her name as if to remind her that they were strangers.

"But I do. I do want to be kissed."

That look again. She recognized it because she felt it too—the slow burn of desire.

"I am too old and too cynical for this conversation," he said. "The days when I could give a girl like you a chaste kiss and send her back to her mama are long gone."

His use of the word "girl" galled her. "I don't want you to send me back."

He seized her arm, and dragged her into the darkness of the trees. Muttering a curse, he pushed her up against the trunk of an oak, planted one hand on either side of her head, and took her lips in a fierce kiss.

She stayed very still. If she didn't move, perhaps she'd feel it more—her first embrace. He'd called himself too old for a chaste peck. True to his word, his kiss was hard and hot.

He tore his mouth from hers. "We have to stop. You can't give me what I want."

"Is that supposed to frighten me?" If so, it had worked, but she managed to speak without a tremor. That small taste of passion hadn't been enough; she wanted more.

"It bloody well should." His muscles tensed, ready to pull away.

"I don't care," she said and pulled him closer. She tilted her lips up for another kiss, pushing her body against his, straining toward his heat.

"Christ." He fumbled with her bodice, his tongue playing at the seam of her mouth, then sliding between her lips. He tugged hard at her neckline until one of her breasts slipped free. He looked down at it, cradled in his hand. "Tell me to stop."

"Kiss me," she said. "Kiss me there."

His breath hitched, and then slowly he took her aching nipple into his mouth. Her legs went limp. She might have fallen if she hadn't been pinned between the tree and his body.

"Tell me what to do," she said.

He gave a muffled groan and pulled her hand to the front of his trousers. His other hand left her breast and reached down to clutch her skirts. He pulled them up, his fingers grazing the top of one stocking. She yelped as he reached between her legs. "Will you touch me?" he asked.

"Yes. Help me." She tugged at the fastening of his trousers.

His fingers tangled with hers. She couldn't see what he was doing, but then he guided her hand between their bodies.

She gasped at the first touch. Part of her couldn't believe what was happening. Her hand flinched away momentarily, but then she reached for him again and took him in a tentative grip. He felt hot and silky smooth. She stroked him gently.

"Sylvia." His breath sighed out against her forehead.

Her heart leaped. He was going to ruin her, and she was going to glory in every second.

CHAPTER FOURTEEN

"Mr. Standish." Mrs. Randle hissed his name in a stage whisper.

"What is it, ma'am?" If he craned his neck slightly to the left, he could see beyond her to where Fran waltzed with Mr. Henley. He didn't know when she'd returned to the ballroom, but he admired her bravery. She didn't have the look of a woman who'd been swindled into a confrontation with estranged and hostile relatives. She danced with grace, her attention fixed on her partner as he whirled her about.

He forced himself to give Mrs. Randle his full attention. Now that he took a good look, her face appeared a trifle pinched.

"Have you seen Sylvia?" she asked, plucking at his sleeve with dainty fingers. The unsolicited physical contact alerted him to the seriousness of her distress. Mrs. Randle was fastidious in her dealings with gentlemen.

"Afraid not." Hardly surprising considering the size of the ballroom and the number of people crammed inside. "I hope nothing is the matter."

She fidgeted, wringing her hands. "I don't know."

Fran said something to Henley that made him throw back his head and laugh; James's shoulders bunched painfully.

"You see, Sylvia had a headache, poor lamb. She doesn't suffer with them often. She is of a most robust constitution." In spite of her obvious concern, Mrs. Randle still spoke like a horse breeder extolling the virtues of a good mare. "But this evening she complained of a headache and took herself off to the terrace. The air, you know. She said she would not stray beyond the steps but she hasn't returned and now . . ." Dramatic pause. "I can't find her."

"Have you tried the refreshment room?"

"She isn't there. I'm afraid she may have wandered off and got lost in the dark." She spoke with such exaggerated horror, he struggled not to laugh. Really, how lost could a grown woman become at a ball? The company, a fallen woman or two excepted, was hardly fast. Even Thorne wouldn't debauch a debutante.

"Don't fret, ma'am. The path is well lit. How long since you last saw her?"

"I don't know." Her eyes beseeched him. "But it seems like hours."

Hours probably meant ten or twenty minutes. "I will be happy to look for her," he lied.

"Oh, thank you, Mr. Standish. She is not generally disobedient. I would not wish you to think she makes a habit of this sort of behavior."

He'd heard enough. "Excuse me, ma'am, but we mustn't delay."

Her eyes and mouth formed three near-perfect circles as he moved away with every appearance of urgency.

He hadn't taken more than a couple of steps when another hand on his sleeve detained him. "Excuse me, Mr. Standish, but I'm in need of your aid."

"Mrs. Kirkpatrick." Everyone seemed to want his assistance this evening, yet he hadn't managed to exchange a single word with Fran, the person he most wished to help. "What can I do for you, ma'am?"

Mrs. Randle harrumphed and turned away.

"Nothing, actually. It's just I couldn't help overhearing. I think I may be able to help you locate the person you're looking for. The elegant blonde in gold?"

"Well then, why did you not say so in front of Mrs. Randle?"

She lowered her voice so that he had to lean in to hear. "I was dancing near the doors when I saw Edward follow her out. I think she may still be with him."

"Did you see them come inside?"

"No, and I was paying very close attention."

Bloody hell. "But you were dancing. You may have missed them."

"I may have, but I assure you I didn't."

He thought rapidly. If Miss Randle were with Thorne, then she was not in any physical danger, but her reputation might suffer if anyone discovered she'd been alone with him for an extended period. He swore softly. "Perhaps they're part of a group."

"I think we should look for them."

He scanned the room but he couldn't see Fran anymore. The thought that he might not get to her before she left made his gut twist, but what if something really had happened to Miss Randle? And under Miriam's roof. As thoroughly disgusted as he was with his aunt, he didn't want her publicly shamed.

"All right," he said.

Out on the terrace, Mrs. Kirkpatrick took his arm. They ambled along, just a couple out for a promenade in the open air. No need to advertise their errand to the rest of the guests. She had no reputation left to lose. If people saw them and drew false conclusions about the nature of their relationship, it wouldn't hurt either of them, and the extra pair of eyes might come in useful.

They followed the lantern-lit path in the hope of meeting Thorne and Miss Randle somewhere along its length. Crickets chirped from their hiding places in the dark. The sounds of carousing faded to a whisper, softer even than the muffled thud of James's footfalls and the subtler shushing of Mrs. Kirkpatrick's skirts against damp grass.

They didn't speak until they reached the last of the lanterns on the far side of the rose garden. He peered into the gloom. "What now?"

"We must look for them before it's too late."

"You don't fear for Miss Randle's safety, surely? Thorne wouldn't hurt her."

She met and held his look. "Not deliberately maybe."

Perhaps she knew Thorne even better than he did. Together with his dwindling faith in his friend, the unmistakable concern in her eyes convinced him to take this seriously.

He reached up and detached one of the lanterns from its branch. With pale yellow paper stretched over its metal frame, it would provide better illumination than the more flamboyantly colored lights. "Let's go."

She accepted his arm again, and they took the path leading away from the rose garden. It curved out and traced the circumference of Aunt Miriam's arboretum. Thorne and Miss Randle might have completed the circuit ahead of them. If so, they might already be on their way back to the ballroom.

"Should we call out?"

He shook his head, then realized she probably couldn't see him. "No. Someone else might hear us. We can't risk drawing any more attention to their absence. Perhaps we might when we're further away from the rose garden."

"What if they didn't stay on the path? What if they went in through the trees?"

"It's only a small arboretum. We shouldn't have too much trouble finding them."

"Do you think we'll need breadcrumbs?"

"Breadcrumbs are no good. Hansel and Gretel got lost when the birds ate them, remember? Pebbles are more the thing."

"Well, in that case, you can be the one to scrabble about in the dark looking for them."

Eventually, they arrived back at the beginning of the path. Next, they'd have to strike out into the trees.

"Don't worry. I used to play here all the time when I was a boy. This won't take long." He guided her over a gnarled tree root barely visible in the shadows. She swore, lifting her hem clear.

It made sense to conduct a thorough search. He didn't intend to traipse all the way to the ballroom only to find them still missing and have to traipse all the way back again. After only a few minutes, he stopped. Over the sound of branches creaking in the wind, he heard rustling and something else.

"Miss Randle?" he called softly.

The noise separated into distinct and all too familiar sounds—moaning, panting, whispering—the unmistakable sounds of sensuality. Mrs. Kirkpatrick's fingers dug into his arm. He called again and rounded the trunk of an oak.

They—the lovers—sprang apart. He caught the small, telltale movement as Thorne refastened his trousers. Despite the deafening roar in his ears, James still found the presence of mind to turn his back, allowing Miss Randle time to readjust the bodice of her gown.

"Miss Randle, your mother is looking for you." Mrs. Kirkpatrick sounded calm and rational. "Will you allow me to walk back with you? If you wait on the terrace, I'm sure we can find someone to assist you. You've had a nasty fall and your gown and hair will need attention."

He admired her composure and, even more, the generous heart that let her speak kindly to this woman she'd found in her protector's arms. She was the voice of reason when he could hardly see straight.

Miss Randle must have thought so too. "Thank you," she said.

He waited until Mrs. Kirkpatrick and the trembling, mortified girl were out of earshot. Only then did he allow himself to look at Thorne, who stood leaning against the oak, his relaxed pose an affront to decency and friendship. "I seem to recall informing you I was considering marriage to Miss Randle." The words sounded laughably tame, but he didn't trust himself to say more. Not yet.

"Are you about to deliver a lecture?" Thorne's tone was glacial. "To be honest, I thought you wouldn't mind. Share and share alike and all that."

"What the hell are you saying?"

Thorne smiled. "I think you know."

The words hung in the air like a challenge. James thought of Fran, of Hyde Park, of his fervid dreams. "I've grown to care for Francesca a great deal over the last few weeks, but I didn't sleep with her. I wouldn't have betrayed you that way."

Thorne shrugged. "Perhaps."

"Are you actually comparing my private thoughts to what you've done to Miss Randle after a single hour's acquaintance?"

"What I've done to Miss Randle?" Thorne lurched forward, his face a mask of fury.

James stood his ground. "For all you knew, I might already have proposed. I might have been in love with her."

"But you're not." Thorne pushed past. "And she certainly didn't behave like an engaged woman."

Spikes of rage broke through James's control. "What were you going to do, just take her up against a tree? She's practically a child, for God's sake."

Thorne spun to face him. "That's bollocks. If you must know, she was begging for it and I was happy to oblige. When all's said and done, they're all the same—aching for a good, hard fuck just like my wife."

James grabbed him by the throat and shoved him hard against a tree. His hands shook from the effort, but somehow he stopped himself smashing Thorne's head against the trunk. "You disgust me. You have no honor. Everything between us is ended, do you understand?"

He let go, and Thorne fell to all fours, coughing and spluttering.

James didn't stop to savor his triumph. He stalked back toward the house, his long, ground-eating strides doing little to calm his raging temper. He saw no sign of the ladies as he crossed the terrace.

He stopped just inside the French doors, sifting the crowd for Fran. She sat by herself in one of the straight-backed chairs, watching the dancers and fanning herself with a sparkling lace fan. She smiled as though something amused her. He'd never seen her look so merry, but he didn't trust her hard, bright gaiety after what she'd been through tonight.

Thorne slipped in, calm and dignified, as if nothing had happened. James couldn't go to Fran, not here, not with Thorne so eager to gather evidence against her, but he meant to offer her all the comfort she could stand later. In the wake of his fading anger, there rose a strange and near-giddy gladness. Nothing stood between them.

CHAPTER FIFTEEN

Francesca closed her front door and leaned her head against the wood paneling. She couldn't wait to collapse into bed. The ball had gone on and on, and she'd stayed for as long as she could stand it. Set after set had gone by without a glimpse of Aunt Helena or Uncle Arthur, but of course they wouldn't remain under the circumstances.

The strain of forcing herself to laugh and smile under the glare of everyone's pity and scorn had left her brittle, as though the slightest pressure might shatter her. That Edward had witnessed her humiliation . . . she could hardly bear to think of it.

"Oh, Mrs. Thorne, I must have dropped off." Barker struggled out of the chair facing the door. She always sat there when Francesca stayed out late.

"It's quite all right, Barker. I'd like to go straight to bed now, I think."

"Please, ma'am, Mr. Standish is waiting in the parlor."

"At this hour? God, what does *he* want?"

Seeing him at the ball had been more difficult that she'd imagined because her nerves were in shreds after the encounter with her aunt and uncle. Had he seen them cut her? Even if he hadn't, someone would have told him. Juicy gossip spread like wildfire in a ballroom. His absence in her hour of need had hurt, despite their agreement to stay away from each other. When he'd disappeared midway through the evening, she'd tried not to look for him.

The thought of seeing him now, when she'd thought the night over and done with, threatened to overturn the outward calm for which she'd struggled all evening. Her emotions roiled, a confusing tumult of anger, sadness, and guilt. When those feelings finally exploded, she didn't want anyone to see.

"He didn't say what he wanted, ma'am, but he insisted on waiting."

"I hope no one saw him come in. What can he be thinking?"

Barker shook her head as though James's thoughtless behavior only confirmed what she'd always suspected; no friend of Edward's could be trusted.

"You'd better go and lie down, Barker. It's late and I don't know how long this will take. I'll ring for you when I need you."

As Barker made good her escape, Francesca straightened her shoulders and lifted her chin. She'd indulge in self-pity later. Whatever he wanted, she'd hear him out, then send him packing. Despite her better judgment, she'd started to fall for him. He'd made it clear—and she agreed with him—they didn't have a future. The first goodbye had been difficult enough without rehashing things again and again.

Upstairs, James sat sprawled in the saggy, old armchair she'd begun to think of as his. A single oil lamp turned down low was the parlor's only source of light apart from the embers smoldering in the grate. It took her eyes time to adjust.

"Jemmy?"

He made no attempt to rise.

She walked to the mantel and fiddled with the lamp, trying to turn it up. Smudges of soot on the glass obscured most of the extra light, and the scent of smoke tickled her nose. She'd have to remind Barker to see to its repair.

He still hadn't made a sound. It wasn't like him to be rude, but a peculiar tension emanated from him. How long would he maintain this ridiculous silence if she didn't say something to end it?

"Well?" she demanded. It was difficult to remember her manners when he'd evidently forgotten his. "Aren't you going to greet me?"

More of that steady stare from serious eyes, no censure or judgment in them.

"For goodness' sake, it's late and I'm too tired for games. Either tell me why you're here or get out."

He stood up, the movement so abrupt it startled her.

"I'll summon Barker to show you out," she snapped.

Moving quickly, he stepped into her path. Far too close. A strange, wanton thrill simmered through her. He smelled of sandalwood and the faint but sweet tang of champagne. When he spoke, his lips grazed her ear, making her shiver. "I'm here to spend the night," he said.

If she didn't know better, she might think he tortured her on purpose with his indecision. She didn't need this, not tonight. "You said it was impossible because of Edward."

"Things change."

Deliberately, she raised her eyebrows and hoped she looked suitably unimpressed. "Things change? Well, they don't change for—"

He kissed her. The taste of him, the warmth, transported her back to that day on the Serpentine Bridge, as if she'd been waiting seconds for his next touch instead of weeks. His hand cupped the back of her head, holding her still. Not preventing retreat, but discouraging it, overwhelming her senses. It seemed like he was all around her, enveloping her.

"No." She stiffened until he released his hold on her. "No," she said again.

Her lips felt unusually sensitive as she covered them with her hand and closed her eyes. Soon this foolish trembling would subside.

He stayed close, his breath stirring the loose strands of her hair. "You want this as much as I do."

"Perhaps, but you were right. It's impossible. I'm not divorced yet and unlikely to be if Edward's lawyers hear anything about this." The way he looked at her . . . Like he wanted to consume her. "Besides, our friendship is too precious to risk, remember?"

She raised her arm, meaning to push him away, but he took her hand in a warm clasp and tugged her gently forward.

"You're so cold." Whether he meant in temperament or temperature, she couldn't tell. "It doesn't have to be that way. I won't let you down, Fran. We can find a way to keep you safe."

Despite the sick, frightened fluttering in her stomach, she let him pull her close. "How?"

"Discretion. Subterfuge. We'll find a way. I promise." With little teasing nudges of his lips on hers, he persuaded her to let him in. How could she resist when it was all she wanted?

"See?" he said. "Friendship still intact."

Despite good sense, she softened, her body naturally fitting itself to his. "And Edward? You may be close, but he'll never forgive you for this."

"That doesn't matter now."

"Liar." She grasped the lapels of his coat and pulled him down for another kiss. A kiss that became a promise and left her drunk with wanting.

"I've wanted this for months," he whispered.

Her body thrummed with sensation, his soft voice seeming to echo down to her soul. Leaning her forehead against his shoulder, she squeezed her eyes shut once more, clinging to his still, solid form even as he set her entire world spiraling into chaos. *Everything will not be all right. This is a mistake that can only end in misery.*

But every time she'd pulled away, the air had felt cold where his body had been. After an evening—No. After *years* of rejection, of loneliness and self-denial, of coldness, she wanted one night with someone she . . .

She wanted one night—just one—with James.

"All right," she said.

In the end, the decision was that simple.

* * *

She took him to her bedroom, but he was too intent on kissing her—her face and neck, the glorious swell of her breasts—to pay any mind to his surroundings. Greedy and demanding, he crowded her, deliberately driving her until he'd trapped her against the wall. The need to possess was all the more powerful for the long weeks of denial.

He reached round and found the row of hooks at the back of her gown. The first gave, then a second, but it took too long. Sick of fumbling, he wrenched the last few fastenings apart. The short, sharp sound of tearing fabric ended the near silence and, before he could stop her, she slipped past.

Seizing one of the carved bedposts, she faced him, her breaths ragged. He expected her to start arguing, to list all the reasons they shouldn't do this, reasons that had once seemed compelling but were in truth as insubstantial as sea spray. Instead, she slid the dress off her shoulders and allowed it to fall. It settled in a red silken heap at her feet. The taffeta petticoat and stiff crinolette followed, then her camisole.

He stood rooted to the spot. Never had he seen anything as beautiful as Francesca Thorne in those two remaining layers of undergarments, lips plump from his kisses, breasts rising and falling with every inhalation.

"Now you have to help me," she said.

Happy to oblige, he stepped forward and turned her so he could see the lacing of her corset. She wore her hair swept up and the exposed nape looked soft and fragile. He must have seen the tiny expanse of skin a hundred times or more, but tonight it enticed him until he had to reach out. His hand closed high on her shoulder, thumb resting at the place where the back of her head met her neck. She leaned into the touch as he massaged her skin in slow circles.

When he bent and pressed his lips there, she gasped. The faint sound made him ache with wanting.

As he continued to unlace her, his hands shook. He'd never felt this nervous with a woman before. It was just Fran, but somehow that made it worse. A woman he knew so well. A woman he liked more than any other person on earth. He couldn't imagine anything more terrifying.

The unlaced corset sagged. She unhooked the front, and the garment fell to the floor. Finally, nothing remained of her clothing but a single thin layer of cotton. Easing her combination down, he bared her upper body.

At last he knew: Francesca Thorne had perfect breasts. High and full, tipped by large, pale pink nipples. He cupped one, running his thumb over the peak.

"Are you all right?" she asked.

"God, Fran. Yes, perfect." His voice sounded odd, husky. "*You're* perfect. I've dreamed of this."

He wanted to tell her she felt like silk. A dozen equally ridiculous thoughts and sentiments occurred to him, each jostling for primacy. Fortunately, the foolish words wouldn't come, and he parted her lips with another kiss instead. Where before he'd been fierce, now he took his time. She tasted sweet, like fruit and wine, and she made the most seductive noises—tiny moans and soft panting.

She brought her hands up to frame his face, her gaze so tender that emotion welled in his chest. As he pushed the combination all the way to the floor, he went down with it until he rested on his knees, then pulled her forward and leaned his cheek against the gentle curve of her stomach.

"Jemmy?"

He glanced up, flashed her a grin, and then pressed a hard kiss between her legs. Fingers tangling in his hair, she pulled hard as he sucked and nibbled, grazing her with his teeth. Her inner thighs grew damp as she shuddered and pushed against him.

"Not yet," he whispered, and dragged her onto the floor.

She made a tiny noise of protest as he stood.

"Let me look at you," he said. He never wanted to forget a single detail. Fran naked except for black silk stockings, her dark hair escaping its pins, her eyes clouded with passion. He intended to carry that picture for the rest of his life.

His mind spun with all the things he wanted to do to her. He could keep his clothes on, just unfasten his trousers and take her from behind, or lie down on the floor and have her ride him. They would do those things soon, but tonight what he desired most was to feel her skin against his.

He stood up, towering over her, still fully dressed in his black evening finery. Francesca had never felt more vulnerable, more exposed than she did now kneeling on the floor, practically nude. He seemed different—dominant. His eyes glassy with desire, her sweet friend had transformed into a stranger, overwhelming her. And she delighted in it.

He crossed the room to the ramshackle old sofa near the fireplace, his movements relaxed and unhurried. She felt a leap of anticipation as he sat and began removing his footwear. Her gaze never wavered as she watched him undress, first his dress coat, then his white marcella bowtie and collar. The V of skin beneath his neck showed dark against the stark, white cotton of his shirt. He kept going, shedding the trappings of culture one by one.

Standing there naked before her, he looked stronger than she'd imagined him, with powerfully built arms and thighs, and broad shoulders. Some men needed the tricks and disguises of clever tailoring. Such men appeared diminished in their nudity, but with

James the reverse was true. Clothing civilized him, made him appear urbane and insouciant. She never felt nervous with that man, but this one . . .

He came back to her, stopping no more than a foot away. "Look at me," he said.

She knew what he wanted. Slowly, she allowed her gaze to travel lower. His already generous erection seemed to lengthen even further under the scrutiny. She wanted to touch it. Instead, she shifted onto her knees and touched the fingertip of one hand to her collarbone, trailing it between her breasts. She savored the prickles of sensation spreading outward from that small point of contact. She knew what he saw—a dazed and lustful supplicant kneeling before him.

Moistening her lips, she leaned forward and brushed a kiss against the tip of his cock. His breath hitched and she could feel his stomach muscles bunch beneath her fingertips. A quick smile up at him and she grasped him in one hand, licking at the spot where her lips had just been. His fingers clasped the back of her head as she made a trail of gentle kisses.

His balls felt soft and cool against her lips. He cried out in surprised pleasure as she opened her mouth over the left testicle in a long, wet kiss. He shifted restively, torn between ecstasy and unease. She might be on the floor, but he was the vulnerable one, panting and squeezing her shoulder, his body begging hers. She gave him what he wanted, took as much of his cock into her mouth as she could manage, and used her hands too, establishing a rapid rhythm as he moaned for release.

"Wait." He eased her to her feet and rested his forehead against hers. "I need a moment."

He led her to the bed and sat with his back against the headboard, positioning her in the space between his legs, facing away from him. The press of his chest against her back felt like safety. His big hands slid around to cup her breasts, lean and graceful, yet dark and hard against her soft skin. He pinched a nipple gently between two fingers. When she gasped, he did it again, hard enough that she felt the beginning of an exquisite pain.

"Turn round," he said. She did, but before she could straddle him, he rolled her beneath him so that the pillows cushioned her head. "Tell me you want me."

"You know I do."

His hand wandered from her collarbone through the valley between her breasts, mimicking hers when she'd touched herself. He kept going along her rib cage, down the length of her stomach, and lower until he cupped her mons. "I want you, too."

Arching, she met his stroking fingers. He slid one deep inside her, but it wasn't enough and she tugged at his hand.

"I think part of me always wanted you," he said. "The day I met you, you sat in your aunt's parlor looking so prim and coy. I didn't know. How could I? And then you laughed and everything changed."

She moved against his hand, shaking her head from side to side, lost to the tension building within her.

He slid in a second finger. "I wonder what would've happened if I'd pursued you then? Would you have let me take you like this? How many times would we have done this by now? A thousand? Five thousand?"

"Please."

"Tell me you would've let me," he urged. "You don't have to mean it, but I want to hear you say it. Tell me you would have let me."

"Yes." She would say anything, do anything, if only he'd stop tormenting her. She groaned as he rocked his palm against her.

"Tell me you want me to fuck you."

The coarse, vulgar word sent an extra jolt through her. "Please," she begged again.

"Say it." He withdrew his hand, positioning himself between her thighs where she felt the welcome press of him.

But still he waited. She reached between their bodies, taking him in a strong grip. "Now."

He seized hold of her hips. "Say it," he demanded, and slid into her in one hard thrust.

She couldn't think straight. His cock filling her, his words, the things he wanted her to say—all of it excited her to the point of madness. She framed his face with her hands and looked into his eyes. "Please. Please fuck me. Now."

He kissed her neck and at last began to move. With each long, deep stroke, his pelvis brushed her swollen clitoris. She threw one hand back to grasp the headboard and met every thrust.

His teeth grazed her throat as he moved harder and faster. He bit down, and the delicious pain drove her over the edge.

"Christ," he muttered.

She held him as he shook with the sudden power of his release.

CHAPTER SIXTEEN

James began the next day in the usual way, blinking back the light as his valet pulled open the drapes. "Bloody hell, do you have to?"

"Good morning, sir," Stephens replied, always confoundedly cheerful at such times. "Another beautiful day."

"Perfect," he said through gritted teeth. Though he'd wanted to stay with Fran last night, she'd gabbled something about appearances and bundled him out without so much as a goodnight kiss. She'd actually averted her face so that his lips got her cheek. Talk about a blow to one's pride. Obviously, they had things to discuss.

Stephens had already set out today's clothes: a stroller made up of a double-breasted coat, striped trousers, necktie, and waistcoat, all in varying shades of gray. The sight made James groan. "A bit formal, isn't it? Where exactly am I going in that getup?"

"I assumed you'd be calling on Mrs. Price."

"Bugger. I forgot all about that."

After leaving last night's ball without a word, he needed to smooth things over with Miriam. If things with Fran went the way he hoped, they'd spend the next few days in bed. His aunt wouldn't brook so long a delay.

Once Stephens had him turned out to their mutual satisfaction, James took the carriage to Belgrave Square. Inside the white stucco, the servants scurried about in the final stages of a grand clean-up operation. One would hardly know a ball had taken place.

The lady of the house wasn't so forward.

Though he'd arrived a few minutes short of noon, she received him in her wrapper. Swathed in what looked like a dozen layers of linen, lace, and white feathers, she resembled a dandelion gone to seed. "Oh, it's you, is it?" she said. "And where did you disappear to? As if I didn't know perfectly well."

After her machinations last night, she didn't deserve the upper hand. Too bad he'd provided her with a legitimate grievance by deserting his duty as de facto host. He would've appreciated those brief, righteous hours in possession of the high ground.

He kissed her cheek and sat down in the nearest chair. "I do apologize. I found I had important business. Nonetheless, I should've informed you before I left. It was unpardonable." Apologizing was the gentlemanly thing to do even if one wasn't in the wrong. So, why did he feel like a villain charming an old lady out of her fortune?

The tight line of her mouth softened, but only slightly. "We both know the phrase 'important business' is nothing more than a polite euphemism. When a man disappears, one may be sure there's a woman involved."

His valiant efforts at gentlemanly evasion were clearly wasted on Miriam. She could be annoyingly blunt at times. One thing, perhaps the only thing, she and Fran had in common.

"Your gathering seemed to be a great success," he said. *The music was excellent, the flowers a triumph, and, as for the entertainment . . .* even Emperor Nero would have been impressed by the way she'd thrown Fran to the lions.

"It went splendidly, but don't try to distract me when I have a bone to pick. What's going on between you and Mrs. Thorne?"

"I have no idea what you mean."

"Oh, come now, James. You don't fancy little Sylvia Randle and, while I might question your judgment, I accept it. But I must tell you, any involvement between you and Mrs. Thorne would be extremely unwise."

Was it a threat or a warning? He laughed as though the question never occurred to him. "Even if I were *involved* with Mrs. Thorne, as you put it, why should it concern anyone but me?"

"You are more worldly wise than that naive remark implies. After all, marriage is marriage. No matter how badly a husband treats his wife, no matter how bitterly he betrays her, her duty remains. It's her lot in life."

He tried and failed to imagine his redoubtable aunt demonstrating the forbearance she prescribed. If Mr. Price had behaved like Thorne, she'd have made his life a living hell.

"Mrs. Thorne is not free to remarry and may never be," she went on. "She's still a wife—a *de jure* wife perhaps, but few will care for the distinction."

"A fact which might sway me if I had the smallest intention of proposing." Fran had a shocking reputation; he couldn't propose to her even if he wished—but he hated saying the hateful words aloud.

Instead of puffing up and ordering him from the room as he half expected, his aunt sank back in her seat like a falling soufflé, her relief almost tangible. Happily, he'd hit upon the very thing she wished to hear. "You're just dallying with her then?"

"Of course," he said, but Miriam's evident glee sickened him.

"Because one ought to be careful. A woman such as Mrs. Thorne has allurements. You might find yourself hooked, my boy. A liaison of that sort cannot go on indefinitely. You may reject Miss Randle as a possibility, but you'll want a wife who can give you lots of strong boys. Mrs. Thorne is too old. You *are* going to provide me with heirs, aren't you, James?"

He felt his future closing in, a noose tightening about his neck. Toe the line, say the right thing, follow the path Miriam carved out for him, and inherit, inherit, inherit.

Money, land, and influence—all he'd ever wanted. What else existed for a man like him? A gentleman inherited his wealth and, sometimes, as in James's case, certain unspoken conditions needed to be met. Miriam did nothing wrong by expecting him to make choices of which she approved, and he ought not to feel ashamed for doing his duty in that regard.

Yet lately he found it difficult to meet his own gaze in the mirror.

One couldn't always have what one desired. Last night was a mistake—a wondrous, thrilling, joyous disaster.

Francesca followed Caroline's butler into the Ashtons' breakfast room. She needed tea and sympathy, perhaps a swig of something to stiffen her resolve, so she could do what needed to be done. Much as she wanted to see where this madness with James would lead, she couldn't risk exposing herself to further scandal. Even if the thought of letting him go made her heart throb and her stomach cramp.

Both Ashtons were still at breakfast, but Caroline took one look at Francesca and turned to her husband. "Philip, do you think you might find something to do elsewhere?"

"There's no need for that," Francesca said. "Stay and finish your meal." Civilized manners weighed heavily when one needed to unburden oneself.

"Nonsense," he said. "I can see you and Caro have things to discuss." He swiped a bun from the table as he left.

Caroline gestured to an empty chair. "Are you hungry? Sit down and have something."

Francesca hadn't eaten all morning because she had no appetite. Now she helped herself to an omelet but only managed a few bites. Even though the eggs were a perfect creamy yellow, even though they felt soft and springy on her tongue, her stomach roiled in response.

"How was the ball?" Caroline asked, stirring sugar into her tea.

"Terrible." Francesca impaled another bit of omelet with her fork. "I'm afraid I've done something foolish."

"Oh?" Caroline waited. When Francesca didn't immediately continue, she took up the tongs and procured herself another lump of sugar. "Go on. I'm all ears."

"Remember how my lawyer cautioned me to be circumspect?"

"I do."

"There's been something of a hitch. You see, when I got home last night, Mr. Standish was waiting for me."

The tongs clattered against the edge of Caroline's saucer. "Oh! Does this mean what I think it means?" Francesca's countenance must have provided answer enough. "Well, what an affront to my middle-class morals. You quality are exceedingly decadent."

"I'm not sure I qualify as quality these days. Not strictly speaking."

"I hope you aren't feeling guilty for Mr. Thorne's sake. But why else would you look so dejected? Was it so very bad?"

"For someone supposedly shocked by upper-class depravity, you seem quite eager for details. I have no . . . concerns regarding Mr. Standish's prowess."

"I'm relieved to hear it. I do apologize for prying, but that's the problem with us stolid, middle-class types. We are insatiably curious about other people's sins."

"Edward could use this against me."

The teasing glint that hardly ever left Caroline's eyes vanished. "He could, but only if he finds out."

"He's bound to, isn't he?" All it would take was one careless word and her case would fall apart. The petitioner in a divorce case had to appear blameless. Even though she didn't live with Edward, she still bore his name. Until a court set her free, he'd always have a claim on her. A tiny part of her would still be his. She couldn't jeopardize her one chance of escape.

"Not if you're discreet."

"I'm never discreet."

Caroline sipped her tea and recoiled. She always took one sugar, not two. "Is there anything stopping you from trying? You and Mr. Standish seem like good friends."

"I suppose that's all ruined now." Francesca glared at the omelet. She hated the damn thing with all her soul. "Do you mind if I don't eat this?"

"Leave it, by all means. But why must your friendship be ruined? I've always believed such attachments an excellent foundation for love."

"I don't think Mr. Standish is in love."

"Are you?"

Francesca's stomach gave an uncomfortable lurch. "I don't know. I don't think so. How can I be?" She felt happier concentrating on the issue at hand. "I don't understand him. What can he be thinking? Why now? What about his so-called friendship with Edward? Is this his idea of loyalty? Because, if it is, I think I'll keep away, thank you very much."

"All very good questions," Caroline allowed. "But your chance of receiving reliable answers would increase dramatically if you put them to Mr. Standish instead of to me. Don't you think?"

The omelet sat on Francesca's plate, no longer perfect, its surface pocked with tine marks. "I suppose so."

"That's the spirit." Caroline reached across and took her hand. "You are the most direct, most honest person I know. Why should your behavior differ in this situation?"

Though she had a point, all Francesca wanted was to go home, shut herself in her room, and ignore the problem in the vain hope that it would somehow go away.

* * *

Twenty minutes later, Francesca froze in the act of removing her hat. "Say that again, Barker."

"Mr. Standish is waiting for you in the parlor, ma'am."

Of course he is.

"I told him you were out," Barker continued. "I even said I didn't know when you'd return, but if you'll pardon me for saying so, he's a right stubborn one."

"Thank you, Barker."

Reluctance made each stair step a challenge. It was hard to walk toward the problem when instinct told her to run and hide. She'd forgotten to remove her gloves and tugged at the brown kidskin fingertips of one as she climbed. In the parlor doorway, she stopped, the glove half off, her most recent footsteps still echoing in the silence.

The little room was just as she'd left it. Her book lay face down on the window seat. The chairs by the fire were empty.

"Barker, where is he?" she called without moving from the threshold.

Swift footsteps sounded on the stairs and the maid appeared at her back, craning her neck to peer over Francesca's shoulder into the vacant room. "I don't know, ma'am. He was here. I showed him in myself. Perhaps he left without telling anyone."

"I don't think so." In fact, she had a shrewd idea where she might find him.

"Do you wish me to help look for him, ma'am?"

If she was correct as to his whereabouts, she didn't want Barker with her when she located him. "No, thank you. You can go now."

She trudged up another flight of stairs and pushed open the door to her room. Sure enough, there he was, stretched out on her bed and looking for all the world as if he belonged there. At least he wasn't naked.

Thank you, Jemmy, for keeping your clothes on.

* * *

Fran looked far from thrilled to see him, but James wouldn't let a little thing like that affect his manners.

"Hello, Fran," he said sensibly. "Nice morning?"

She went to the dressing table and dropped a pair of gloves onto the surface. "What the blazes are you doing here?" Her voice sounded flat despite the challenge in her words.

What was the point of hiding in a woman's boudoir if she wasn't going to evince surprise? "Revisiting the scene of course. Remembering, visualizing, that sort of thing."

Her dark brows arched up almost to her hairline. "Well, you can stop right now."

Oh, now that was more like it. Just the sort of reaction he'd expected. He heaved an exaggerated sigh. "It's just as I thought, then. I knew, as soon as I left you on your own for five minutes, you'd start panicking. How like a woman."

She picked up the gauntlet, as he'd known she would. "I most certainly am not panicking. I've merely had time to think."

"Never a good thing."

Her lips thinned with annoyance. "Clearly, we lost our heads last night."

Lost their heads? She spoke as though they'd have to be out of their minds to touch one another. Yet, in Berkeley Square, when he'd ended their connection, she'd seemed distraught. She felt as he did, he knew it.

With a deliberately blithe smile, he lounged back against the pillows. "I'm not so sure. I confess it isn't as clear and obvious to me. Why don't you explain? Do you want things to go back the way they were before? Because, fair warning, I intend to do everything in my power to convince you otherwise."

He liked her usual fighter's stance, the way she held herself straight and proud, but it crumbled before his eyes. "Why won't you let this go?" Her trembling voice turned the demand into a plea, and she stared down at her feet instead of at him.

Such a heartfelt question deserved an honest answer. He stopped teasing and spoke in all seriousness. "Because you've become my dearest friend, because I like you tremendously, and because last night, I fucked you and you enjoyed it."

She flinched, but he didn't regret his choice of words. He needed her to reconcile her teasing friend with the man who whispered wicked things with his cock buried deep inside her.

"You're right." She lifted her chin, rallying magnificently as always. "I enjoyed last night." He waited for the inevitable *but.* "But I make it a rule to avoid gentlemen whose affections are engaged elsewhere."

Sudden comprehension propelled him forward to a sitting position. "There is nothing between Miss Randle and myself, nor will there ever be."

But she'd already turned away again toward the dressing table. It looked as though she'd recently removed a hat or bonnet. Doing so had left her hair in slight disarray. The loose locks and wisps looked adorable, but she started pulling out pins, doubtless intending to make repairs. Well, he'd see about that.

"And Edward?" she asked. "What would Edward say if he discovered what you and I did last night?"

James didn't give a toss.

"I don't owe him anything," she went on. "But aren't the two of you supposed to be friends?"

"Supposed to be? An interesting choice of words. Perhaps we were *supposed* to be, but in truth, I think we haven't been friends in quite some time."

She let go of the curl she'd been pinning and spoke without turning. "What happened?"

"My friendship with Thorne has been failing for a while now. Last night, it came to a decisive end. I can't tell you everything because it involves another person."

She stayed silent. The seconds ticked by, but he waited. This obviously made a difference, and he didn't want to interrupt her thoughts and send her running scared again.

"So, Edward behaved dishonorably toward someone," she said at last. "Was it a lady?"

"Yes."

"Were you and the lady—?"

"No. There's no one but you, Fran."

Another long silence. "You want me to become your mistress?"

He swung his legs onto the floor and sat on the edge of the bed. "No. I don't want that." A mistress was someone to set up in a house, someone who existed to satisfy a man's whims with no thought to her own. He went to her and set his hands on her shoulders. "I want us to be lovers."

She faced him and shivered as his hands skimmed the rose-colored taffeta of her sleeves. He touched her lips with his, the merest hint of a kiss. "Let me," he whispered. His breath sent strands of unpinned hair dancing. "I need you."

Her arms came round him in a tight embrace.

At last. He closed his eyes and breathed her in.

CHAPTER SEVENTEEN

James was accustomed to furtive, nighttime encounters. Afterward, one put out the light and went to sleep or simply gathered one's clothes and left. When a gentleman took a lady to bed in the middle of the day, escape became problematic and one had nowhere to hide.

With the right woman in his arms, he preferred it so.

The sun warming his naked skin, he traced stripes of shadow across Fran's body. He'd never known her to be so quiet. She was too thoughtful, that was the trouble, and he couldn't see her face. "Not still worried?"

"Honestly? I can still hear the voice of common sense, but I'm choosing to ignore it."

"That's what I always do."

She laughed. Not much, but still . . . "James—"

"Wait." He had to interrupt. "Did you just—? I'm sorry, but did you just refer to me as James? You never call me that. Why now? This seems a strange time to introduce greater formality into our relationship."

She propped herself on one elbow and looked at him, her eyes piercing, dark brows drawn together, but at least he could see her expression now. "I need time to get used to things. I feel as though everything is changing."

Lifting her gently, he eased her forward until she straddled him. Face to face, he felt the luscious press of her and hardened. "Not everything has changed. We're still who we were yesterday." He kissed her—a small, almost chaste peck on the lips.

Her eyelids fluttered shut. "What about the day before?"

He kissed beneath the lobe of one ear. "Then too."

"And what about the week before?"

This time he lingered, trailing slow, open-mouthed kisses across the base of her throat. "Yes, the week before and the month before." He cupped one perfect breast and grazed the pink tip with his mouth. She gasped, so he did it again to the other, teasing the plump nipple with his tongue. "My dearest, my sweetest, my darling friend."

Her breaths were fast and urgent in his ear. "Jemmy," she whispered.

"Let me show you, Fran." Easing between her legs, he found her slick and wet. "Let me show my friend how very much I care." And he entered in one slow thrust, savoring the simple sensation of joining. She moaned and rocked on top of him while he covered her face, neck, and breasts in kisses. The gentle back-and-forth of her body gradually intensified into a long, unhurried push and glide.

She whispered his name again and the tiny sound filled him. He wanted to go on and on forever, but she drove forward, reaching and reaching for completion. Gripping her hips, he looked down at the place where their bodies joined.

Only when her cries became one long, drawn-out groan, did he allow himself release. The last thing he saw before he lost himself was the intense green of her eyes gazing into his. The eyes of his lover. The eyes of his dearest friend. Eyes he wouldn't mind looking into for the rest of his life.

The question came in the quiet calm that so often followed passion.

"Were you in love with Trafford?"

Francesca lay with her head pillowed on James's chest, one hand absently stroking the trail of dark hair that arrowed down from his navel. She could answer with a simple yes or no, but maybe "were you in love?" was his oblique way of asking another question entirely.

He pressed a tender, reassuring kiss into her hair.

"No," she said at last. "No, I didn't love him."

"But you cared for him?"

"Yes."

The steady thump-thump of his heart, and the rise and fall of each breath, soothed her as she waited for him to say more.

"Was it . . . was it a passionate relationship?"

She squeezed her eyes shut. "I don't think you'll like my answer."

Silence. She forced herself to relax, to remain where she was, curled against him. If he suspected how important his response was—perhaps more important than anything else that had ever happened between them—the temptation to tell her what she wanted to hear might be too much. She'd rather have his honest reaction. Even if the truth hurt, it was better to know.

One of his hands began to move in long, soothing strokes over her back. "Tell me anyway."

She considered refusing. If she tried, she might tease him out of this curious mood. She didn't owe him an explanation and instinct told her he'd respect that, except . . . her past was part of who she was and she wanted to share it with him, wanted to share all of herself.

The realization came as a complete surprise. To be seen, *really* seen, for who and what she was, and for him to want her anyway. Such a thing would mean everything.

"I'd been married for eight years or thereabouts." How dispassionate she sounded, as if it didn't matter at all. "Edward had been gone for almost six. Tommy—" She hesitated. He'd flinched ever so slightly when she'd said the name. "*Tommy* was a guest staying with one of our neighbors. He and I were thrown together at various social engagements. Eventually, we became lovers." A cold recitation of the basic facts when she wanted to say so much more.

His hand paused in its rhythmic motion, but then continued as before. She really ought to turn and look at him. It was cowardly to lie here like this so that she wouldn't have to see the expression of—what? Disapproval? Distaste? Disgust?

"How long did it last?"

As if from somewhere outside, she saw herself lying in the arms of her new lover discussing a previous liaison. She thought of the girl she'd once been, the girl who'd wanted to marry Edward, and knew what *she'd* say about a woman who'd taken, not one, but two lovers. How would she explain her conduct to that girl if they met now face to face? *Edward doesn't love you. Edward will never love you. You're going to be very lonely.* Would that silly nineteen-year-old understand? Would anyone?

"It lasted several weeks," she said.

"You ended it?"

"No. He left. His visit was over and he left."

"Oh."

Why did that little syllable hurt so much? "I'm afraid I'm not what they call a good woman."

He stopped stroking. "Oh?"

"Didn't you hear me? I carried on an illicit affair while my husband was in London. I crept away to meet my lover in secret and I let him do what he pleased with me." She forced a carefree note into her voice. "So you see, everyone was right about me. I'm not respectable. I'm not virtuous. And now that everyone sees that, I'll—"

He rolled over, reversing their positions so that she found herself quite unexpectedly pinned underneath him, her back flat against the bed. He glared down at her, his gray eyes cold with anger. She'd only seen his face this way once, the day he'd seen her with Tommy.

"What a load of old tosh," he said, to her surprise. "If you took a lover, I dare say you thought you had your reasons. You don't have to tell me what they are, although I hope you will, but please pay me the compliment of believing me capable of hearing you without putting the very worst interpretation on every word you say."

She half-opened her mouth, but he wasn't finished.

"We both know you're not perfect, just as we both know you *are* respectable and you *are* a good woman. The best woman I know, in fact. And, just so there are no misunderstandings, I respect you more than anyone I've ever met. If you decide to tell me what happened, what *really* happened between you and Thorne to make you do what you did, can we please manage it without all this ridiculous tension?"

She stared up at his scowling face and thought she'd never liked anyone as much. He was really quite wonderful. Just when she'd braced herself for condemnation, he gave not only his acceptance, but his good opinion. "Are you truly this angry because I said those things about myself?"

"Why else would I be angry? If anyone else said those things about you, I'd have to hit them." Then, still looming over her, he furrowed his brow as though he hadn't a clue how he came to be in that position. "I do realize that my shouting at you and nearly crushing you might not be the best way to relieve your anxiety," he added.

"Actually, it was." Though he hadn't really shouted. As for crushing her, she felt quite delightfully squashed.

"Good." A lock of hair had fallen over his left eye. When she brushed it back, he caught her hand and brought it to his lips. "So, Thorne was in London all the time having lots of very public affairs, and you, understandably, got fed up. What then?"

She wasn't used to talking about her past. God knows no one had ever wanted to hear about it before, except Caroline. Once, early on, she'd tried to confide in Helena, but her aunt always seemed determined to turn a blind eye to anything unpleasant.

James made it so easy. He waited patiently as she arranged her memories, trying to form them into a cohesive narrative. "I was fed up, as you put it, and very, very lonely. By marrying Edward, by not being the woman he mistook me for, I thought I'd ruined my life.

"I'd always known about the affairs. Word travels and Hertfordshire is sufficiently near London that it didn't have far to go. The first time I heard about one of his . . . little friends, I confronted him. He denied it, but I didn't believe him. I wouldn't accept the lies meekly, and in the end, he admitted everything. The worst part was when he told me he wouldn't stop."

She still remembered Edward's exact words. *As it happens, this isn't the first time I've strayed, and it won't be the last,* he'd said. So matter of fact. As if she meant nothing to him.

"By the time I met Tommy several years later, I was at the end of my strength. I hated my life, how empty it had become. No affection, no freedom, no escape. He was kind and attentive, everything Edward wasn't. At first, we were just friends, though I admit I thought him handsome. I suppose I felt flattered by his attention. The neighbor he was staying with had several pretty young daughters, but he wanted me. Anyway, one day, we . . . you know."

They'd gone walking together in the woods between the two estates. She'd been unhappy about something, though now she didn't remember the specific cause. She never cried in front of people. Aunt Helena had taught her to suppress her grief and tears until she was in the privacy of her own room. But Tommy's kindness was her undoing, and she broke down.

It began as comfort, but, starved of physical affection for so many long years, she'd let him make love to her right there in the open air.

"Was . . ." He shook his head and smiled as if at some private joke.

"What? What were you going to say?"

"I was going to ask if he . . . if you and he . . . Was he a proficient lover?"

Until that day, she'd never known anything like it. "I don't think you'll like the answer to that question either."

"Oh." He smiled. "Well, that's good." But he sounded thoroughly disappointed.

"With Edward, when we . . . I felt so much guilt. I have a passionate nature, and he didn't like it. I was very young when we married and, in those days, I cared what he thought."

He played with a coil of her hair, twisting it around one finger. "Why didn't he like it? I don't understand."

"Nor do I. Perhaps I'm wrong. Perhaps he liked my passion well enough, but it made him lose respect for me or think less of me." Cheerful acceptance and submission—those were desirable traits in a wife. But not lust.

"But Trafford didn't think less of you?"

"No, he didn't. And it was very freeing."

"Oh."

"I'm sorry if this is painful to hear."

"No, it's not that. I just wish it had been me."

She stayed silent, tracing small spirals across his chest and stomach with her fingertips. Her feelings for Tommy were complicated. It wasn't true to say he'd awakened her sexually, because she hadn't needed awakening. He'd allowed her to be herself without recrimination. For that she would always be grateful. She would never regret the affair, but she was not so unconventional that she could easily separate sexual intimacy from love, and sometimes she felt vague pangs of guilt.

"You said you didn't love Trafford. Do you still love Thorne?"

Given the nature of the story she'd just related, his question surprised her. "If I still loved Edward, I wouldn't be here. I'd probably be in Hertfordshire wishing he would change his mind and come back to me. We knew one another for all of six weeks before we got engaged and, in all that time, we'd never once been alone. We didn't get to know each other until after we were married. I'm afraid we disappointed one another from the beginning, and not just in bed." If it had just been bed, they could have fixed things. "He wanted me to be sweeter, more acquiescent."

That raised a smile. "He really was doomed to disappointment, wasn't he?"

She laughed, his gentle tease helping to dissolve the last of her tension. "He wanted me to think as he thought and believe as he believed. We quarreled constantly, which was bad, but then we stopped and that was even worse."

"There's no accounting for taste." He leaned forward and touched his lips to hers. "All I know is the more I get to know you, the more I—" A strange, almost scared look flickered across his face. "Let's just say Thorne's a fool and leave it at that."

It was customary, on the day following a grand entertainment, to pay one's respects to the hostess. Ordinarily Edward contented himself with leaving a card, corner turned down, but today he made an exception. Today he'd decided to pay a personal call on Mrs. Price.

He arrived at four o'clock, as late as he could without a breach of etiquette. He hoped to find her alone or, if not, soon to be so.

After the ball last night, he'd played *rouge et noir* at a new gaming house, and the sun had shone high in the sky by the time he'd made his way home. Consequently, he would much rather sleep through this hangover, but he had a thing or two to say to Mrs. Price about her precious nephew. He hadn't staggered out of bed and all the way to this cold mausoleum just to say thank you for the party.

A liveried footman ushered him into her august presence. Two additional ladies, seated on a two-seater sofa with their backs to him, occupied the huge oval drawing room. He considered this an inconvenience, but he'd simply have to outstay them, whoever they were. He had nowhere important to go until this evening's round of entertainments.

"Well, well, Mr. Thorne, this is a pleasure. How glad I am that you've chosen just this time to call." And she did sound glad, suspiciously so. As he neared the sofa, she gestured to her guests. "You'll recall my introducing Mrs. Randle and her daughter to you last evening."

In the cold light of day, his head clear of its usual alcoholic fog, he might have expected the girl to prove less alluring, but no. She still had the face of a Madonna—just as lovely, if a little wan.

The mother stood. "Well, we really must take our leave." It was the height of rudeness to depart the instant he arrived, a fact of which she was no doubt aware.

Mrs. Price smiled, her gaze flitting between them. "Oh, no. Surely not."

"Sylvia is out of sorts today, and you have *other* company now."

Sylvia got up too, her face ashen.

Without meaning to, he reached out, only just preventing himself from touching her arm. "I hope you're feeling better today, Miss Randle."

Though it hardly seemed possible, Mrs. Randle's expression grew even stonier. The last thing he wanted was to get the poor girl into any more trouble. "I happened upon your daughter last night when she was unwell. I do hope she is recovered."

Sylvia's beautiful blue eyes met his at last. "I am very well, Mr. Thorne. You mustn't be concerned for me. After all, no lasting damage was done. I feel very fortunate." She smiled sadly, and he knew she referred to their near miss in the garden, not a headache. "But, thank you," she added. "Thank you for your consideration."

Each word touched a chord deep within him. Most girls in her situation would blame him, and rightly so. She'd thanked him and tried to set his mind at ease. Last night, she'd been ardent and yet . . . artless. A rare woman indeed.

The mother, curse her, was already at the door. "Come, Sylvia," she said as if ordering a dog to heel. He wanted to roar at her to leave her daughter alone, but Sylvia wasn't his to protect and never would be. And perhaps that was fortunate. He damaged things; he didn't repair them.

Mrs. Price waited until the door closed behind the two ladies before delivering her verdict. "Nonsensical woman. She'll ruin that girl if she doesn't take care. If one holds the reins too tight, the horse is bound to bolt eventually."

She might be right. He remembered Sylvia's urgency as she tugged at his clothes, the desperation that, in his drunkenness, he'd mistaken for eagerness. She'd tried to throw off the restraints binding her in the most self-destructive manner possible for a lady. To think he might have been the agent of her destruction. What a feather in his cap that would've been. Yet another dubious accomplishment.

"Pretty little thing though," she said, offering him a seat. "Don't you think?"

"Very." He saw no reason to hide his admiration.

"And how is your dear mother?" As she spoke, she poured the tea.

"Quite well, I thank you."

"Overset by this business with little Francesca, I suppose?"

One could always depend on the old girl to ignore the social niceties. No subject was so indelicate that Mrs. Price felt uncomfortable declaring her interest over a cup of tea and a cucumber sandwich.

"She was at first," he replied. "Now I think she's angry."

"Quite right."

"She's angry a great deal since my father died. Disputes among the servants, irregularities in the household accounts, seating plans. These are all things that vex her just as much as *little Francesca*." As much as he detested his wife at times, he hated to hear anyone else bandying her name about with so little respect. It reflected as badly on him as it did on her.

Mrs. Price raised both bushy brows and handed him a cup on a dainty saucer.

"What an extraordinary brooch," he said, after he'd taken a sip. Actually, *brooch* didn't seem the right word for what was in fact the stuffed and severed head of a hummingbird, its beak dipped in gold, pinned to the breast of her lemon-yellow tea gown. It must have been a beautiful creature once. Even now, its feathers shone red and gold in the light.

"You like Freddy, do you?" She stroked the bird under his chin, pursing her lips in thought. "And now, Mr. Thorne, suppose you come to the point of this visit of yours?"

Ah, he'd almost forgotten why he'd come. He'd nursed his anger all night and part of the morning, but as soon as he'd seen Sylvia, he'd forgotten all about revenging himself on Standish. Even now that he'd remembered, he seemed to have lost his taste for it. What was the point?

"I wanted to congratulate you on a wonderful evening," he said.

She stared blankly. "I see. How very interesting. I've never known you to suffer from an excess of politesse before. At least, not since you were a young pup. Are you sure there's nothing else?"

I was hoping, if I poured enough poison into your ear, you might disinherit your nephew and disappoint all his long-cherished expectations. I hate him, you see. Although, now that he considered, he didn't know why. It wasn't as if he gave a damn about Francesca.

He thought about Sylvia, about how it had felt when she'd held on to him so tightly, how the soft skin of her breasts had tasted, and of how lost she'd looked a moment ago as she left the room.

"Quite sure, ma'am." After all, he could always come back tomorrow.

He could ruin Standish any time he chose.

CHAPTER EIGHTEEN

"Are you nearly ready over there?" James lounged in the middle of Fran's bed, his knees drawn up to his chest and his bare feet resting on the soft, white counterpane.

"Almost. This isn't easy without Barker." Her voice issued muffled from behind a folding screen. Why she felt the need to dress out of sight after everything they'd done together, he couldn't begin to fathom. Women were strange creatures.

A length of green fabric, possibly a sash, appeared over the side of the screen. "I'm still having trouble deciding what to wear."

As if she needed to tell him. Every so often, an item of discarded clothing appeared over the top of one of the gold leaf panels, left to dangle over delicately painted cherry blossoms. He found the sight of the rejected garments strangely arousing—frothy linen and lace petticoats, a silken chemise, and, most tantalizing of all, creamy white stockings with pink rosebuds embroidered about the tops. Hence, he himself had progressed no further with dressing than trousers and shirtsleeves.

"Do you want me to help?" he asked, ever the optimist.

"Certainly not." Her voice was all starch and vinegar. He liked it when she waxed indignant.

And I might be in love with her.

He pushed the errant thought aside. The feeling was too new, too terrifying to contemplate. Love, once acknowledged, meant complications. For now, he wanted to enjoy simply being with her.

Once he'd dressed, and despite his frequent lapses of attention, he still had to cool his heels for several minutes. He peered at his reflection in the mirror on top of the dressing table and adjusted his ascot tie. Not quite as well turned out as usual, but considering he'd had to manage without a valet, not bad. "Have you at least chosen a dress?"

"I'm sorry. The first one I chose buttoned in back. When I realized I couldn't fasten it myself, I had to find another." She emerged in a simple ivory silk with yellow piping at the seams, and a straw hat tied under her chin with a wide, glossy yellow ribbon. Sunflowers peeped out from the underside of the brim. She looked so fresh and happy that he felt a strange squeezing in his heart.

He cleared his throat. "Shall we go?"

"Are you sure this is wise?" She had a way of looking down and to the side when she teased him. It made her look coy.

"I've been your escort before."

"Yes, in Hyde Park. I almost forgot. Hmm, you make it very difficult for me to remain circumspect."

"I certainly hope so."

"Even so, I think we should arrive separately at the party. We mustn't be seen parading through the streets together."

"Thorne was the one who threw us together. He can hardly complain if we're seen out in public. It's my visits here we need to be careful about." That was why he'd brought a small bag of clothes for his stay, thereby avoiding too much coming and going. Why he'd walked instead of taking the carriage. Why, from now on, he'd enter via the mews instead of the front door.

"We're very lucky I have such loyal servants. I think Barker found it quite difficult to pretend obliviousness while she dressed my hair."

For the second time in three days, they happened to have invitations to the same entertainment—a garden party being held by Mr. Walsh, the owner of a well-respected newspaper. James didn't know him well, having conversed with him briefly at a dinner party. He hadn't intended to prolong the acquaintance, but he changed his mind when she told him she couldn't spend the day with him, committed as she was to attend today's gathering. He'd dashed off and dispatched a belated acceptance only a few hours ago.

Fran stood in front of him and fiddled with his tie. It must be slightly askew, although he hadn't detected anything amiss when he checked his appearance a moment ago. "There," she said. "Now you are quite presentable."

Their eyes met. He saw the affection in hers and wondered if possibly, just possibly, she might feel a little of what he did.

She shook her head as if to clear it. "Let's go."

Before her *descent into infamy,* as Aunt Helena called it, Francesca had attended dozens of Mayfair garden parties. Here in Bloomsbury, such an occasion occurred on a smaller scale, but with no less assurance.

She followed her hostess, Mrs. Walsh, fresh and cool in printed muslin, as she led the way across the lawn. The setting was suitably refined yet informal. Someone had arranged chairs, no doubt borrowed from the dining room and the drawing room, in small groups in the shade of silver birch and lilac trees. Pinks and sweet Williams, foxgloves, and crimson petunias bloomed, creating a sea of color and a heady fragrance. A string quartet, discreetly tucked away in an arbor, finished tuning and began to play.

They reached a fluttering white canopy beneath which Caroline sat with several other guests, including her husband.

Ashton stood. "Mrs. Thorne." He kissed her hand, all formality. "Caro is dying to talk to you," he whispered. "Mrs. Walsh, your garden is looking especially lovely this year. Are those perpetual roses?"

With Mrs. Walsh out of the way, Caroline barely waited for Francesca to sit before speaking. "You look radiant. I take it you resolved matters with Mr. Standish to your satisfaction."

Francesca smiled. She couldn't seem to stop today.

"My goodness, I'll take that as a yes."

James arrived twenty minutes later. He spent several minutes with Mrs. Walsh, no doubt apologizing for his eleventh-hour acceptance. Judging by her flustered, laughing appearance, his charm found a receptive audience.

Afterward, still on the far side of the lawn, he smiled at Francesca in that lazy way that always warmed her from head to toe. With every appearance of inattention, he started toward her, strolling in the general direction of the canopy under which she sat. If not for that brief yet devastating smile, she might think he truly hadn't seen her.

A lady intercepted him, her hand on his arm.

"Who's that?" Caroline whispered.

Francesca had no trouble recognizing the tall, sophisticated widow. "Her name is Elizabeth Harding." She'd caused something of a scandal within the upper echelons. Of low birth, she'd married well but received only the grudging acceptance of her husband's peers. Since his death several years ago, her conduct had been declared *too fast,* a fact Francesca found easy to believe. The way she touched James's arm . . . so familiar, and slightly possessive.

"Harding, you say. I've never heard of her, but she seems very . . ." Caroline searched for the right word. "She seems very tactile."

Francesca agreed, though she couldn't fault James. He didn't allow Mrs. Harding to delay him longer than good manners dictated. He caught Francesca's eye again and raised his hand to his lips, as if drinking from an imaginary cup. She nodded and watched him disappear through the gathering crowd.

When he returned several minutes later, he brought two glasses of champagne, one of which he placed on the small table next to her chair. "Mr. Ashton, Mrs. Ashton, how nice to see you both." He turned to her as if he'd just noticed her. "And Mrs. Thorne as well. How pleasant."

As he settled on the rug at her feet, a sense of peace and well-being overtook her. It felt natural to have him close. It felt right. Her momentary disquiet over Mrs. Harding seemed foolish. Even so, while the footmen busied themselves distributing cold cuts, lobster patties, and salad, she leaned forward and spoke into his ear. "How do you know Mrs. Harding?"

"We used to be . . . friends."

"Oh." The meaning of his pause hadn't escaped her, and she almost laughed out loud. Preoccupied with her own lurid past, she'd forgotten James had one of his own. She appreciated his candor. If her affair with Tommy hadn't already been the talk of London, she didn't know if she'd have shown the same level of frankness. "Just so there's no confusion, when you say friends, you mean in the same way that you and I are friends?"

He swigged his champagne. No sipping or quaffing—just one big, crude glug. "Actually, I've never been friends with anyone the way you and I are friends."

His words sent a thrill chasing through her. She was special to him, just as he was special to her. Perhaps what Caroline said was true. Perhaps friendship made the best foundation for love. Perhaps this was what a marriage of true minds felt like.

On the other hand, perhaps too much Shakespeare addled the brain.

Gentlemen of his standing didn't marry women of hers. She'd always known that, and even if the thought made the sun shine a little less brightly, she was too old to lie to herself.

What a shame that was. The cherishing of romantic delusions was one of the best parts of an infatuation. New lovers ought to build castles in the clouds and dream romantic dreams, but she had no illusions left. The clouds were mist and romance was best confined to fairy tales.

Their host, Mr. Walsh, had been conversing quietly with Ashton. Now Walsh grew sufficiently animated that his voice broke into her contemplations. "Yes," he said. "But one cannot compare real journalism to what your men do at *The Review*. Serious news, that's what our publication is about." He and Ashton, both owner-editors, had a great deal in common, but Walsh considered Ashton's specific area of interest quaint and trivial, and he was blunt enough to say so.

Ashton took it all in good part. "But really what can one expect from a philistine like you?"

"Ha! What rot."

"Art uplifts the soul, you know."

Mr. Walsh lit a cigar and puffed contentedly away. "Well, I'm a simple man. My father started out as a humble bookseller. We built the business up together. What I and the more rational of my readers are interested in is hard facts. If it were up to me, I'd drop the art section altogether."

Ashton regarded him narrowly. "You don't have much of one as it is. Besides, it *is* up to you."

"Got to think of the public. Unfortunately, not all of them are sensible."

James glanced up from toying with the tassels on the rug. "How did you get your start, Ashton, if you don't mind my asking?"

"My story is similar to Walsh's, except my father owned a manufactory. He did well enough to buy me an education and, when I came home, I started at a provincial rag and worked my way up."

It was hard for her to imagine, her life having been what it was. "Your father must have been very proud."

Ashton flushed slightly. "I hope so."

His wife took his hand. "*I* certainly am."

Francesca recognized the tightness in her chest as envy. The Ashtons hadn't started out with the same advantages as she and

Edward, but they loved and supported one another. After several years of marriage, the affection between them was obvious to anyone who met them.

James frowned down at the little bit of fringe in his hand. To him, this must seem like a very vulgar conversation. His upbringing had been similar to hers, and like her he would've learned to disdain the notion of meritocracy. To people like them, hard work for financial gain or increased status was not something of which to boast. One was born to privilege and, if one advanced, it ought to be as a result of some great and noble feat, and not the simple earning of money and worldly success.

Yet to her mind what Ashton's father had done—working hard so he could afford to educate his son—seemed the height of nobility.

No wonder poor Aunt Helena despaired of her.

The afternoon had started to go wrong.

As James watched Fran sip champagne and laugh at Caroline's remarks, he knew he had to escape.

"*Your father must have been very proud,*" Fran had said to Ashton, and James couldn't help contrasting those words with what she'd once told him: "*You, my friend, are a victim of your own desires.*"

The respect in her voice when she spoke to Ashton, the admiration in her eyes . . .

When she looked at James, he saw affection and lust. He wasn't so certain about respect.

She placed no value on rank; that was the trouble. As an outcast, she had no use for hierarchies. Most people esteemed him for his breeding alone, but Fran . . . she'd had the trappings of class and privilege torn away from her. Perhaps she'd ceased to value them out of necessity. How else could she have borne social ostracism so cheerfully?

But perhaps that didn't matter. The woman she'd become, the woman he cared for above all others, prized hard work and industry over genteel indolence. How did he ever hope to preserve her regard? If one ignored lineage and the expectation of future wealth, what was there in him to admire? He didn't *do* anything. He'd wasted every gift God and nature bestowed.

He remembered the path that led from the house down through a laburnum walk. She wouldn't think it strange if he went for a stroll without her. It was important that no one guess their connection, and time apart would help conceal it. She looked happy, cheerfully oblivious to his wild thoughts.

"Back soon," he said into her ear. He didn't look back as he crossed the lawn to the path.

Gravel crunched underfoot as he passed through the tunnel of yellow blooms. He emerged in a small sunken garden filled with crimson petunias and phlox. A small fountain trickled in the center. He sat on its ledge and stared into the water, wondering what the hell was wrong with him. When had he started to doubt himself like this?

Despite Fran's disapproval of his mercenary streak, she'd never once asked him to change. One of the million things he liked about her was that she accepted him for who he was with all his faults. And yet he felt this need, this imperative to impress her, to be more. For years, he'd felt oppressed by the sameness of his life, the inevitable, inexorable routine. Now the sense of oppression intensified into a feeling of deep unworthiness.

Once, Fran had been like him. She'd spent her youth and the years of her marriage cosseted and infantilized. To hear her tell it, she'd never even glanced at the account books, but now look at her. She ran her home, struggled to manage her meager income, and stood up to anyone who shunned her. He could never hope to deserve a woman like her.

"James, what are you doing here all alone?"

He wanted it to be Fran—as desperate as he'd been to put some distance between them, he felt a powerful need for closeness—but he knew it wasn't. He turned and found Mrs. Harding right behind him, as though she'd materialized out of thin air. Too busy feeling sorry for himself to notice the sound of her approach.

"How are you, James?"

"Wonderful. Couldn't be better."

"Is that so?" Her beautiful catlike eyes regarded him with amusement through the half-veil of her blue hat. "I couldn't help but notice your preoccupation with Mrs. Thorne. I take it we won't be renewing our friendship, or at least not for a while."

"Mrs. Thorne is an old friend of the family," he said without missing a beat. Glib responses came naturally to him. If one behaved as though everything were in order, people generally followed suit.

Mrs. Harding knew him too well. "Oh come now, James. You can hardly take your eyes off her."

"Elizabeth, my dear, forgive my rudeness, but you don't know what you're talking about."

He tried to pass her, but she stepped neatly into his path. "Why, about Mrs. Thorne of course." She laid one elegant hand across the front of his coat. "I confess to some surprise. I would never have thought she was your sort of woman."

"Well, precisely," he said, although he felt the words like a knife to the ribs in light of his recent anxieties. "She isn't my sort at all, but we've known one another for years. I can hardly drop the acquaintance now."

"From what I hear, everyone else is dropping her. It's not like you to go against the prevailing wind." She moved closer, her lips pouting beneath the veil. "I think I'll call your bluff."

As she gazed up at him, he stood very still, his face relaxed and, he hoped, expressionless. If he allowed her to kiss him, would that satisfy her? Would she leave Fran alone?

Her eyes drifted shut. She tilted her face up, her flowery scent enveloping him.

At the last moment, he stepped back. "Mrs. Harding, your doubts wound me. Please allow me to escort you back to the party."

She smiled. Her pleasure at being right outweighed any sense of rejection she might otherwise have felt. "Thank you, Mr. Standish, but I am quite capable of finding my way." She walked back up the path, her skirts swaying. "What a waste."

He heard her laughing even after she'd disappeared from view.

CHAPTER NINETEEN

During the years of her marriage, Francesca had perfected the art of polite conversation while fixing most of her attention on what her husband might be up to in the next room. She'd noticed Mrs. Harding follow James through the laburnums, and though she told herself she'd be a fool to allow her past with Edward to rule her, she counted every minute that passed during their absence.

Mrs. Harding came back first, looking smug about something. She smiled and raised her champagne flute in silent salute. Francesca returned the smile, feeling all the while as though she'd stepped back in time. Several minutes passed during which she made idle conversation and ate strawberries and cream as if her life depended on it. When she saw James, she'd know; she could always tell with Edward.

James emerged from the walk and made straight for her. He didn't look guilty or sated or any of the other adjectives she associated with Edward's infidelity. Neither did he seem like his usual self. The weary lines of his expression reminded her of that night at Covent Garden when she'd met him in the crush room. Something had been troubling him then too.

She smiled in welcome, her own worries fading somewhat in the face of her concern.

Caroline, however, did not smile. "Mr. Standish, at last. I thought you'd got lost. How rude you are to neglect us for so long." Francesca detected a distinct chill in her friend's tone.

"My apologies, Mrs. Ashton," he said. "I fear I was very badly brought up. What do you think, Mrs. Thorne?" The serious expression in his eyes undermined his easy smile.

"About your upbringing? I think Mrs. Price probably overindulged you."

He took one of the strawberries from her plate and bit into it. "That she did."

Mrs. Walsh stood up. After so much good food and champagne, a certain lassitude had overtaken everyone. Some of the older gentlemen looked in danger of nodding off, which would never do. "If everyone would please proceed toward the west side of the house, I do believe it's time for the lawn tennis to begin."

As guests migrated toward the improvised courts, servants busied themselves clearing away plates and half-eaten platters of food. Francesca rose to follow the Ashtons, but James stopped her with a hand on her elbow. "I'd like to talk to you if I may."

The general exodus made it easy for them to slip away. They reached the house without attracting particular notice. She followed James through the cool, quiet corridor until he opened the first door they came to and led her into a small drawing room. She waited for him to speak, but he shook his head and tried one of the four inner doors. "Ah, much better. Come on."

The new room wasn't large enough for a library, though books lined the walls. She walked to the nearest shelf and scanned the titles—novels mostly, and a few scattered biographies. The little drawing room they'd just left was probably a family sitting room and this book room housed the volumes the Walshes liked to keep close at hand.

She turned as the door clicked shut behind her. James stood with his back flat against it, resting his head against the polished wood. "Alone at last."

It amazed her how reassuring she found those three tiny words. Her residual fears and insecurities melted away when he looked at her with so much warmth. All she had to do was ask and he'd tell her the truth. "What did the lovely Mrs. Harding have to say for herself?"

He grinned. "Spotted that, did you? She congratulates herself on having noticed my partiality for you."

"She knows?"

"She suspects. I didn't admit anything." He turned and glanced at the door. "Ah, good. There's a key." He turned it, sealing them inside with another decisive click.

"Why did you . . ." Why was she even bothering to ask? She knew exactly why he'd locked the door. "You must be joking. Here?"

"Why not? Everyone's outside anyway." The room had only one window. He drew the moss green drapes.

"We'll be missed." But she didn't move.

The key still protruded from the lock, but he might as well have swallowed it. She waited—she always waited—for him to come to her. As he crossed the small space toward her, she felt excitement build within her like fear, as if she might pick up her skirts and run. Instead, she leaned her hip against a small reading table.

Slowly and deliberately, he untied the thick yellow ribbon under her chin. She tried to swallow but her mouth had gone dry. His fingers brushed her hair, sending little sparks of sensation flying across her scalp. Removing the hat, he set it down carefully on the table, then tilted her chin up until her lips met his. His control seemed to collapse in an instant, as if all that restraint and care had been pretense. Greedy kisses stole her breath. Grasping hands encircled her waist and hauled her up against him.

Her backside hit the surface of the table as he trapped her, his arms forming barriers on either side of her, his body inescapable in front. He eased back slightly and looked deep into her eyes. She waited, anticipation building, but he didn't kiss her. Instead, her skirts rasped against her stockings as he pulled the fabric up, bunching it around her thighs until cool air caressed her exposed skin. He nudged her legs apart and eased into the space, forcing them even wider.

His gaze finally shifted down as he reached between her open thighs. Clever fingers stroked and fondled while she tipped her head back and sighed.

"Fran, I'm terribly sorry," he whispered. "But I don't think I can wait. It has to be now." His other hand undid the front of his trousers. Then he tore at her drawers, tugging the flimsy silk aside, reaching round to cup and squeeze her backside.

He pushed into her. She was tight, but she didn't care. She wanted him inside her; she wanted to believe that he was hers and hers alone, if only for an hour. She clutched at him, nails digging into his shoulders as he lifted her to meet each hard, fast thrust. She smothered gasping cries against his throat and hooked her legs around his waist, bringing him in deeper. She couldn't bear it. Just a few more moments and she'd . . .

He shuddered with the force of his release and collapsed against her.

It took a while for her mind to clear, but she held tight to him, her hands stroking and soothing. She was disappointed, but these things happened.

He eased back and met her gaze. "Not my finest performance."

At least he had the grace to look contrite. "That's quite all right," she assured him. "You have form."

He laughed. "You look extremely prim for a woman with her skirts up around her chin." He stepped back and lowered her dress back into place. "I wouldn't have believed I could laugh in the circumstances. Physical pleasure is the one thing I can offer you dependably, but today even that is beyond me." As he spoke, he refastened his trousers. "I promise I will make this up to you as soon as we get home."

Part of her wanted to ask him what he'd meant by "the one thing I can offer," but she sensed he wasn't ready to elaborate. Instead, she reached for her hat. "Is that so? In that case, when do you think we may decently leave?"

Francesca stripped down to her shift and lay on top of the bed covers. Fortunately, she kept the drapes closed on days as hot as today to make the nights more bearable. The bud between her legs throbbed with unsatisfied arousal, but she wouldn't touch it. James had caused this hot, frustrated feeling. It was only fair that he be the one to assuage it. She covered her aching breasts with her hands and closed her eyes.

She heard him on the stairs. Rapid, eager footsteps. He must have waited a scant five minutes after her departure from the party before he made his own excuses. She ran to the door and pulled it open just as he reached it. He'd already removed his jacket and unknotted his tie. Its ends hung loose about his neck. His gaze scorched her, and she felt as if something momentous was about to happen. A foolish notion on her part, no doubt.

She let him step past her into the room. His presence filled the small space in a way it hadn't this morning. As she closed the door, he shoved her against it, his breath tickling the back of her neck. His hands roved urgently over her skin and the thin layer of cotton. Pushing back against him, she exulted in the feel of the prominent hardness pressing against her buttocks.

Her hands shook as she reached down and grasped the hem of her shift. In one fluid motion, she drew it off over her head. He scooped her up and carried her over to the bed, setting her down next to it. She reached for him, but he turned her again and teased her neck and shoulders with his lips and tongue. Gripping one of the four bedposts for support, she arched back.

"Still aching for me?" He spoke low, his breath cool on her ear.

She couldn't answer. His clothes rubbed against her bare skin, sending out little shocks of perverse pleasure. It felt wicked to be naked when he remained fully dressed. She felt vulnerable, as though she gave everything while he withheld.

His hand found the wetness at the apex of her thighs, and, heedless, she pushed against his seeking fingers. His other hand fumbled behind her, but he wouldn't let her turn and help him with his trousers. "Face the bed," he ordered.

She did so and cried out as he pushed inside her. The relief. The glorious fullness. "Yes," she whispered.

"That's it. Let me hear you." He withdrew and thrust again and again, each movement hard and clumsy. His grip on her hips tightened painfully.

Every exquisite jolt against the bed brought her closer to release. She hugged the post. "Harder," she cried. But he pulled away and forced her down onto the mattress. The sudden softness left her dizzy.

His touch was rough and uncompromising as he pushed her legs apart and mounted her again, rocking hard against her, reaching forward to grab and squeeze her breast. She gave herself up to the frenzy as tingling waves of joy swept away what was left of her mind. Just for a moment, she saw stars.

He lay half over her, his face buried in the counterpane, his hair clinging to his scalp, damp with perspiration.

"Well played," she said into his ear.

His soft laughter made her shiver.

"You weren't worried, were you?" James asked. "I mean, when I was with Mrs. Harding."

His own worries seemed very distant with Fran lying naked in the crook of his arm. Her room had become a world unto itself. No barriers separated them here. Society's dictates could be set aside like clothes.

She turned onto her stomach so that she could see him. "A little."

After what she'd been through with Thorne, he wasn't surprised. "It's you I can't stop thinking about. There's no room for anybody else."

"Now you just have to convince Caroline."

"No need. She'll soon realize I'm besotted."

He was edging dangerously close to a declaration, but Fran gave no sign she'd noticed. Her lips quirked in a smile. "Did Mrs. Price really spoil you?"

"It's how she shows affection. She's not one for pretty speeches or warm embraces."

"How old were you when you came to her?"

"Five," he said and almost left it at that. But why shouldn't he tell her? She'd placed so much trust in him when she'd told the story of her past. Why shouldn't he reveal what he'd never told anyone else?

"I thought it was to be a short visit," he admitted. "My father rang the doorbell, shook me by the hand, and that was the last I saw of him. He left it to Aunt Miriam to explain the change in my circumstances."

"Poor little boy. You must have missed him terribly."

"Not really."

He waited for an exclamation of surprise or perhaps disapproval. Instead, Fran merely raised her eyebrows in mute enquiry.

"We'd never really had a lot to do with one another. Aunt Miriam made such a to-do about how she'd always longed for a little boy of her own. I'm afraid I barely noticed that my father didn't want me. I think the gifts probably helped. Even then, you see, I was easily distracted by expensive baubles."

He'd meant it as a joke, but now he wondered if there wasn't an element of truth in his words. Had he allowed riches to become a substitute for affection?

"You truly didn't miss him at all?" Fran's tone seemed devoid of censure. James sensed she was merely trying to understand.

"I'm afraid not." Then, because he didn't want her to think him unfeeling, he added, "I missed my mother when she died. I was only four, but I still remember her."

"What was she like?"

"Pretty. She had fair hair she wore in ringlets. She used to sing to me."

"She sounds wonderful."

"She was. I'm grateful for the time I had with her."

Talking about his mother, a rare enough occurrence, usually made him maudlin. He couldn't help but wonder how different his life might have been if she'd lived. Yet telling Fran had been different. By sharing that small piece of his past, he'd somehow brought her closer.

He pulled her back against him. "Do you know what else I'm grateful for?"

"Tell me." She sounded wry, and he realized he'd cupped her breast without thinking.

"You didn't get all dewy-eyed and weepy when I told you my sad story."

Her laugh—rich and husky—was the best sound in the world. "That wouldn't do you much good, would it? There's nothing worse than telling someone one's troubles only to end by having to comfort *them*."

"Actually, I'd quite like to comfort you. I wanted to the other night at the ball. I'm sorry I didn't."

Her hand covered his over her breast. "It's all right. You've comforted me very well since, even if you didn't realize that's what you were doing."

"Were you very upset?" But what a stupid question. He'd seen for himself how pale she'd turned when the Lyttons cut her.

She stayed quiet for a long time. James didn't push. He stroked her hair, content simply to lie with her if she didn't feel like talking.

"You see," she said, "I don't remember my parents at all. My aunt and uncle took me in when they died and they were all I had."

Thorne had told James as much once. It hadn't mattered then that he and Fran were both orphans, but it did now. Judging from the Lyttons' behavior at the ball, there hadn't been much love in her childhood either. Yet another bond between them, and he meant to forge new ones.

"What happened to them?"

"Typhus when I was just a baby."

"I'm sorry. About the Lyttons, too."

She smiled wistfully, and he could tell she'd reached her limit. "You really mustn't comfort me," she told him. "Otherwise, I might as well have cried after all."

I love you.

He wasn't ready to say the words aloud yet and perhaps she wasn't ready to hear them, but he meant them with all his soul.

CHAPTER TWENTY

James set his pen aside in disgust. Due to some perverse quirk in his nature, his deepest feelings transformed into schoolboy smut when he tried to commit them to paper. He glanced at the bed where Fran still slept, one hand tucked under her pillow, the other resting on the cover beside her. She deserved more than the paltry rhyme he'd just scribbled on the back of a calling card.

He needed to go now, before it grew light. The longer he waited, the more likely someone would spot him exiting the house, but the need to express his love kept him rooted where he sat at the dressing table. He couldn't write *I love you*. He didn't know precisely how one went about declaring oneself, but he was certain one didn't do it via a note.

Thank you was too grateful, *Until later* too clichéd, *Gone for more clothes* too mundane. The spindly, feminine chair creaked under him as he tugged at his hair in frustration. Nothing tied the tongue like love.

He got out a fresh card and took up his pen once more, determined to express some small part of what he felt. Ten minutes later, he read through his efforts. His first love poem, but it had turned into a dirty limerick. It wasn't even a good one. He couldn't put his heart on paper.

He left the card next to her on his empty pillow.

At home, he found three letters waiting, all from Miriam and each more strident than the last. She interpreted his continued absence as a personal affront. He neglected her. He owed her a better apology for deserting her on the night of her ball. She expected to hear from him the second he returned from wherever he'd hidden himself.

He set the letters aside with a sigh.

There was nothing for it; he would have to see her. Today, if possible.

He glanced at his pocket watch. It was a few hours before he might decently call at Belgrave Square. He'd spent a great deal of time in Fran's bed, but precious little of it sleeping. A few hours of shut-eye would fortify him for what lay ahead.

Stephens expressed a certain skepticism when told to awaken him at eight, but for once James rose before his valet arrived. He'd slept alone for most of his life, yet his bed felt cold and lonely. How easily he'd grown accustomed to Fran's presence.

At a quarter to nine, Miriam's startled butler admitted him. He waited while the servants scurried to inform his aunt of his presence. She wouldn't be thrilled to see him at such an ungodly hour, but one might construe three letters as an urgent summons and, therefore, justification for his unorthodox behavior. In truth, he wanted to get the thing over with.

He'd always acknowledged the possibility that one day he and his aunt might disagree on a subject dear to both their hearts. This might well be it. What he'd never considered before now, because he'd never had to, was how he would conduct himself in an out-and-out conflict.

She received him twenty minutes later, upstairs in her private sitting room. A fire burned in the grate even though it was a warm morning and promised to be a hot day. She sat enthroned in an armchair, a blanket draped over her knees. "James, you wicked boy, where on earth have you been? Your man told me you were missing."

"Not missing." Confound Stephens anyway. "Merely absent." He sat down and allowed her to clutch both his hands.

"Wretched boy, what nonsense you talk. You didn't answer my question and it's not the first time. Don't think I haven't noticed. When a gentleman engages in obfuscation, one assumes he's been up to something not fit for a lady's ears. Were you with Mrs. Thorne?"

What a curious blend of concern and command. She made for a most benevolent dictator. At least she spared him the trouble of finding a tactful way to raise the subject. "Can I depend on your discretion?"

"I have no intention of spreading this abroad, you may be sure."

"Then, yes, I was."

She closed her eyes, absorbing the blow. "The last time we spoke on this subject, you claimed you were dallying with her."

Might as well be hung for a sheep as a lamb. "I lied."

She raised imperious brows. "Indeed? And are you truly so foolish as to nurture a serious attachment to such a creature?"

She relinquished his hands. Not a good sign, but he was sick of prevaricating. She relished plain speech and he intended to speak very plainly. "If you call it foolishness to admire a woman who is as kind and brave as she is lovely, then yes."

"Do not speak to me of Mrs. Thorne," she snarled. "She is infamous, as you well know. What I wish to know is what you intend. Do you mean to set her up in a house?"

She made it sound so sordid. Perhaps she even did it on purpose since he'd made the depth of his feelings clear. "Mrs. Thorne doesn't require setting up."

"You do realize, should you continue with this idiocy, Mr. Thorne might name you in court? It's bound to end up in the papers." All trace of warmth had left her tone.

It was now or never. "I do and, in all honesty, I don't care. My intentions toward Mrs. Thorne are honorable."

She spluttered. "Are you—*Can* you mean marriage? To Mrs. Thorne?"

He hadn't said marriage, not even to himself. Strange that Miriam should be the person to give his true desire voice. He'd always thought any sane man contemplating matrimony, no matter how enamored, must fear the loss of his freedom. All he felt was an ineffable sense of rightness. How many men were lucky enough to spend the rest of their life with their best friend?

Having waited in vain for a denial, Miriam ran out of patience. "Well, this is absurd. Mrs. Thorne is already married."

"She is soon to be divorced."

"That remains to be seen. If word gets out about this nonsense, no court in the land will grant her freedom. The petitioner is supposed to be blameless."

"She was. She is. The marriage has been over for years."

"Well, however it may be, let me make my position on the matter absolutely clear." Her face was no longer pale but mottled with rage. "If you persist in this, I will cut you off without a penny. You will get nothing, do you understand? Not one farthing. Furthermore, I will make it generally known that anyone who receives either one of you will find my doors closed against them."

"I see." It was no more than he expected and, after a sick lurching in his stomach, he felt calm. "I'm sorry for it, ma'am."

It was almost worth losing a fortune to see the look on her face when he rose to leave. Obviously, she expected him to come to heel immediately. Everything she knew about him and the choices he'd made so far led her to expect it. Even he felt a vague sense of surprise as he walked toward the door. That and a surge of triumph.

This is who I am now. This is the life I want.

"James, think. Think about what I've said. Think about what you stand to lose."

He didn't look back. "That's all I think about."

This time, she let him go.

* * *

Francesca smiled from ear to ear as she read James's note:

My dearest sweet mistress and lover,
Homeward must I to recover,
When again I can come,
To your house I will run,
For your bosom I wish to uncover.

How juvenile. How bawdy. Without doubt, the most wonderful communication she'd ever received. But how fortunate his livelihood didn't depend on his poetic talent. He'd certainly starve.

She tucked the little card into the bottom of her jewelry box next to her other treasure, a locket containing pictures of her parents. She knew so little of the man and woman in those tiny paintings. Had they loved each other? Had her mother ever played the fool for love like her daughter? For undoubtedly that's what Francesca had been doing.

Common sense was not one of her virtues, but even she knew she risked her chance of freedom. Meeting James in public, entertaining him alone in her home—her behavior lately went far beyond indiscreet. But courting this particular disaster felt wonderful.

She summoned Barker to dress her. As she stood before the mirror, mechanically stepping in and out of garments, she longed for things to be simple. If only she could stem the tide of feeling.

Before Edward had sent James to bargain with her on his behalf, she'd thought of him, if she thought of him at all, as a minor irritant; a troublesome, if fashionably dressed, gnat in need of a good swatting. He'd needled her and teased her, then forgotten about her as soon as she left the room, and she'd repaid him in kind.

Now everything had changed. *They* had changed, and people were bound to notice. She'd never been adept at dissembling her feelings, and society always believed the worst, particularly of a woman in her situation.

"Barker, fetch my hat. I've decided to go for a walk."

Once Barker had twitched the last curl into place beneath the brim, Francesca headed out.

The crisp morning air of Bloomsbury was almost entirely devoid of coal dust during the summer. Why, it might almost be called fresh. She inhaled deep into her lungs, then struck out toward Bond Street. She did her best thinking wandering through the city. There was something about the sensation of the pavement under her feet and the proud old buildings rising up around her. Besides, if she couldn't reach any satisfactory conclusions, she could always comfort herself with one or two small purchases. A hair ribbon or two wouldn't bankrupt her.

The clear blue of the sky promised another hot day. Perhaps she should have brought a parasol. James eyed them with distrust ever since she'd almost unmanned him with one, but it wouldn't do to get sunburned. That blasted parasol. Perhaps if she hadn't hit him with it, they'd never have crossed the line from polite friends to true intimates.

Why must human beings always yearn for forbidden fruit? She wanted to love in the open, free from shame and condemnation, but it wasn't to be. No use crying about it. Discretion must be her watchword.

How did one go about this discretion business anyway? Must they arrange secret trysts in hotel rooms and darkened corners? The notion seemed unspeakably squalid, yet she could think of no viable alternative. She might never be free and, even if she were, he could never marry a woman of her reputation. She doubted he wanted to.

What if he does?

The question popped into her head, seemingly of its own volition, and caused her step to falter momentarily.

A second marriage? My God, the fact that she even contemplated it proved how besotted she was. Only a few short weeks ago, she'd told her lawyer she had no wish to remarry, yet the joy of being with James—for joy is what she felt—made her question everything. He called her his dearest friend. Might they not remain that way forever?

No. He stood to lose everything. She mustn't torture herself with silly dreams.

Oh, she was no martyr—she was selfish enough to let him throw it all away if it was possible for them to marry—but he wouldn't want that, not really, not deep down, and eventually he'd come to resent her. One disastrous marriage was enough for a lifetime.

She stopped walking. Where was she anyway? She hadn't been paying attention to her surroundings. She recognized Tottenham Court Road. Not the most savory route she could have chosen, albeit direct, but she wasn't in the mood for shopping anymore.

James was right. As soon as he left her alone for five minutes, her fears assumed titanic proportions. If she went to Bond Street in this mood, she'd probably buy everything she saw.

She'd go back. Home was almost always the least expensive option. She could do a bit of weeding and think in the garden.

As she turned into Tavistock Street, she sensed someone behind her. The person didn't make a noise, or at least nothing she heard consciously, but she felt a presence as surely as if his breath tickled the back of her neck.

She glanced back. A gentleman out for a walk. Nothing more. Even so, and despite the respectful distance he maintained, she quickened her pace.

He stayed with her as she turned into Caroline Street. She reached Bedford Square, where two early birds strolled together on the green. Another gentleman sat on one of the benches, perusing a newspaper. She kept to the path, careful to stay in sight of the other walkers. Her pursuer matched his speed to hers whether she went slowly or quickly. Sense dictated she apply to a passerby for help, but as was so often the way with her, anger got the better of wisdom. She turned and blocked his path.

He kept coming. He didn't look her in the eye, just gazed through her. A gentleman out for an early morning walk. A nondescript personage, neither handsome nor ugly, tall nor short, fat nor thin. Not the sort of man one would ordinarily notice. No threat to anyone. Yet she remembered where she'd seen him—on Bond Street the day she'd run into Tommy.

"You," she said. "I saw you before."

His confident step faltered, but only for a moment. He sauntered forward as though he meant to walk past.

"Why are you following me?" she demanded, raising her voice nice and loud.

He stopped, his mouth hanging open in surprise. Ladies didn't cause scenes, a fact he clearly depended on. An unfortunate mistake. She excelled at scenes.

"Tell me."

Instead of answering, he snapped his mouth shut, turned, and walked rapidly in the opposite direction. She had to break into a trot to keep up. "Who are you? What do you want? Answer me!" She gripped the sleeve of his plain brown coat, but he shook her off with ease. She knelt and scrabbled with her hands for a stone. Her fingers found grit and pebbles, nothing substantial.

People began to take notice. The young gentleman left his newspaper on the bench and crossed the green toward them. The couple ceased strolling and watched with shocked faces. Perhaps she was fortunate there were no stones to hand. If she hurled one at her quarry, she might bring him down, but she might also find herself charged with assault. Surely the last thing she needed.

Her would-be victim broke into a sprint. She couldn't hope to emulate him, even if inclined.

"Are you all right, madam?" The young man looked at her with concerned eyes.

"Thank you. I—Yes, I'm fine." She watched in impotent fury as the spy made good his escape. She ought to go to the police, and yet this had Edward Thorne's citrus reek all over it.

If only she'd found a stone after all. Perhaps if she was fortunate, she'd find a really big one on her way home. Next time she saw her dratted husband, she'd aim said rock straight at his head.

James was shaking, actually shaking. The shakes was something that happened to old women and debutantes, not grown men.

He'd felt fine when he left Belgrave Square. After all, he hadn't done anything irreversible. He could make things right with Miriam, walk back in there tomorrow and overwhelm her resistance with charm. She wanted him to promise not to marry Fran and, as that wasn't an option anyway, why not give the old girl what she wanted?

Or perhaps I won't. Perhaps that life really is over.

"Damn!" he muttered as his whisky sloshed over the side of the glass. So far, spirits had failed to steady him. The next one might do it, though. He leaned against the mahogany sideboard and took another big gulp from the tumbler. High time he started drinking in the morning anyway.

Miriam had taken him in and raised him in the expectation of wealth and power. He'd been her heir for thirty years. If this was real, if she actually went through with it, disinherited him, cut him off, then his future was a complete unknown. He'd never move into the mansion on Belgrave Square. He'd never own the stately pile in Shropshire. He'd never get her wealth and he'd never wield her phenomenal social influence. Lost in the shuffle, he'd be just another shabby-genteel nobody.

Yet he didn't care. He wasn't going to lift a finger to fix this.

No wonder he trembled like a shy virgin on her wedding night.

What would Fran make of all this? She'd probably advise him to view it as an opportunity. Without the money—no, without the *lust* for money—he could make his own choices. *I wonder what you'd do then,* she'd said once.

Well, they were both about to find out.

He had a small inheritance from his mother, but it wasn't much. He had savings, but again not much. If he were very frugal, he could live on it, but frugality had never been his strong suit. He stood in great peril of poverty, but the thought didn't scare him nearly as much as it should. At least he had enough to keep him going until he decided what to do.

Perhaps the reason he'd put that money aside was because part of him had known this day might come, the day he and Miriam reached their final impasse. If his early life had taught him anything, it was that people had a tendency to leave. First, his mother had died, then his father had abandoned him without a word. Deep down, he'd always known Miriam's favor came with conditions. So he'd kept a life jacket on hand just in case his little ship got wrecked.

To rely on his own talents, to earn his own money like one of the lower classes . . .

A small part of him found the idea repellent, but another part, long dormant, rose up out of his ruined hopes to meet the challenge.

When had this happened? When had he come to value freedom more than the easy life he'd always wanted? A year ago, if someone had asked him to name the worst thing that could ever befall him, he'd have described something a lot like this. Until now, he'd never realized how trapped he'd been. Miriam hadn't destroyed him; she'd liberated him.

He tossed back what was left of his whisky and put the glass aside. He wouldn't mind starving if it meant he could look the woman he loved in the face without shame.

CHAPTER TWENTY-ONE

"God, that's filthy!" Edward spluttered, trying not to choke. In his time, he'd sampled a great variety of foul morning-after tonics, but this one capped them all. What *was* that taste? "This better bloody work."

He took several large gulps of the strange green liquid, paused to shudder, and then downed the rest before his courage could fail him.

His butler, Lambert, watched, utterly unmoved. "My father always swore by it, sir."

Perhaps Lambert senior had been an arch-prankster, or perhaps Edward's servants hated him. How else to explain this taste.

"What's in it anyway?" Cloves? Cabbage? Sulphur? "No, don't tell me. I'm better off not knowing. I can barely keep it down as it is."

He pushed the empty glass away in disgust and turned his attention to the pristine copy of the *Times* awaiting him on the breakfast table. He didn't give a toss about the news. In truth, he'd much rather go back to bed and sleep this off, but he settled into his chair with every appearance of a man anticipating a good long read. Lambert quite correctly interpreted this as a dismissal and withdrew, taking the glass with him.

Edward scanned the first few announcements until he heard the door close with a click. Alone at last, he was about to put the paper down again when a familiar name caught his eye. His stomach, already queasy from last night's revels, began a painful churning as he read on.

Mr. and Mrs. Henry Randle are pleased to announce the forthcoming marriage of their daughter Miss Sylvia Randle to Mr. Charles Biddle, the son of Mr. and Mrs. Frederick Biddle.

Christ, what could the girl have been thinking to agree to such a match?

He knew the Biddles. Land rich and cash poor, but one of England's oldest families. An alliance with the Randles would replenish their dwindling coffers and, in exchange, Mrs. Randle could boast about her daughter, the new mistress of one of the largest estates in the land. Never mind that Charles Biddle was a bloody fool.

Sylvia Randle possessed beauty and intelligence as well as wealth. She might have her pick of all the youngbloods, and this was the fellow she chose? She was worth ten Biddles.

Disgusted with himself, he threw the *Times* down so hard his cutlery rattled. Worth ten? Of all the maudlin, sentimental rubbish!

He hardly knew the girl, but he knew she didn't love her fiancé. Otherwise, she wouldn't have played the trollop at the Price ball. The naive little fool would do what all so-called ladies did. She'd marry a man of her mama's choosing, then six months or a year from now she'd realize what a mistake she'd made. Out of pure desperation, she'd drag some complete stranger into a dark corner in a garden somewhere and open her legs. Perhaps he'd be fortunate and she'd choose him again.

Until that time, this had nothing whatsoever to do with him.

After the debacle with the spy, Francesca decided not to go home after all. Instead, she went straight to Mr. Flint's office, where she endured the most humiliating interview of her life.

At first, when she described her encounters with the stranger, the old lawyer reassured her. "Mr. Thorne is trying to gather evidence against you, but we won't provide any," he said.

"But, you see . . . the thing is . . . who knows how often and how long this man watched me? He *may* have seen something." Even this delicate admission made her cheeks burn.

Mr. Flint's expression remained placid as a cow's, but the increased rigidity of his posture signified a powerful disturbance of his sangfroid.

Now that she'd prepared him, she told him everything. To formulate a strong defense, he needed to know every damning detail, and so she told him, a conscious act of self-abasement.

"I've shot myself in the foot so spectacularly, I wouldn't blame you if you didn't want anything more to do with me or my case," she said, when she'd finished.

"My dear Mrs. Thorne," he said, his usually remote eyes regarding her kindly. "I think we might both benefit from a cup of tea."

"Thank you." Taking tea seemed like an utterly pointless activity when her world was falling apart, but good manners prevailed even in a crisis. At least this meant he didn't intend to throw her out onto the street. Not yet anyway.

He summoned a maid. "A pot of strong hot tea, please, Mary." Then he excused himself, ostensibly to fetch something, but Francesca suspected he really wanted to give her time to compose herself.

In his absence, she struggled to clear her mind. She focused on the leaves patterning the wallpaper and the mass of papers littering the desk in front of her. Anything to keep her mind from dwelling on what a mess she'd made. Nothing worked. Nothing could calm the panicked fluttering in her chest.

After several minutes, Flint came back, preceded by the maid bearing a tray. "Thank you, Mary. You can go, now."

He didn't ask how Francesca liked her tea, adding a splash of milk and three lumps of sugar. "This will help," he said, handing her the cup on its matching saucer.

He thinks I'm in shock . . . and perhaps I am.

Edward had set a spy on her. Why was she even surprised? A shabby trick like this was completely in character. When Edward didn't know how to get what he wanted, he resorted to underhand tactics. Like sneaking around with lovers while his wife waited at home. Like cutting off her funds in an attempt to starve her back home.

The old lawyer made a steeple with his fingers, and peered over it, waiting until she'd taken several sips of the sickly-sweet brew. "Better?"

"Yes, thank you." She wasn't, though.

If only someone would volunteer to horsewhip her for stupidity. *That* might help. Perhaps she'd apply to Edward. No, what was she thinking? Edward was the one in need of a whipping.

"Mrs. Thorne, I assure you, I have no intention of abandoning you. I will continue to help you, provided you understand how this turn of events alters matters. Your unwise conduct has damaged your chance of obtaining any sort of divorce."

She didn't need a lawyer to tell her that. *Till death us do part* indeed. She and Edward bound for life and hating one another cordially until the bitter end.

She forced herself to look at Mr. Flint's face. "I understand."

"If the gentleman you saw was engaged in some sort of surveillance, he may well have gathered sufficient evidence to prove you as guilty as your husband."

"Guilty of criminal conversation," she said dully. "No difference between Edward and me."

He shook his head. "In the eyes of the law, you are worse than your husband, because you are a woman. A higher standard is demanded of wives."

She couldn't speak past the sudden constriction in her throat. She nodded and waited for him to continue.

"If such proves to be the case, if Mr. Thorne proves in court that you committed adultery, the most for which we can hope is a legal separation. Even if we are fortunate and the judge awards you a divorce a mensa et thoro, you will not be free to remarry." He hesitated, the pause so tiny she almost missed it, yet it warned her to expect a blow. "A divorce a vinculo matrimonii is now beyond our reach."

Worse was to come.

That afternoon, too agitated to eat, she'd just pushed aside a perfectly good plate of mutton stew, when she heard someone at the door.

She stayed where she was at the dining table, listening to the distant sound of Barker's footsteps on the stairs, a muffled exchange, and then footsteps again. Somehow, she knew the news wouldn't be good.

The door opened and Barker came straight to her. "A messenger came with this, ma'am." She held out an ordinary, inoffensive brown paper package. "He's waiting for an answer. He says he's from Mr. Flint."

"Thank you, Barker." Gingerly, she prized it open. Inside she discovered a thick sheaf of papers, the uppermost penned in Mr. Flint's spidery hand.

For the attention of Mrs. Thorne,

It is as you feared. These documents arrived by courier not long after you left this morning. I regret I am unable to bring them to you myself as my presence is required in court. However, I knew you would wish to see them as soon as possible.

The messenger will wait. Do not fear. He is entirely trustworthy.

Yours, etc.

The letter fell to the rug as she turned to the next page, then the next and the next. Her eyes skimmed the words as she looked for dates.

The document covered several weeks. Every time she left the house, where she went, who she saw, sometimes even what she talked about—every detail preserved in ink. And there, on page seven, James kissing her for the first time.

She felt sick. This was a violation of the grossest kind. A beautiful memory, one she'd believed hers and James's alone, noted down here to be read aloud in court as evidence of her depravity.

It took her over an hour to read through the entire bundle properly. She saw plenty to damn her. In particular, one tiny notation near the end: *Mr. Standish arrives. Seen leaving with Mrs. Thorne approximately twenty-four hours later.* That sentence sounded the final death knell of her hopes.

She sent the wretched document back with the messenger, but how she wished it were the only copy so that she could burn it and put an end to her misery. Even then, it wouldn't do much good. The spy would testify to its contents. Edward had her at his mercy.

Francesca was sitting in her little parlor, legs tucked up under her, when James came back. He breezed in unannounced, a liberty she found inexplicably touching. She'd tried to read, but the biography she'd selected lay untouched on the armrest of her chair.

"There you are," he said. "You wouldn't believe the morning I've had. I missed you even more than I thought I would." He knelt next to her chair. "I feel as though I haven't seen you in weeks."

She felt the same. So much had happened since she'd found his smutty poem on the pillow beside her. She had so much to say, but she didn't know how. Instead, she threw her arms around his shoulders and buried her face in the warmth of his neck. The familiar, freshly laundered scent soothed her like a long soak in a hot bath. She closed her eyes and breathed him in.

"It's my poem, isn't it?" He sounded rueful. "You didn't like it."

"Actually, I thought it was wonderful."

"Oh dear." He eased her back and peered at her. "I'm afraid that doesn't speak well of your taste. Still, as the beneficiary, I shan't complain."

She still clung to his shoulders but now she forced herself to release him, sinking back into the plump depths of the chair. She despised clingers. "It was very sweet. I almost wept when I read the part about uncovering my bosom."

"I meant every word. Although, I give you fair warning, if you ever again refer to me as sweet, I shall gag you."

"Now there's an idea."

His cheeks turned pink. She'd actually succeeded in shocking him, but he recovered quickly. "You are an endless source of delight." He traced her smile with his finger. "That's better. Do you suppose you're ready to tell me what happened while I was gone? Whenever I leave, I come back to a long face and hollow eyes. Perhaps I'd better live here."

She couldn't tell him. Not yet. "How desirable you make me sound."

"You'll hardly know I'm here," he said airily. "It's just me, two dozen or so cases of fine tailoring, two or three books, and one small valet. Oh, and I'll need to turn your second parlor into my study."

"You are an incorrigible tease," she told him. His words evoked bittersweet visions. Waking up next to him every morning, arguing over who got to read the paper first, his things cluttering the house, mingling with hers. The domestic minutiae most married couples took for granted. "You'd soon get bored with me if you had to live with me. I'm very cross first thing in the morning."

"I wouldn't mind," he said. "If you really are cross every morning, I could always douse you with cold water until your temper improves."

"I'm not sure how effective that would be as a remedy against crossness. Perhaps it's fortunate for both of us that cohabitation with one's lover is frowned upon."

He took one of her hands and pressed it. "Marriage isn't though."

She burst out laughing. "Good God, why would anybody in their right mind want to marry me? Have you been drinking?"

"Well, now you're just fishing for compliments. I can think of a hundred reasons why even a sane man would want you for a wife."

Somehow, she'd lost control of the conversation. There was no point talking about something she could never have. She needed to wrest things back onto familiar territory. Less painful territory. "You know, Jemmy, generally when people marry, it's for money or status or, very occasionally, love."

"How about as a remedy against sin?" he suggested. "Come on, Fran. You've had your way with me and now it's your Christian duty to make me honest."

She wished he would stop. Though he didn't know that the events of the day had made marriage impossible for her, he knew damn well he needed to choose someone more suitable than her as his wife. Under the circumstances, she found his humor cruel.

"Is that it? Is that your proposal?" Hopefully, she sounded amused and disdainful. "Be still, my heart. When I was a girl, I dreamed of a declaration such as this."

"Is that a yes or a no? It's cruel to keep a fellow in suspense." He gave her his most charming smile. "Are you going to make me the happiest of men or not?"

With a horrible inner lurch, she realized he wasn't joking.

James had made a complete mess of proposing. Well, of course he had. He wrote dirty limericks instead of love poetry. Naturally this was how he asked the love of his life to marry him. What a fool!

She stared at him wide-eyed. "Now I know you've been drinking."

A thousand glib remarks sprang to mind. He could pretend this never happened, and try again another day, but instead he took a deep breath, and looked deep into her eyes. "I mean what I say."

She stiffened and pulled her hand away. The fragile light he'd kindled in her when he'd first come in dwindled to nothingness. "You're serious."

He didn't nod. He didn't say anything. She understood him now.

"Oh, Jemmy. What are you thinking? You know we can't."

He usually loved hearing her say that name, but not this time. She sounded like an adult talking to a small child. "Can't we? I don't see why."

"There are a thousand reasons."

"So many? Why don't you explain them to me?"

"You could marry anyone. You don't have to settle for someone like me."

"Settle for you? I never knew you had so little regard for yourself."

"You know what I mean."

"No, I don't. I can't imagine anything more wonderful than spending the rest of my life with you."

Her shoulders sagged. He'd tried to prepare himself for the possibility of rejection, but he hadn't anticipated a reaction like this. He wasn't sure what it meant.

"I'm entirely unsuitable." She held up one hand and counted on her fingers. "I'm an outcast, I'm thirty, and I can't give you children. Mrs. Price will cut you off without a penny if you so much as consider marrying me."

At the mention of Miriam, he couldn't help flinching. He couldn't tell Fran what had happened, not when she was this upset.

"You see?" she said. "There's a whole host of reasons."

"You are perfectly suitable," he insisted. "There's no one for me but you. I'm in love with you, you silly woman." There. He'd said the words with almost no fanfare at all. During a row, too. So much for romance.

She stood and pushed past. What a fool he felt, on his knees proposing to an empty chair. With a sigh, he rose and followed her to the window.

Just like their first day. He'd upset her then too. He'd actually offered her money to stay with Thorne. How impossible that seemed now.

He reached out to touch her shoulder, but he couldn't.

If she shrugged his hand off, he didn't know what he'd do. "You must have known."

She leaned her forehead against the glass. "Jemmy—"

"If you don't love me, just tell me."

"Not love you?" Her voice was barely audible. "I didn't know until this moment how utterly and completely in love with you I am."

His heart soared even though he knew something must be very, very wrong. "Then, if you love me—"

"You don't understand." Her voice trembled. "I had no idea you felt this way about me."

"If this is because of Mrs. Price, please believe me when I tell you I don't care about that."

"Don't." She whirled around, cheeks wet with all the silent tears she'd cried. The woman he loved returned his feelings but, for some unknown reason, it was breaking her heart. "Please don't lie to me. I know how important the money is to you. You told me that day we went riding. You said you couldn't give it up. Not for anything."

That particular conversation was seared into his memory. "I did say that," he admitted. "But things change. I've changed."

"When? Why?"

"I've been unhappy for a long time. I know now that the money's not important. You are. Soon, you'll be free and—"

"Stop. Please." She held out an imploring hand. "I'm not going to be free."

"You don't know that."

Her bleak look sent a chill through him. She spoke quickly, the words tripping over each other. "Edward knows about us. He had me followed. I saw the spy today. I've seen him before too. Edward's lawyer confirmed it."

Once, as a child, James had fallen down some stairs. He'd flown forward, landing flat on his stomach. For several, terrifying seconds, he hadn't been able to breathe. He felt just like that now.

"I'm so sorry, Jemmy."

Even red and blotched, her cheeks swollen with tears, he thought her the loveliest sight he'd ever seen. At last, he felt able to reach for her, gathering her into his arms. "No. I'm the one who's sorry. This is my fault. This is happening to you because of me."

She shook her head; he felt it against his chest. "No, please don't say that. They've been watching me for a very long time. This isn't only about us. I'm responsible for my own actions. But you understand now why we can never marry."

He wanted to tell her she might be wrong. That she couldn't know for sure what the outcome of the trial would be, but he shouldn't raise her hopes. He stroked her hair. "I love you, and if you love me as much as you say, we can still be together. We don't need a judge or a jury to give us permission for that."

Gently, she pulled away. Her eyes were still red, but she'd stopped crying. "What about Mrs. Price?"

"I told you, it doesn't matter."

She frowned. "You say so because you think it's what I want to hear, not because it's true. And, anyway, it matters to me. One day you'll regret losing your inheritance and everything that goes with it. It's not just the money. If you throw in your lot with me, countless doors will close against you. I can't let you go through that."

"For God's sake, stop protecting me. You don't suit the role of martyr. It just isn't you." Despite the careless words, he wasn't angry with her. At Thorne, yes, and the law, but never with her. His deepest contempt and purest rage he reserved for himself; he'd told her he'd keep her safe and he'd failed.

He opened his mouth to apologize but, before his eyes, her soul retreated inward beyond his reach. The intimacy he valued vanished in an instant, destroyed by what he'd said or perhaps because she too began to realize how blameworthy his conduct had been. A curtain had descended between them.

"I'm not playing the martyr," she snapped. "I assure you, my motives are purely selfish. I refuse to place my happiness in the hands of a man who loves money and status more than he could ever love me." She sounded stiff and formal, as though he'd never held her, as if he'd never looked into her eyes while they made love. "You would almost certainly regret it and come to resent me. I'm too much of a coward to take the risk."

She had it wrong. When he'd told her those things, he hadn't known himself. Yes, he'd cherished certain expectations, but couldn't she see they were all he'd had?

She stood with her shoulders thrown back, stubborn chin up. "I think it's a good thing this happened. It's forced me to face what I've always known deep down. We don't have a future together. Our connection was always going to end in pain. Someday you'll have to marry someone else, and I won't be the other woman. I couldn't live with myself."

He waited. He knew what was coming, but he couldn't think how to stop it.

"I think it's best if we make a clean break of it now. I'd like you to leave, please."

He closed his eyes. She went too fast. Half an hour ago, he'd comforted her. She'd let him hold her. How had they come to this?

"Don't do this," he pleaded.

She turned her back again. "Just go."

He should. Yet he couldn't bring himself to leave when there might be something he could say to bring her back. Several seconds passed, neither of them moving or speaking, both caught up in the same hellish inertia.

"Don't break with Mrs. Price for my sake," she said. "I have nothing to give you to make up for what you'd lose. Now, go. And don't come back."

The last vestige of hope inside him died. Incredible as it seemed, there was nothing here for him anymore.

The door clicked shut.

Francesca waited until James's muffled footfalls faded to terrible silence, then returned to her chair on shaky legs. She sat on the edge, her spine ramrod straight. A few seconds later came the opening and closing of the heavy front door.

She imagined him taking a last look up at the window. She counted the seconds as they passed. Only after several minutes did she allow herself to believe he'd truly gone. If he'd come back, she couldn't have borne it. She'd have thrown herself at him and begged him to give up everything just for her, but she knew how that would end.

In the oppressive silence, the ticking of the clock on the mantel made her want to cover her ears.

It was supposed to be an infatuation. He wasn't meant to love her.

She pressed the back of one hand against her mouth just in time to muffle a colossal sob. She hadn't felt it coming, but another followed, and then another, loud and undignified, shaking her whole body.

Years ago, she'd cried for Edward. She'd cried rivers and oceans of tears until she could hardly stand herself. She resented every one. What was crying if not the sign and symbol of submission and defeat? And so she'd remade herself. She'd become someone who knew her own mind, who wasn't afraid of expressing her opinion, and who didn't allow herself to show weakness.

But James . . . Oh, James was worth the tears, and for once she didn't try to stop them—noisy, guttural sobs that made her head ache.

Tomorrow she would pick up the pieces of her shattered life, and the pain would end sooner or later. She'd been living in a dream but now the dream was over.

CHAPTER TWENTY-TWO

James stood on the doorstep of his house, staring at his hand on the doorknob. He couldn't make himself turn it and go in, didn't want to think about what he'd lost, didn't want to feel the pain clawing at his heart. What was there to do inside a cage but think and feel, or tear the place apart?

He wasn't a violent man, but he needed to hit someone.

Then he knew. He knew exactly where he needed to go and what he had to do. Curzon Street was just round the corner. When he got there, he'd find Thorne, and when he found him, he'd knock him through a wall. It had to be the best plan in the world.

He walked briskly, his feet pounding the pavement. He closed his mind to Fran, purged his thoughts of anything soft, letting the anger build within him. Better to unleash it all when the time was right.

A fine coach waited outside the townhouse, four matching chestnuts idling in harness. Two footmen worked next to an enormous pile of luggage, lugging cases and hatboxes onto the imperial.

How fortunate he'd come when he had. It looked like Thorne was about to leave on a long trip.

"Mr. Standish." A woman's voice, but it didn't come from the vehicle. Mrs. Kirkpatrick stood in the doorway of Thorne's house. "Are you quite all right?"

He looked past her, his vision shrinking until it took in only the open door. Several seconds passed, but Thorne didn't emerge.

"Mr. Standish?"

He forced himself to look at her properly and noticed her chic gray traveling dress. "Are you and Thorne taking a trip together?"

She moved down the steps toward him. "No. Just me actually."

"Ah. I hope you have a pleasant time. I'm sure we'll meet again when you return." He didn't want to stand here exchanging pleasantries. He wanted to go in and confront his erstwhile friend.

"I'm afraid we won't." She glanced over her shoulder at the front of the house. "You see, I'm not coming back."

After Thorne's behavior at the ball, James wasn't surprised. In his happiness with Fran, he'd forgotten that Mrs. Kirkpatrick too had been betrayed. "Are you all right?"

"I'm fine, but Mr. Thorne and I are no longer friends."

"I'm sorry to hear it." James liked Mrs. Kirkpatrick. He hoped Thorne had the decency to make a proper settlement on her.

"When a man calls me by another woman's name, it's time to find another protector. If I know anything, it's that."

Her candor in a personal crisis reminded him of someone else, but he pushed the pain away. "I'm glad you told me." Another reason Thorne needed punching. "Whoever your new protector is, I hope he's worthy of you."

"I hope so too."

As she searched his face, he tried to summon his best polite smile. It wouldn't come. For once, he hadn't the strength to pretend.

Her brown eyes took in everything. "Edward's in his study, but . . ." She touched his arm. "Are you sure this is wise?"

Wise? He couldn't care less. "Thank you, Mrs. Kirkpatrick."

She nodded. "Good luck, Mr. Standish."

Seized by a sudden impulse, he followed her to the carriage and grabbed her hand. "Take care of yourself. And if you ever require assistance . . ."

"Thank you." She returned the squeeze of his fingers. "I wish we'd had a chance to know each other better."

Ever the gentleman, he handed her in, but he wouldn't watch her depart. He needed to slip in now, before someone closed the door. He doubted they'd let him in if he stayed to request admittance.

The entrance hall was empty, but servants chattered somewhere nearby. He crept unerringly through corridors in which he'd played as a boy, past the dining room where he and Thorne had spent hours skidding across the bright polished floor. On reaching the study, he didn't bother to knock—just shoved the door open and strode in.

Thorne froze in the act of pulling a slim leather volume from one of the shelves. He abandoned the book, pulled just clear of its fellows. "Standish, do come in," he said, his tone laced with sarcasm. "To what do I owe this—?"

Pleasure. But he never got a chance to say it.

James's knuckles collided with Thorne's jaw, a most satisfying—if painful—sensation.

Thorne staggered back, too stunned by the unprecedented attack to react quickly. "What the bloody hell are you doing, you insane bastard?" His hand fumbled at the portion of his face soon to sport a spectacular bruise. "What was that for?"

"Well, let's see, shall we? What have you done lately?"

"Is this about Francesca?" His mouth twisted up at one corner. "It was actually my lawyer's idea to have her followed. They do it all the time in cases such as these. I really don't see why you're so upset. After all, if she hadn't been behaving like some tuppeny whore—"

James slammed into him with all his weight. They went down, grappling clumsily. Jabbing outward with his elbow, he caught Thorne's face by luck as much as design. By the time they'd scrambled to their feet, both were breathing hard.

"Never talk about her that way again."

"She's my bloody wife. It's none of your damned business how I talk about her."

"She isn't your wife. You haven't acted like a husband in years."

"And now you want her, is that it? Well, you're welcome to the faithless little trollop."

James understood now as never before what it meant to see red. The five senses seemed to suspend until he was pure rage. Before he had time to think, he'd grabbed his onetime friend by the lapels, holding on with all his strength.

Thorne struggled and flailed, but he couldn't break free. "Now what?"

"I'm glad you asked." James jerked his head forward, smashing Thorne full in the face. He saw stars. He supposed they both did.

They sat side by side on the floor in front of Thorne's desk.

James's head pounded. His left eye must be swelling shut, because everything on that side of the room looked fuzzy, and he could see the pinkish bulge of his own puffy skin. He hadn't got the angle of his head-butt quite right. The pain had been worse than anything his opponent inflicted. Worth it, though. He particularly enjoyed the wary glances Thorne kept tossing his way.

"That eye looks terrible. Still, I definitely came off worse. My hat's off to you, Standish."

"You sound very cheerful for someone whose nose might be broken."

"Do I?" Thorne tilted his head back and pinched an already blood-soaked handkerchief over the bridge. "I'll probably summon my minions to throw you out in a moment, but just now I'm a bit busy trying not to bleed to death."

"Oh, don't be so melodramatic." James took his own clean handkerchief from his pocket and passed it to Thorne. Anger had dulled to resentment. Like smoldering coals, a little prodding would probably set the feelings blazing again. In the meantime, James only wanted Thorne to stop complaining.

"Thank you," Thorne said, and cast the old handkerchief aside. "Look, the fact is, I deserved it. I was never comfortable having Francesca followed. But let's face facts. No one is precisely lily-white here."

James had to admit the truth of it. None of the three of them had behaved well according to society's dictates, to say nothing of morality. "You do realize, of course, that nothing would've come of my attraction to Francesca if you hadn't attempted to seduce Miss Randle? Honor would have prevented me from acting on my feelings."

Thorne grinned, a ghastly sight through all the bloodstains. "You know, I think I believe you. I can just imagine you pining away out of misplaced loyalty to me."

James itched to clobber Thorne again, but he wasn't sure he could stand yet. "What happened to *your* loyalty?"

"Yes, sorry about that. But Miss Randle's a pretty little thing. Haven't been able to stop thinking about her as it happens."

Strangely, James didn't doubt it. Thorne had a peculiar lilt to his voice when he spoke of her, despite his outward facetiousness. "And yet you're still determined to hang on to Fran."

"It's not about hanging on to her, not anymore. I simply refuse to let her drag my name through the mud when she's as guilty as I."

James had heard all this before, but now he wondered if Thorne was being sincere. "Do you actually believe that? You've had countless lovers."

"While she's only entertained herself with Trafford and your good self? Yes, I know. The thing is, it's different for women. Infidelity is a failing in a man and I hold my hands up. In a wife, it's unforgivable, especially when she's yet to provide an heir."

That was all very well, except for one small detail. "Fran says she can't have children."

Thorne sighed. "So it would appear."

"Then why not let her go? You could marry someone more to your liking and have a nursery full in no time." Then Fran would be free to remarry if she cared to. James still wanted that for her, even though she'd made it abundantly clear what she thought of his marriage proposal.

A man who loves money and status more than he could ever love me; that's how she regarded him. When he considered what his life amounted to thus far, he didn't blame her for her lack of faith in him.

"Such probing questions." Thorne might have raised an eyebrow; the gore made it difficult to tell. "You know I've never been analytical. But, as you're pressing me, I suppose I'm still angry with her. She didn't accept me. She refused to turn a blind eye, and I can't forgive her for it."

Silence descended as they lost themselves in thought.

James began to understand Thorne's bitterness, and while his attitude might be completely unreasonable, a lot of men would sympathize. James could name twenty without even thinking.

"Anyway, why should I set her free just so she can go running to you? I take it you'd marry her?"

"Hardly." He had to force the word out.

"Ah, yes, I forgot. You'd lose out on Aunt Mim's fat pile of cash. Strange how money becomes so much more vital to one's happiness than love as one grows older."

James allowed himself a grim smile. How like Thorne to take a one-word response and interpret James's feelings as his own. It wouldn't occur to him the reason James would never marry Fran was because Fran had already refused his proposal.

Naturally, he didn't correct the error. "If money truly made people happy, you'd be one of the happiest men on earth," he said.

Thorne twisted his body until they faced one another. The bleeding had slowed, but he still needed to apply pressure with one hand. "But you do love her, don't you?"

James stilled in surprise. "Are we really going to talk about this?"

This time, Thorne definitely arched an eyebrow. The tiny movement made him hiss with pain.

Good. I hope I broke something. "Yes, I love her."

"And she *is* your mistress?"

He had to swallow past the lump lodged in his throat before he could reply. "No." *Not anymore.*

Before Thorne could ask any more searching questions, James dragged himself to a stand, noticing several new bruises in the process. The study looked exactly the same as always. No overturned chairs. No scattered papers. No smashed glass. Their brief bout of violence hadn't changed anything. "Unless you're desperate for another round, I think I'll go now."

Thorne shrugged. "I'm quite happy with things as they are."

James saw himself out for the last time.

He had to walk home, and judging from the shocked and disapproving looks he received, his face probably resembled a plate of raw offal. Stephens confirmed it when he met him at the door to his lodgings. The usually unflappable valet's face was a picture of horrified amazement. Wisely, he didn't comment, just stepped back to let James pass.

He went straight to his study and sat down, fully intending to drink himself into oblivion. A small, white envelope waited for him on the desk. He recognized the stationery. Inside was a single sheet of paper. Written on it was one sentence in Miriam's elegant hand:

Come at once before you do something I cannot forgive.

He leaned back in his chair.

The bars of his cage—the cage Fran had prized open—were closing in around him again, but he wouldn't see Miriam today.

Come at once . . .

He'd go tomorrow or the next day, but not today.

* * *

Sylvia couldn't sleep. She'd spent the last hour staring up at her bedroom ceiling, trying to find a way out of the horrible situation she'd fallen into.

In the days after Mrs. Price's ball, she'd felt restless and fretful. Mama's constant nagging, though no worse than usual, had seemed unbearable after those brief hours of rebellion with Mr. Thorne. Mr. Biddle's unexpected proposal came at precisely the wrong time. He'd caught her at a moment when she'd have done anything to escape Mama's pestering, and she'd accepted him out of desperation. Now the moment had passed, and she had to live with the consequences of her actions.

She couldn't simply retract her acceptance, not when Mama and Papa had already made the announcement. They'd notified the papers as soon as she'd told them, barely pausing to seek Mr. and Mrs. Biddle's approval. If Sylvia changed her mind, everyone would call her a jilt. The Biddles might even bring a lawsuit against Papa, if they had a mind to.

But why not marry him? She had to marry eventually. She had a duty to her family. And Mr. Biddle—she really must get used to calling him Charles—*Charles* claimed to care for her. So, why not?

She heard something—a faint rattle. The sound of the house settling, perhaps.

How stuffy it was. Throwing off the covers, she struggled to make herself comfortable. No wonder she couldn't sleep with this heat and thoughts of Mr. Biddle going round and round inside her head.

They were to have a long engagement—more than a year. Perhaps as she got to know him, she might grow fonder of her fiancé. He seemed pleasant enough.

That sound again. The beginnings of rain? They certainly needed it. The last week had been so humid. So hot and sticky. She turned the pillow so that the cool side faced outward. It felt wonderful against her cheek for those few seconds before her body heat warmed it. She looked with longing at the closed window. Mama didn't like her to sleep with it open in case she took sick.

Mama will suffocate me if I let her.

She rolled out of bed and crossed the room. After undoing the catch, she raised the sash as high as it would go. Fresh air rushed in.

She closed her eyes and took deep breaths. If only she'd done this hours ago. Why was it so hard to resist even Mama's silliest dictates?

When she opened her eyes again, she almost screamed.

Edward Thorne, his beautiful features marred by a nasty-looking black eye, stared back at her over the sill.

"Mr. Thorne!"

He shushed her very loudly, and she smelled liquor on his breath.

"What are you doing here? You have to go." She ought to call for help. Heaven knows what he intended. But if they were found like this . . .

"I can't go now," he said, his words slurring. "I've been trying to get your attention for the last twenty minutes. I felt ridiculous standing there in the street hurling gravel at your window like some lovelorn swain."

That sound. Not rain and not the house settling. A shower of pebbles. "Did anyone see you?"

He considered, his head tilted to one side. "Don't think so."

"You have to go now."

"But I just risked life and limb climbing up here. The least you could do is invite me in."

He must be insane. No, not insane. Just three sheets to the wind. He was lucky he hadn't fallen and killed himself. Her room was on the third floor. "Climb down at once."

"You sound just like the nanny I had as a boy, all strict and caustic. Very amira—admirable qualities in a woman."

He began shuffling along the sill, she hoped preparatory to descending. When he'd gone perhaps four steps, his foot slid out from under him. He didn't fall, but her heart raced so fast it ached.

"Wait!" she cried.

He stopped and sent her an inquiring look.

"You probably did that on purpose."

"Indeed, no, I assure you."

She didn't want his death on her conscience. "Come in and sober up, but then you have to go."

"Thank you," he said, boosting himself forward on his arms. He hit the bedroom floor with an ignominious thud. "After all, imagine the headline. 'Gentleman of dubious reputation found dead outside deb's window.' You'd never live it down."

If he came too close, she'd call out. He presumed too much on her unpardonable behavior at the ball. She fumbled on the floor for her wrapper and quickly slipped it on over her nightgown. What a view she must have given him standing at the window. "What are you thinking coming here? Do you have any idea what this could do to my reputation?"

"Is it true? Are you really going to marry Biddle?"

"What? Yes, of course I am. It's been in the *Times*."

"But he's an ass."

"And you're drunk."

Proving her words, he tottered slightly as he struggled to his feet. Without stopping to think, she stepped forward and took hold of his arm. Silly girl. As if she had the strength to keep him from falling.

He slipped one arm around her and leaned. He didn't do anything shocking, just stood there accepting her support. He felt so hot. His nearness reminded her vividly of the other time he'd been this close. Impossible not to think about it. Her skin prickled with awareness.

His blue eyes focused on her properly for the first time since he'd materialized at the window. When he looked at her that way, she could almost believe he knew her.

Perhaps Mama was right about that window.

"You can't marry that fool."

"Why not?" Then, a moment too late, she added, "And he's not a fool."

"But he won't give you the life you want. He won't like you or understand you. He won't let you paint naked men. He'll stifle everything that makes you unique and wonderful." In the grip of some powerful emotion she couldn't identify, he scowled. "Believe me, I know the type."

Absurdly, she felt like crying.

He dipped his head and kissed the first tear as it fell.

She couldn't help it; she wanted to feel the way he'd made her feel before. Leaning in, she tilted her face up for his kiss. She knew the taste of brandy—she'd stolen the odd nip from the decanter in her father's study—but despite his obvious drunkenness, he kissed gently, his mouth teasing hers.

Something caught fire in her; the passion he'd stirred at the ball had merely lain dormant. One touch reignited it, and she seized his shoulders and pulled herself flush against him. He groaned, and they grew frantic. His hand cupped her breast through the thin fabric of her nightgown. His mouth followed, tracing damp circles over her nipple.

"He won't touch you like this," he whispered. "Or if he does, you won't want him to."

Somehow, she knew it was true.

He pushed her toward the bed, his hands all over her. She wanted to let him. She wanted him to ruin and expose her. When she was nothing and nobody, everyone would finally leave her alone.

"You're a liar," she said. It took every ounce of willpower she had left, but she pushed him away. "You can't give me anything better, and you know it. All you offer is destruction."

His eyes held hers, and she felt that connection, that closeness. But then he smiled, and it was gone. "To be fair, sweet, I never said I could."

"Then you came here simply to destroy my happiness."

"You're not happy."

For a moment, she hated him. How dare he come here and expose her for a sham?

"One day you'll tire of Biddle," he said. "And when that happens, I'll be waiting."

"Get out," she said, her voice breaking.

Still wearing that horrible smile, he obeyed.

CHAPTER TWENTY-THREE

"Ladies and gentlemen of the jury, I am confident, once you have heard the evidence presented here today, you will be only too willing to release the petitioner from what has become an intolerable union."

Francesca listened from the back of the courtroom as her barrister, Mr. Pimlico, delivered his opening speech. In his black robe and horsehair wig, he looked the twin of the opposing council. Only his spectacles and his sonorous voice distinguished him.

The courtroom, indeed the whole magnificent structure that housed the Royal Courts of Justice, was brand new. The Queen had presided over its grand opening shortly before Christmas. From outside, it resembled a palace from a fairy tale, its multitude of neo-Gothic spires pointing proudly to the sky, and the ornately carved stone walls, as yet, unmarked by smog.

Inside proved just as grand. The main hall, through which she'd walked earlier, reminded her of the inside of a cathedral with its vaulted ceiling arching what must be a hundred feet overhead. The courtroom itself was slightly less formidable, its oak paneling lending it a comparatively cozy air. Sunlight streamed in through enormous windows, shining on spectators packed onto rows of benches.

Though no longer a rarity, divorce cases still had the power to bring society out in force, especially when the estranged husband and wife sprang from within their own ranks. Today's events would provide fodder to keep them gossiping for weeks. Those fortunate enough to hear all the salacious details firsthand would be sought after guests over the next few days.

This crowd would go into a collective frenzy if they knew Francesca was there. What sort of lady would opt to appear at her own divorce proceedings unless compelled to do so? Why, no sort of lady at all, and there lay the rub.

Though no rule explicitly barred her attendance, Mr. Flint permitted it with reluctance and only if she did her best to avoid detection. She'd slipped in quietly, dressed plainly in a sensible gray suit. A full veil would be too theatrical and invite speculation as to her identity. She'd opted for a hat with a half-veil, and tried her best to seem insignificant but not furtive. So far, it appeared effective. But really, what was a little more disapproval? Today's outcome was a foregone conclusion. She couldn't sit at home while judge, jury, and legal council decided her entire future in her absence.

Edward sat in plain sight—no hiding in the crowd for him—next to his barrister, Mr. Snow. He looked supremely uninterested in the proceedings as Mr. Pimlico continued to speak. His nonchalance had to be deceptive. According to Mr. Flint, he'd dismissed the family solicitor in favor of his current representation at the eleventh hour. No one seemed to know why.

"Mrs. Thorne—Miss Francesca Heller as she was then—was barely nineteen years old when she married Edward Thorne on the strength of a mere six-week acquaintance. Various witnesses will testify to her impeccable good character throughout the many years of her marriage. You will hear no convincing evidence to the contrary. She was an exemplary wife."

If Edward burst out laughing, she wouldn't blame him in the least. How many exemplary wives existed in the world? Not many, she'd wager.

Opening statement complete, Mr. Pimlico called various witnesses from among her and Edward's acquaintance and servants.

All of them conceded she was of good character. Typical of these was Mr. Cholmondeley, an old school friend of Edward's who she remembered vaguely. He spoke about what a nice girl she'd seemed and how happy they'd been during their engagement. But by far the most important of these early witnesses was Aunt Helena.

Until the name Helena Lytton was called, even Francesca had been in danger of nodding off as witness after witness repeated more or less the same testimony. Now an excited hum of conversation rose up among the spectators. The judge peered at them severely through his pince-nez and called for silence. Her aunt was not there willingly—they'd had to issue a subpoena—and she looked mortified as she took her place in the witness box. She gave her oath with the appearance of one who might weep.

"Mrs. Lytton," Mr. Pimlico began, once he had dispensed with the preliminaries. "You and your husband were the petitioner's legal guardians subsequent to the deaths of her parents. Is that correct?"

"Yes." The single word was uttered so quietly that the judge had to ask her to repeat it.

"You were the closest thing she had to a mother?"

"I suppose so, yes."

Pimlico smiled kindly. "This must be very upsetting for you. It is fair to say, I think, you did not approve of your niece's decision to leave the marital home?"

"No, I did not." This time, she spoke up. She wanted everyone to know she didn't condone such behavior. Francesca almost pitied her. She knew how it felt to fear what people thought—the fear of losing the love of one's family and the respect of one's peers. As someone who'd lost both, she knew such a burden should never be assumed lightly.

That was one of the many reasons she'd broken with James.

Even now, so many weeks later, the thought made it hard to breathe.

"You disapproved so much you disowned her?"

"Yes."

What hurt most was the pride in Aunt Helena's voice, pride that she'd cut her own niece out of her life. And yet she'd trembled with shame merely admitting their kinship to the court. If Francesca had allowed James to turn his back on his inheritance, surely the day would've come when he too would turn his back on her. The resentment would've torn them apart in the end.

"But you were close once?"

"Yes. We were together every day."

"And before her marriage, was she ever a cause for concern?"

A slight hesitation. "No," she admitted. "She never gave me a day's trouble."

"She was a dutiful niece?"

"Yes, she was."

He paused, giving the jury time to ponder these admissions from a witness clearly not on his client's side.

"Were you pleased with the betrothal?"

"Yes, I was."

"You did not consider it rather sudden coming after so short an acquaintance?"

"No. Many successful marriages have been made in half as much time."

Was it Francesca's imagination or did Helena protest a little too much?

"Can you name any?"

Helena spluttered. "None spring to mind at this particular moment, though I feel sure there are many."

"That's quite all right, ma'am. Perhaps you will think of some later," Pimlico said with quiet humor. "Let's talk instead about the marriage itself. Did you see your niece with any frequency after the wedding?"

"Yes, several times a year."

"Did she seem content?"

"Of course she did. Why shouldn't she?"

"You noticed no difference in her demeanor?"

"I . . . well, nothing significant. I suppose she sometimes seemed a little subdued."

"Did she ever confide in you regarding any suspicions she entertained as to her husband's constancy?"

Aunt Helena looked down at her lap, the very picture of dejection. "Once."

"In what circumstances?"

"Shortly after Mr. Thorne left for London. I was concerned and I asked if anything were the matter."

"And what was Mrs. Thorne's response?"

"She broke down and . . . confided certain suspicions. She wanted to know what to do."

"And what did you advise?"

"It was of a personal nature."

"I appreciate your diffidence, ma'am, but it is important."

"I told her most men enjoy a . . . dalliance from time to time. As a wife, it was her duty to understand, not to censure."

"Thank you, Mrs. Lytton. No further questions."

Helena left the stand, visibly relieved to escape so soon. The pain of losing her would never ease completely, but Francesca watched her walk away with a strange sense of calm. If she'd ever truly had her aunt's love, then she had it still, and one day they would reconcile.

Mr. Pimlico held something aloft. A small paper subtly yellowed with age. "It was in the April of 1874 when, approximately two years after the wedding, the petitioner made a discovery that shook the very foundations of her happiness. This note, which I now enter into the record, is dated February of that year."

Francesca braced herself as the lawyer began to read the letter she'd kept for over eight years, first as a reminder of what her husband was, then with this very day in mind.

"*Teddy dearest*," he began and got no further. A ripple of laughter from the spectators greeted the words. The silly salutation, pronounced in Mr. Pimlico's serious lawyerly voice, had proved too much.

Mr. Snow whispered something to Edward.

The judge cleared his throat. "May I remind the ladies and gentlemen present of the seriousness of the occasion?" Though said in mild tones, this was enough to quell the slight disturbance.

Order restored, Mr. Pimlico continued to read. "My husband sends word he is to return from Bristol sooner than expected. We must postpone our rendezvous. Please be assured, I long to hold you in my arms again." He gazed sternly at the jury. "It is unsigned."

Francesca sank back in her seat. She'd known he intended to read the letter, a vital piece of evidence in her favor, but she hadn't realized how uncomfortable she'd feel. Her feelings made no logical sense. Why should she feel guilty for humiliating Edward? If he hadn't betrayed their vows, she wouldn't be able to hurt him this way. Of course, that's probably what he said about her.

Mr. Pimlico was already calling his next witness.

Barker looked terrified as she took the stand, then cast an uneasy glance at the judge high up on the bench.

"You have been Mrs. Thorne's personal maid since before her marriage. Is that correct?"

"Yes. That is, yes, sir."

"You're doing very well, Miss Barker," Pimlico said, trying to be kind. "Now, tell me, did your mistress ever confide in you about the letter just read out in court?"

"She did, sir."

"Did she tell you what she believed it to mean?"

"She did, sir. She thought Mr. Thorne was being untrue to her."

"Did she tell you what she intended to do?"

"No, sir. But I know for a fact she confronted Mr. Thorne."

"And how do you know that?"

"She told me afterward, sir. One afternoon, they shut themselves away in the study. They argued until he got fed up and admitted everything."

Mr. Pimlico waited while the spectators murmured among themselves. This time, a look from the judge sufficed to silence them.

"Did Mrs. Thorne suspect the identity of the note's author?"

Barker considered carefully before answering. "If she did, she didn't confide in me, sir."

"Mr. Thorne left for London shortly afterward, did he not?"

"In June of the same year, sir."

"He removed to London, but rumors of his liaisons with numerous ladies of dubious respectability traveled back to Hertfordshire, didn't they?"

"Yes, sir. It was no secret in the servants' hall. Everyone knew about Mr. Thorne's lady friends."

Edward's barrister, Mr. Snow, saw fit to intervene. "My Lord, this is pure speculation." Until then, he'd been so quiet Francesca had almost forgotten him. "This letter, even if genuine, does not prove illicit intercourse ever took place between my client and the author. Thus far, we have heard no convincing evidence to suggest Mr. Thorne was unfaithful during this time."

The judge considered for several seconds. "Mr. Snow, you are correct from a legal standpoint, though not necessarily from a commonsense one. The jury is free to infer for themselves what significance attaches to this letter. Carry on, Mr. Pimlico."

"Thank you, My Lord."

Mr. Snow sat down again, somewhat crestfallen.

Francesca sympathized. One would think in a court of law the legal standpoint would carry the day. How fortunate for her that this judge showed himself such an advocate of common sense.

"Did Mrs. Thorne believe these rumors?" Mr. Pimlico asked.

"Yes, sir. I was at the end of my tether."

"You were concerned for her?"

"Yes, sir."

"Did she ever confront Mr. Thorne again?"

"Many times, sir. She wrote letters and whenever he came home, which was less and less often, they rowed something fearful."

"When did she tell you she intended to leave?"

"In 1881, sir." Barker thought for a moment. "I'm not sure of the month."

"1881 will do very well. What was your opinion of her decision?"

"Oh, sir, I was so relieved when she told me."

"You thought it the right thing to do?"

"Yes, sir. It was no life for a young lady. She'd been unhappy for a long time. I didn't see why she should sit at home waiting for a husband that didn't want her. And when she started planning for it, her spirits were better than I'd ever seen them."

Francesca remembered. With something to plan for, she'd felt better than she had in years. Barker had been a phenomenal ally in those days, just as she was now. All this time, Francesca had been busy mourning the loss of her aunt; Barker was just as much of a mother to her, perhaps even more. Helena had been a close companion, particularly once Francesca had come of age, but Barker had been her nursemaid before she'd taken on the lofty mantle of personal maid. She'd taken care of Francesca through everything from a childhood bout of measles to a broken heart. Wasn't that true motherhood?

Mr. Pimlico had no further questions. "Thank you, Miss Barker," he said, his voice snapping Francesca out of her reverie.

Now Mr. Snow came forward. "Was Mrs. Thorne entirely alone in the Hertfordshire house?"

"No, sir. Mrs. Thorne—that is, the elder Mrs. Thorne, her mother-in- law, lived there too. But they weren't exactly what you'd call close."

"Did she never have visitors?"

"Sometimes, sir."

"I am thinking of a particular visitor. Do you happen to recall one Mr. Trafford?"

Barker looked honestly puzzled, bless her. "I do, sir."

"Do you think it fair to say he and Mrs. Thorne were particular friends?"

She hesitated. "Yes, sir, but—"

He turned to the judge. "No further questions, My Lord."

Mr. Pimlico got up again. "Did you suspect anything untoward in Mrs. Thorne's friendship with Mr. Trafford?"

Barker looked close to tears. "Oh no, sir," she said, horrified. "They were just friends."

Remorse swept Francesca as she listened to this heartfelt defense. At the time, deceiving Barker had seemed like a kindness. Why implicate her? But now Francesca felt like the biggest liar in the world.

To her surprise, Mr. Snow permitted Barker to step down without further questioning. Why hadn't they asked about James? What game was Edward playing?

Next, several servants testified regarding the rumors of Edward's affairs. Most of them had moved on to new positions and didn't need to fear the elder Mrs. Thorne's displeasure.

After what seemed like hours, Pimlico called his final witness. The judge had to reprimand the spectators again when Mrs. Kirkpatrick swept regally up the aisle toward the box. She looked entirely too sultry as she peeled off a single glove to lay her bare hand on the Bible.

Francesca hadn't seen Mrs. Kirkpatrick since Mrs. Price's ball, but Mr. Flint claimed the courtesan had expressed herself happy to testify on Francesca's behalf.

"Mrs. Kirkpatrick, can you please specify the nature of your relationship with Mr. Thorne?"

She smiled. "I was his mistress for more than two years."

As an excited murmur rose up, the judge addressed the crowd again. "This room will be cleared if there are any further interruptions."

Pimlico tried again. "Forgive me for asking, but I wish to make things quite plain to the jury. During those two years, did you bestow your sexual favors upon Mr. Thorne?"

"Many, *many* times," she said, her tone low and intimate.

The old lawyer's ears turned a telling shade of pink. "He committed adultery with you?"

"He most certainly did."

"Did he ever discuss his wife with you?"

"Very rarely."

"To the best of your recollection, did he ever imply he wished for reconciliation with her?"

"Oh, no. On the contrary, he disliked her quite intensely. He said he never wanted to live with her again." She delivered this last remark so airily, one might almost think she didn't know she'd dealt Edward's case a hefty blow.

"Thank you," Mr. Pimlico said.

As Mrs. Kirkpatrick glided back down the aisle, her gaze traveled over the rows of spectators, halting when it reached Francesca. She nodded almost imperceptibly as she passed on by.

James was not among the throng of voyeurs at the law courts, but he woke already thinking of Francesca, his body still tingling from the wraithlike touch of her double.

Whenever he stopped to rest, particularly when he slept, peace fled. She always came to him like a ghost, sometimes a succubus. The dreams disturbed him. Worse, they made his heart ache. He knew her too well, remembered every curve, every line of her face and body. The apparition his mind conjured was too vivid, too real. Her taste, her smell, the timbre of her voice—when he dreamed, he wallowed in them all.

Now he groaned as the real world came into focus. A new day. *Her* day in court. He knew straight away that he'd slept late. It must be ten o'clock at least, judging by the light, a time he'd once considered unfathomably early. Things changed and, in the several months since he'd last seen Fran, things had changed enormously. For one thing, he no longer needed to be dragged from his bed against his will.

He rang for Stephens. By now, proceedings at the Royal Courts might already be underway, but he needed to stop thinking about her. No good came of dwelling on the past, and the Ashtons expected him.

At first, he'd spent time with them because they were *her* friends. He'd wanted to be where he'd hear news of her or where he might see her. Their paths never collided, and now he went for simple friendship's sake or for business.

Ashton had found room for him at *The Review*. To James's surprise and, he suspected, to Ashton's, he enjoyed his work as assistant editor. Sometimes he succeeded in losing himself in one task or another completely. On those occasions, he felt a peace bordering on contentment, something he'd never known before. With *her*, he'd experienced dizzying highs and the worst lows and, before her, boredom and dissatisfaction with himself and his life. Now, he preferred to be busy.

"Shall I pour your bath, sir?" Stephens glided in, dignity undaunted by their move to smaller, slightly shabbier quarters.

"No time for that today. Bring me hot water and I'll wash."

Stephens returned with soap and water. "Mr. Thorne is appearing at the Courts of Justice today," he said, just by way of conversation.

"I believe so."

"If you'll forgive me for saying so, sir, I thought you might attend. I couldn't help but notice you've been following the newspapers."

"These things are always more diverting when one knows the players."

In truth, those few minutes James allowed himself each day with an open paper had become his guilty pleasure. He read about her, but then he cast the newssheet aside and thoughts of her with it. It was that or run mad.

About a month ago, Caroline had confessed that she always sent Fran a note warning her when he visited Bedford Square. She *chose* to avoid him. Had she ever been there at the same time as him, hidden away in another room or disappearing out of the back door? Perhaps she'd never really returned his feelings; he'd always been the one in pursuit. The thought would plague him if he let it.

"Then you don't mean to attend, sir?"

"Certainly not. Mr. and Mrs. Ashton are expecting me."

"But I wonder—"

"Confound you, Stephens! Are you angling for the afternoon off so that you can attend? By all means, enjoy the show." An unfortunate outburst, yet an effective one because it ended the conversation.

James walked to Bedford Square—it wasn't far now that he'd made the move to Bloomsbury—and a servant showed him straight to the comfortable room where Ashton worked when he wasn't at his office.

"Come in, Standish. Care for a drink?"

"It's only half past ten. Bit early, isn't it?"

"Ah, but today is no ordinary day. I thought you might need fortifying."

"My God," he couldn't help exclaiming. "It's a conspiracy. First my valet, now you." He should have known she'd be inescapable today, but surely Ashton of all people would understand and respect James's wish to avoid the subject. "As a matter of fact, the outcome of today's trial is a matter of supreme indifference to me."

"Oh?" Ashton sat down and poured two brandies. "You surprise me. I thought you'd be on tenterhooks."

"I hope, for her sake, she gets her freedom, but it has no impact on me or my life either way." And he'd keep reminding himself of that until the words penetrated his thick, stupid skull.

"I see," Ashton said, his tone stiff. "So, you no longer care for her."

Precisely what James had meant to suggest, yet now he felt irrationally angry that Ashton, that anyone, could believe it of him, even for a moment. "I wish to God I didn't! I wish to God I could get through even a single day without thinking of her, but I can't. I hope for her happiness more than anything."

Wasn't that why he'd sent her lawyer word of the estrangement between Thorne and Mrs. Kirkpatrick? If there was any chance he could help Fran to her blasted freedom, he'd take it, even if he could never share a life with her. Even if, when all was said and done . . . "Our futures are destined to remain separate."

Ashton pushed a tumbler of brandy across the width of the desk. This time, James didn't argue; he just drank.

"I've always been suspicious of destiny myself," Ashton said quietly. "I think we make our own fate."

James nodded because, in some ways, it was true. He hadn't been destined from birth to work in journalism, or to work at all for that matter, yet here he was and, heartbreak aside, he was thriving. Yes, his rooms were in a less fashionable part of town now, but he had a comfy chair, a window overlooking the park, and interesting work to occupy his mind. To his surprise, he'd discovered he didn't need more than that. Thoughts of Francesca lingered and would always linger, but if he'd managed to scrape his way through those first few weeks after she'd broken with him, he could survive anything. "A man can't force a woman to love him."

"Is that what you think? That she doesn't care for you?"

He thought back to their last day. He still remembered everything she'd said, every reason she'd given. "I think all Fran's fine talk amounts to little more than petty excuses. I would have done anything for her. Anything. The truth is she didn't want me as much as I wanted her."

The slow ticking of the clock on the mantel seemed far too loud. Bloody clocks accentuating every silence, every pregnant pause.

Ashton regarded him thoughtfully from his plush wingchair. "But it must have occurred to you that her reasons for rejecting you are no longer relevant. Even if the outcome of today is the misfortune we're all anticipating, Mrs. Price is no longer in a position to control you. Surely the two of you could reach some sort of understanding?"

He shook his head. "Fran was very clear on that point. She didn't want me to give anything up. *Don't break with Mrs. Price for me.* Those were her exact words."

"Yet you still told Mrs. Price where she could stick her inheritance."

"Not in so many words. I simply . . . never went to see her. My work here is far easier on the soul than catering to an old lady's whims simply to lay hands on her fortune. I refuse to perform like a circus monkey. It has nothing to do with Francesca, not that she'd believe me, and that's precisely what I mean when I talk about excuses. In her heart, I don't think she wanted to marry me." The admission, uttered aloud for the first time, brought a pang.

Ashton opened his mouth, no doubt intending to argue, but James cut him off. "Only a boor would force his attentions where they're not wanted."

If Fran didn't need or want his love, the least he could do was respect her wishes.

CHAPTER TWENTY-FOUR

After the lunchtime recess, Mr. Snow took his turn.

"Mr. Thorne does not dispute the charge of infidelity, but he contends his wife's coldness and lack of womanly feeling are partly to blame. Furthermore, far from abandoning her, my client provided for her handsomely throughout the years of their marriage and for many months after her departure from their home. Only when he began to suspect her of unfaithfulness did he withhold further financial support."

How clever of Edward. He'd admitted everything except the weakest charges. The grounds for abandonment were flimsy. That, coupled with her lapses with Trafford and James, might be enough to win him the day.

"Mr. Thorne too is dissatisfied with the marriage. However, as a man of good sense, he realizes such a solemn union ought not to be dissolved merely because one or both parties are no longer happy. Instead, it is their duty to make the best of things."

She clenched her hands into tight fists, her nails digging into the flesh of her palms. She'd spent *years* making the best of things while he caroused in London. If he'd made even the smallest effort, they might not be here today.

Mr. Snow called his first witnesses.

His opening gambits were similar to Mr. Pimlico's. He called numerous old friends and trusted retainers to testify to Edward's good character prior to the marriage. He asked the same questions repeatedly, inviting a contrast between Edward then and Edward now. A picture emerged of a well-intentioned young man who, disappointed in his wife, turned to other women to give him all he lacked. Much as it galled her, she had to admit the truth of it. Although she'd done what she could, their incompatibility had left them both unfulfilled.

The most important of these early witnesses turned out to be Edward's mother. Francesca didn't know the elder Mrs. Thorne had come to court until the clerk called her name. She hadn't changed. As she swept up the aisle toward the witness box, she held herself as straight and tall as ever, her silver hair partially hidden under a peacock-blue hat. Never, in all their years of living under the same roof, had Francesca managed to penetrate beyond her patrician reserve.

Snow started with the same question he'd put to every other witness. "Mrs. Thorne, how would you describe your son's character prior to his marriage?"

"He was my mainstay," she said, in her clear, clipped tones. "No mother was ever blessed with a kinder, more thoughtful son. He was always good-tempered, always dutiful."

"But that changed?"

"Shortly after the marriage. He became quiet, even sullen. I knew something had gone wrong between them. I noticed a certain . . . coldness."

How strange to hear the collapse of her marriage described in this concise manner by a third party. Mrs. Thorne—the *real* Mrs. Thorne, Edward's mother—had seen that her son wasn't happy and blamed his wife. But surely Edward might have striven harder to overcome his life's first grave disappointment. Were her early crimes—sexual curiosity, resentfulness of temper—so great they justified his response? Francesca didn't think so.

"Did you ask your son what the trouble was?"

"He wouldn't talk to me. I believe he meant to protect *her* from censure." Never had a simple pronoun been spoken with so much scorn.

Quite possibly. Edward wouldn't have wanted their private affairs talked about, even within the family.

"Were you aware of your son's affairs?"

Her lips thinned. "No, not at first. Of course, nothing remains hidden from a mother for long. Once I discovered his . . . amours, I found I couldn't blame him."

"A mother's partiality, perhaps?"

"Indeed, no. A woman's role in life is to marry. It is my firm belief that, once married, she must fulfill certain obligations. She must endeavor to satisfy her husband and provide him with heirs. My daughter-in-law failed at both."

Once such an indictment would have brought Francesca to tears. Now it meant nothing. Just the faint, momentary throb of old scar tissue.

Mr. Snow continued. "And after she left, when she notified you of her intention to seek a divorce . . ."

"It disgusted me. I always thought her undutiful, but to go to these lengths . . . a wife should forbear no matter how her husband treats her, but my son was never cruel. She owed him her loyalty and fidelity."

A damning indictment. And worse was to come. Mr. Snow still hadn't raised the subject of what Francesca had been up to with James.

Next the clerk called Mr. Fisher, Edward's secretary. A dull but scrupulously loyal man, he reeled off figures from his account books until her eyes glazed over. Each represented a sum provided by Edward for her support. She might accuse him of desertion if she liked, but this proved he'd sunk plenty of money into her support over the years. The more she listened, the more she felt like an expensive courtesan.

At last, the witness ran out of numbers. Now Mr. Snow would dismiss him. What else could he have to say?

"Did Mr. Thorne confide in you regarding certain suspicions he harbored about his wife?"

"He did."

"Of what nature were they?"

"He suspected her of infidelity."

Her face grew hot as she realized what was coming. Thank God she'd worn the half-veil.

"Did he attempt to verify these suspicions?"

This was it. She'd thought herself prepared. She'd thought she was strong enough. But already she recoiled at the thought of her most intimate secrets spoken aloud in open court. Even so, she leaned forward to hear Mr. Fisher's response just like everyone else.

"He did. He had Mrs. Thorne followed for several weeks."

"And what evidence did he uncover?"

She waited for the final blow to fall. This was Edward's chance. If he exposed her now, she'd never be free of him.

"None," Mr. Fisher said. "Mrs. Thorne's behavior was above reproach."

The lawyers had convened in Mr. Flint's office. They'd been talking for forty minutes now, but for all their verbosity, they couldn't tell Francesca what she most wished to know.

Why had Edward done this?

He slouched in his chair, inspecting his manicure. He looked bored, nothing like a man whose evil schemes had just been thwarted. Observing him offered no clue as to what had possessed him to let her win the day.

Nothing was ever simple.

She tried and failed to catch his eye, and then cleared her throat. "May I speak to you alone?"

Mr. Flint stopped mid-sentence. In unison, both lawyers glanced first at her, then her erstwhile husband.

Edward shrugged. The slight roll of his shoulders proclaimed his complete indifference.

The solicitors made disapproving noises, but decamped to the next room with little fuss.

Edward regarded her calmly, a strange smile playing across his face. She had no confidence in her ability to prize information from him. How utterly foreign he seemed. Yet she'd been his wife for more than a decade. She'd shared his bed every night for two years, but she'd never understood him.

In court, words and phrases had jumped out at her—adultery . . . Abandonment . . . in favor of the petitioner . . . sad duty . . . decree nisi. Her world had tilted on its axis when she'd realized she'd won. Now, more than an hour later, everything still looked askew.

She'd actually won. She was free.

Failure all but certain, she'd come very close to withdrawing her petition. The desire to have her say in open court, albeit using Mr. Pimlico as a mouthpiece, prevented her. She should have lost. Why hadn't Edward used the evidence his spy had gathered? Why, why, why?

"My, my, what can you be thinking?" he mused, his voice low and amused.

"What happened today?"

"What happened? I should think it perfectly obvious. Didn't you hear the spectators as they filed out?"

She fought to keep her temper in check. "Of course."

"And what did you hear?"

Whispered malice, mostly. "That I've sealed my own fate. That no one will receive me."

"Precisely." He smiled. "You got what you wanted."

Something didn't feel right. "And you? Did you get what you wanted?"

"I don't know what you mean." He smirked, deliberately giving the lie to his words. Today had gone exactly according to his wishes.

"You could have stopped me."

"Yes, I could. Obviously, I chose not to."

"Is that why you dismissed Mr. Farrow?" Farrow's firm had handled the Thorne family's affairs for generations.

"The law is a respectable profession. What could I say? 'Farrow, old chap, when we're up in court don't argue my case too vociferously, will you? I find I'd rather like a divorce after all, if you don't mind.'" He shook his head. "It's called collusion, my dear. Fortunately, Mr. Snow is completely ignorant of all your little trysts with Standish, so it wasn't a problem for him."

"But you still had to bring up Trafford?"

"Well, I had to put up a halfhearted defense. Snow assured me, although of course he thought he was warning me, that we didn't have enough evidence to convince judge and jury."

All afternoon, she'd felt numb. Now she felt something stir. Anger, perhaps. Well, just as long as she didn't cry.

"I couldn't let you get away unembarrassed, now could I? That would hardly be fair." He leaned forward, peering into her face. "Oh, don't look so upset. Everyone knew about Trafford. That horse had already bolted."

It happened to be true, but that hardly made it less infuriating. "I see." She stood and walked to the window, raising her face to the graying light, to the drizzle and gloom of another winter day. "Why the sudden change?"

"Perhaps I felt guilty for setting that spy on you."

She laughed, her breath fogging the windowpane. "It's not impossible you experienced a qualm or two, but I'm far from convinced they'd stop you."

"Perhaps . . ." His chair creaked as he rose, but he didn't come any closer. "Perhaps I realized I was punishing myself as much as you. Perhaps I don't want to be trapped anymore than you do. Perhaps I might like to marry someone else, someone I actually like, and have children."

"Oh." She'd dangled those selfsame lures. Why did she feel as though she'd been run over by a hansom now that he'd taken the bait?

"Surprised?"

No, not surprised. Shocked might be a more accurate description. "Do you have a particular lady in mind?" She faced him. "Good God, you're blushing! There is, isn't there? You've found someone else you want to marry."

"Why, sweetheart, you sound almost jealous."

"Why, Edward," she mimicked. "When your ears turn pink like that you look just like a boy again." That wiped the smirk off his face. "But I'm evading the issue. What was the question? Oh, that's right. Am I jealous?" She put a finger to her lips and pretended to consider. "Perhaps I am. I confess it does seem a little unfair after all the times I begged for my freedom." He'd begin again when she never could—a self-pitying thought on a day when she ought to get down on her knees and give thanks to a benevolent god.

It wasn't even true. She *could* start again, just not with James.

Did he think of her fondly? They'd parted on such bad terms, but maybe anger was preferable to indifference. By now, he'd probably realized she'd been right in her refusal. To him, the entire incident must seem like a bout of temporary madness from which he'd since recovered. No doubt Mrs. Price's riches would console him.

"Don't look so glum," Edward said.

She turned her back on him, a childish gesture maybe, but satisfying.

To her surprise he joined her at the window, and they stood side by side, staring out at the bleak day. "If it makes you feel better, I doubt the lady in question will have me," he said after several seconds.

"Yes, that seems very likely. After all, young women reject handsome men with large fortunes all the time."

Her remark startled a laugh out of him. Perhaps he'd forgotten her capable of humor.

"Who is she?"

No answer. She stole a quick glance at him.

He frowned down at the floor, his eyes hidden behind unruly hair. "Look, you've got what you want. It shouldn't matter why. Is there really any reason to prolong this further?"

He had a point. The last chains binding them were broken. After today, she need never even see him again, this man who'd once been her husband. She gazed on the handsome face, once so dear, and tried to view it with an impartial eye.

It couldn't be done. Each line, every strand of hair, every mood, every expression reminded her of past enmity. She couldn't envisage a day when she might look on him without pain.

She crossed to the door, but then looked back over her shoulder. "At least . . . At least, you're free to ask her now."

He nodded. "Don't forget your umbrella. It's raining harder now."

"Oh. Yes, of course." She took her plain black umbrella from the stand. "Thank you."

She walked away for the last time.

CHAPTER TWENTY-FIVE

Every time anyone said the word "wedding," Sylvia wanted to vomit with fear. And since she'd come back to London two weeks ago to order her trousseau, she'd heard the word a lot.

"Do try to express an interest, Sylvia," Mama said as the footman handed her down from the carriage. "It's your wedding gown after all. Aren't you excited?"

They'd just come from the first fitting. White organdie and tulle. "Of course. It's only that . . ."

Her mother paused outside the house, waiting for the servants to open the door. "Yes?"

"Sometimes it's overwhelming." If she had to look at one more version of the seating plan, she'd scream until they sent her to the asylum. At least then she'd get some peace. Since the engagement, Mama had grown more, not less irritating.

The moment the heavy front door closed behind them, the library door opened. Papa stuck his head out. "My dear," he said to his wife. "Join me, if you please."

He must have someone in there. Her father didn't generally use endearments. He must be trying to impress whoever it was with their happy home. He disappeared again.

Mama cast her gloves aside. "How tiresome. Oh, well. We'll just have to discuss the wedding flowers after I'm finished with your father. Orange blossoms for your hair, I think." She followed Papa into the library, still muttering.

Sylvia went to her room and picked up *Metamorphoses*, the book she'd been forced to abandon for the trip to the modiste. At least affianced ladies could read what they liked. As she'd told Mama, no one had the right to restrict her reading matter except Mr. Biddle, and she took great care he never had the opportunity. In his company, she read devotional tracts. They seemed the safest choice. She didn't know for certain he'd disapprove of *Metamorphoses*, but why take the risk? For reasons of her own, Mama conspired with her to conceal her "defect."

She removed the scarlet ribbon that marked her favorite part. Orpheus had journeyed to the underworld to find Eurydice. All he had to do was lead her back to the surface without looking back at her. "Afraid that she might disappear again and longing so to see her, he turned to gaze back at his wife," she read aloud. "One final, faint 'Farewell'—so weak it scarcely reached his ears—was all she said. Then, back to the abyss, she fell."

Someone knocked on her door. She shoved the book under her skirts from force of habit, then retrieved it and set it beside her on the window seat. The knock came again, a firm rapping, not her mother's delicate tap. "Come in," Sylvia called.

She couldn't conceal her surprise when her father entered. In all her life, he'd never once visited her room. He edged in cautiously, as if just as astonished to find himself there.

"Why, Papa, whatever's the matter? Where's Mama?"

"Downstairs. I told her to come to you, but she said I must go myself."

She didn't know what to say. Her Mama never defied her father, or if she did, Sylvia never heard about it. "Is something wrong?"

"There's no easy way to say this. The fact is your betrothal is broken."

She stared stupidly. "Broken?"

He stepped closer, a large, clumsy, bald man completely out of place in this feminine environment. Even she didn't feel fully at home. In many ways, this was still a little girl's room—nothing to do with the adult who now inhabited it.

How bilious Papa looked standing next to those pink bed hangings. She clamped a hand over her mouth to stop a laugh. There must be an appropriate response to getting jilted, but this wasn't it.

"My betrothal is broken," she said, just to have something to say.

Papa opened his mouth to speak, but changed his mind. She'd never seen him lost for words before.

"Did . . ." She searched for the right question—something apposite, something helpful. "Did the Biddles cry off?" There, that ought to get him going again. Really, though, she couldn't imagine why they would. They'd seemed thrilled with the match. The last time she'd seen Charles, he'd been full of honeymoon plans.

"Not exactly."

"Well, what exactly?"

"I've—that is—your mother and I, we've decided on a different match."

For the second time, she stared.

Her parents had made themselves clear. She had to marry, but provided she didn't delay beyond reason, she might choose her own husband from within the preapproved pool. Mama had her favorites of course, but she hadn't meddled beyond her incessant pestering.

"You can't. The Biddles will take you to court."

"It's all taken care of. Young Charles has behaved handsomely in the circumstances. He's told his parents he's changed his mind. He's willing to accept all the blame."

"What circumstances?" It made no sense. Had he changed his mind? Was this her parents' way of softening the blow?

"Now don't make a fuss," he said. "You were never terribly fond of the boy."

True, but that didn't mean she appreciated being pushed about like a tea trolley. "But we've just been to a fitting."

"Your mother is a sensible woman who does what she's told. And this gentleman who's asking for you now is willing to pay through the nose."

Abruptly, the appropriate emotions—anger, frustration, and embarrassment to name a few—manifested themselves and threatened to overflow. If she didn't have so many questions that needed answering, she'd launch Ovid at Papa's head. "Who? Who am I to marry?"

"He's older than you, but not overmuch. Your mama says you've been introduced."

"Introduced? Is that all? Tell me his name, Papa."

"Edward Thorne." He didn't quite meet her eye. "Now, don't make a fuss."

She didn't think. Rage blotted out everything else as she ran out of the room, ignoring Papa's shout, tore down the stairs, and barged into the library.

Mr. Thorne sat facing the desk, his back to the door. He leaped to his feet as she crashed into the room. His cobalt eyes lit with a curious mixture of pleasure and . . . was that fear? "Miss Randle."

"You," she breathed.

When he looked past her, she knew Papa had followed. She didn't turn, but she heard the soft click as he closed the door. He'd left her alone with a divorced man. She'd never felt so abandoned. "This is insane. You can't marry me. You aren't even properly divorced yet."

He took a step toward her. "That gives us plenty of time to get used to the idea, doesn't it?"

He looked far more presentable than last time she'd seen him. In her room, he'd been drunk and disheveled. Now he looked almost respectable, his fair hair tamed into some semblance of order and his shirt freshly pressed. She thought him beautiful in both guises. She'd forgotten how the sight of him affected her.

"I don't want to marry you," she snapped. Given his high-handed interference, she'd be no better off with him than she was with Mama and Papa.

He went still. A muscle twitched in his jaw. "Better me than Biddle."

Biddle wasn't an issue anymore. He'd seen to that. "Is that what your wife would say if she were here?"

"I have no wife."

"I read as much in the papers. How did you convince my father to be a party to this?"

He gestured at a chair just across from the one he'd vacated. "Won't you sit down?"

"I'd rather stand."

He sighed and sat down. "Suit yourself." And now she felt foolish towering over him. Curse him. "Your father is a businessman. I made him an offer. It was better than Biddle's."

She blinked back tears. His attempt to buy her came as no surprise after all she'd learnt about him in the *Times*, but her father's willingness to make the sale disgusted her. "Mr. Biddle will sue for breach of promise."

"No, he won't." He surprised her by taking her hand. How warm and strong he felt.

"I don't believe it," she said. "I don't believe Charles would let me go so easily. You must have done something, threatened him."

"I didn't threaten him."

"Tell me what you did."

He hesitated. "I want to be honest with you."

"Then be so."

"I spoke to him. I dropped a few hints about our past . . . dealings."

She pulled free and sat down heavily on the chair after all. "Oh, you didn't!"

"I know you probably hate me now, but—"

What she hated most was how little she hated him. If he'd gone about this with more kindness and consideration, she might have thrown herself into his arms regardless of the danger. So much for her much-vaunted intelligence. "Is this how you mean to force my compliance?"

"I don't intend . . . Biddle won't talk. He's in a spot of financial trouble—the sort he can't take to his father—and I offered to help."

"Then I've been sold by two men today."

He blanched. "Forgive me, Sylvia. I didn't stop to think about how this would make you feel. I'm not a good man. God knows I made an appalling husband. I destroy everything I touch. But I won't force you to marry me. I just wanted you free. I wanted you to have choices again."

She didn't know whether to believe him. She knew so little about him, and most of it bad. But when he looked at her the way he did now . . . "Tell me the truth."

"The truth." He smiled and shook his head. "The truth is I want you very much."

Such compelling eyes. They said more than his words. She knew he wanted her physically, she'd known it since he'd approached her in Mrs. Price's garden. But his eyes told her that he wanted her in other ways too. With a thrill of fear, she realized she was actually considering his suit. "But I don't know you."

"You can get to know me." His hand flexed on the arm of his chair, but she was glad when he didn't try to touch her.

Yes, she could get to know him better, but would she ever learn to love him? Was it desirable that she should? "You told me you don't know how to be a husband."

"I was telling the truth. I've no idea."

"You don't make a very compelling argument, Mr. Thorne." Though at least he was honest.

"What if I offered a bribe?"

Her breath caught; she'd almost forgotten what he was.

She stood and went to the far side of her father's desk where she sat in the enormous brown leather chair, leaning her elbows on the armrests. "A bribe, you say. Well, why not? You've bribed everyone else today. How much am I worth? Astonish me."

He gazed at her as if seriously assessing her value. "What if I let you arrange my house to your liking?"

Not what she'd expected.

"What if you could spend as much or as little as you liked and make it exactly as you want it?"

"I'm afraid I don't understand."

"What if I gave you leave to read any damn book you please? What if you could paint whatever you like? I'll build you a studio if you want one."

Oh, he was a devil. He'd actually listened to her that night in the garden. And now to distract her from his high-handedness, he offered her everything she wanted. "And what would you expect in return?"

"You," he said. "You in my bed every night."

She remembered his low silky tone from that first night when he'd whispered her name in the dark. "It sounds like you're offering me carte blanche. Perhaps you'd prefer a mistress rather than a wife."

He leaned forward in his seat. "Except that I want all of you, every thought and feeling. I want to be the only man you allow to touch you."

More seduction, more soft words. She closed her eyes, and prayed for strength. "And will I receive your fidelity in return?"

He didn't hesitate. "Yes."

"I don't believe you." She hurled the words at him like an accusation.

She waited for him to rise up with offended pride, or slouch back in his chair and make a joke of her concerns. Instead, he looked down at his feet.

"How could you expect it?" she asked. "I've read the trial coverage. By all accounts, we could fill a village with your lovers."

His cheeks turned pink. Gracious, he was actually blushing.

"What if I told you I'd changed? What if I told you you'd changed me?"

"I wouldn't believe that either."

He stood and strode to the mantel. His fingers traced the flowers carved into the wood, but he stared into the grate. The flames cast flickering orange lights across his features. "I used to think a wife had to be kept in a state of innocence. Mistresses were for pleasure. Wives were for the begetting of children. But since I met you . . . I want you to be yourself."

She remembered what he'd said that first night, his thoughtless words of flattery. "Charming and elegant?"

"Intelligent. Passionate. Occasionally reckless and self-destructive, but no one's perfect. Just you and whoever you grow to be."

"That all sounds wonderful." The words sounded wistful even to her own ears. How she *longed* to believe him.

"How can I convince you?"

His question took her by surprise. She groped for an answer that didn't exist. "You can't. Only time could do that."

He took several steps toward her, his face suddenly full of hope. "Then give me time."

Could he feign such a look? Her heart lifted despite everything she'd learned.

When she didn't answer, he went on. "We don't have to announce anything. In fact, given my circumstances, we can't. I can wait as long as you need."

She must be mad. Nothing else could excuse the tremendous pull his words exerted. She let it carry her across the room, stopping a single pace from him. She peered into his face. If she examined him closely enough, perhaps she'd see something to convince her one way or the other.

But it was just a face—handsome and apparently sincere.

"Will you let me paint you?" she asked.

Edward couldn't tell if she was joking. Ever since she'd burst into the room, she'd been unpredictable. He despaired of her one moment and brimmed with hope the next. Now she asked if she might paint him as if there were nothing irregular in the request.

"As often as you like," he said. If he posed for a portrait, she'd have to spend hours with him.

"You won't try to stop me from painting? You won't try to change me in any way?"

A light shone in her when she spoke of books and painting. He couldn't bear it if that light ever went out. "No," he promised. "I like you just as you are."

She regarded him with the same keen scrutiny as before. "Will you let me paint you naked?"

For a second, he was robbed of breath. She'd said something like this the night he'd met her, but he'd never expected her to allude to it again. Heat flared inside him. "Even better."

"Very well then." She turned and swept to the door, leaving him confused and off-balance.

"Do you mean very well, you'll paint me naked, or very well, you'll give me time to prove myself?"

She'd reached the door, but now she turned and ran back to him. She stretched up on tiptoes and placed a small, shy kiss on his lips. "Both, I imagine."

She'd kissed him before. Powerful, drugging kisses, but this small peck almost sent him to his knees. She tilted her head to one side and touched her fingertips to his lips. Tracing his smile, he realized. He hadn't even known it was there, though he felt a happiness so intense it was like pain. "You should do that more often," she whispered.

He leaned his cheek against her open palm. "I intend to." He had his time, and he intended to make the best of it. "I won't disappoint you."

She backed away toward the door, her eyes alight with mischief. "I'm cautiously optimistic."

It was enough.

CHAPTER TWENTY-SIX

"What will you do now?" Caroline asked.

It was the question Francesca had dreaded. "I haven't had time to think about it," she lied. In truth, she'd thought about little else. "I'm just enjoying my newfound freedom." As soon as she'd finished her sentence, she brought another spoonful of soup to her lips and hoped Caroline would take the hint and let her eat in peace.

"But you've had months and months to plan."

Francesca stifled her irritation and placed her spoon down carefully. The last thing she wanted was to splash Duchess soup all over herself. "This will probably sound ridiculous but . . . what I'd really like to do is help other women in my situation. There must be so many women trapped in terrible marriages, many to men a thousand times worse than Edward."

Caroline might have spoken but Francesca rushed to prevent her. "I know what you're thinking; I'm the most disorganized, ineffectual creature you ever beheld. What makes me think I can help anyone?"

"That's not what I was thinking at all, but do go on."

"Divorce is expensive. Ruinously so. I thought I could raise money for women who otherwise couldn't afford it." For the first time since she'd started speaking, she forced herself to actually look at Caroline. Instead of outrage or disbelief, she saw admiration in her friend's eyes. "I wasn't certain about telling you. I thought I might overfill my allotted scandal quota."

"Impossible. Your quota has no limits. You may of course depend on me for donations and assistance. I can think of several of my friends who'd offer the same, though some will want to keep their involvement quiet."

"Oh, thank you!" Impulsively, she squeezed Caroline's hand. "But if we don't change the subject, I'm afraid I'll burst into tears." Luckily, Ashton chose that moment to appear, newspaper in hand, and join them at table. "How are things at *The Review*?"

"Things are going very well, actually. I've managed to find an investor at long last. He doesn't know much about the business yet, but he's keen to learn and he's proving unexpectedly dedicated."

"That's wonderful." She knew how much he wanted the journal to succeed. It must be difficult to get started. How did one persuade people to try a new periodical let alone subscribe to one? "What about the content? Did you not say some of your contributors were rather behind the times?"

"We're working on it. Apart from his financial investment, my new associate has a few useful acquaintances. I think he may be able to bring in new blood given time."

"Who is this paragon?" He sounded like the ideal business partner.

A chinking sound and Caroline's glass of wine went over, hitting the table with a resounding clunk. The deep red liquid spread quickly, turning the white table linen a vibrant pink. "Oh dear. Sorry. At least the glass isn't broken."

They all concentrated on their food while a footman saw to the spill.

"Oh, I forgot to ask," Caroline said, as soon as the servant had withdrawn again. "You said Edward might remarry. Does he have a lady in mind for the role of next Mrs. Thorne?"

"I have no idea." Her second lie and it was only the first course. "Edward is out of my life. I have no wish to talk or even think about him."

"I can certainly understand that. Poor woman, whoever she is. You won't mind, will you?"

"Of course not. What Edward chooses to do is of no interest to me."

Mrs. Kirkpatrick had told her all about Edward, Miss Randle, and what had happened between them at Mrs. Price's ball. Francesca had only called to thank her for her testimony, but they'd spent hours talking. Strange as it seemed, they were becoming friends.

"Forgive me if I speak out of turn—" Caroline began.

"Which you always do," Ashton said, earning a stern glare.

"Well, I'm sorry, Philip. But she deserves to know."

"Caro," Ashton warned.

"If she isn't in possession of all the facts, how can we be certain she's made the right decision?"

"It's none of our business."

"What facts?" Francesca asked. "For that matter, what business? What on earth are you both talking about?"

Before Caroline could respond, the servants arrived with the fricassee. Always the soul of tact, Ashton extemporized at length about an exhibit he wanted to include in the next edition while Caroline toyed with the little pieces of stewed chicken on her plate. The short wait until the servants departed again was agony.

"Mr. Standish was here on Friday," Caroline said, at long last.

Ashton froze and waited for Francesca's reaction.

"Oh?" She spoke softly, striving for insouciance when her heart clamored for news of him. "How is he?"

"Hale and hearty," Ashton said, looking daggers at his wife.

"Good." She stabbed her fork into a bit of meat. "I'm glad."

"He's Philip's new partner."

"For heaven's sake, Caro, stop interfering," Ashton snapped.

But it was too late. Francesca pushed her plate aside, suddenly too nauseous to continue. She could think of only one reason for James Standish to take up a trade. "What? What did you say? Why?"

"He needed a larger income because he broke with Mrs. Price. He gave Philip his savings. It wasn't a huge sum, but it was enough. Philip is teaching him the business."

"Oh God. He broke with Mrs. Price? When? Why didn't you tell me?"

"We didn't know if he'd stick with it. We thought he might turn out to be lazy or easily bored."

"He is!"

Caroline gaped.

"I'm sorry." Francesca's voice came out all wobbly. "I didn't mean to shout. But he *is* lazy and easily bored. He's a feckless dilettante who invariably sleeps until noon." Where the words came from or what frightened recess of her mind vomited them up, Francesca didn't know.

Ashton glared at her. "As a matter of fact, he's thrived on the challenge. He works very hard. In truth, sometimes I fear he works a little too hard."

Voices clamored within her, demanding to be heard. All of them shouted out questions and more questions. Did this mean he still loved her? Was he happy? Had he forgotten her? Had he done it for her or for himself? *Please let it be for himself.*

"How long has this been going on?" she demanded. Of all the questions she could have asked, she'd chosen the one that made her sound most like a betrayed wife. And, really, she ought to know.

"Since July," Ashton said.

She'd broken with him in June. This was February. Seven months.

"I told him not to do this. He needs Mrs. Price's money to be happy. He said so." But her words rang hollow. He'd said those things before they'd become lovers. Afterward, he'd claimed being with her made him happy; she just hadn't believed him.

"Yes," Ashton said. "But he broke with her anyway."

Caroline's gaze volleyed back and forth between them, her face white and pinched.

Francesca's eyes stung. She blinked back tears of happiness, hoping no one would notice. "Oh, I'm so glad for him." Glad and so very proud.

Caroline covered the short distance between them and set her hands on Francesca's shoulders. "Perhaps I shouldn't have told you, but I've been avoiding the subject for months. It felt like I was deceiving you and . . . was I wrong? Should I have kept my mouth shut?"

"No. No, of course not. It's just . . ." She tried to keep her voice steady, but she felt her composure crumbling. "God, I feel as though my heart will break."

Ashton whispered something to Caroline, then took one of Francesca's hands and squeezed. "I'm sorry," he said, and quietly left the room.

"Do you still love Mr. Standish?" Caroline asked when he'd gone.

"Yes, but I'm so afraid. I didn't want him to give up his inheritance because I knew—or thought I knew—how he'd hate me for it later. I thought I was doing the right thing for both of us." Now, here she was, seven months later, in as much pain as she'd have felt if all her fears had come to pass. "I should have trusted him."

Caroline handed her a handkerchief. "After the way Edward treated you, I'm astonished you trust anyone."

"That's the heart of it." After Edward, she'd lacked the courage to risk her heart again. What she felt for James was infinitely more powerful, but so was her fear. "Perhaps James was right all along; no one is truly free. We're all trapped in prisons of our own making."

Except he hadn't allowed his fears to control him.

Somehow, he'd broken free.

The question remained; could she do the same?

The light had already begun to fade by the time Francesca stepped from the Ashton carriage into the disturbing Sunday quiet of Fleet Street. On a weekday, one couldn't stand still on the bustling thoroughfare for fear of getting in some brash newspaperman's way. Perhaps that was why she'd never noted the strange hodgepodge of architectural styles.

Lofty Georgian edifices towered over much older, ramshackle timbered structures, one so narrow that it appeared squashed flat by the grander constructions on either side. Close by to the east, the distinctive spire of St. Bride's Church pointed straight to God. When the dreaded People Who Wrote weren't in Bloomsbury, they lived and worked right here. They drank here too. Fleet Street boasted almost as many taverns as newspapers.

The Review occupied the first two floors of one of the smaller Georgians. No light shone at the windows. On the doorstep, she fumbled in her pocket for the small, bronze key Ashton had given her. She jiggled it in the lock until it gave with a loud clunk, then stepped into the small lobby.

Several doors led in different directions, but following Ashton's instructions, she ignored them all, heading for the stairs at the far end. She ascended slowly, but her heart beat rapidly. Caroline had promised James would be here, but what if he wasn't? And if he was, what was she going to say? She'd devised a speech on the short journey over, but she couldn't remember half of it and the rest seemed trite.

The first door at the top of the stairs boasted a shiny brass plate. MR. JAMES STANDISH, CO-OWNER. She reached out, tempted to graze the name with a fingertip. Instead, she knocked on the oak panel—a timid *tap, tap, tap*.

No response from within. No wonder. Even if he'd truly chosen to spend his Sunday working instead of sleeping, he'd need an ear trumpet to detect her presence. Mice made more noise. No squeak of hinge betrayed her as she pushed the door ajar.

He sat at his desk, a ledger open in front of him, and several heavy-looking tomes stacked at his elbow. His gray eyes narrowed as he stared at the page, mouth turned down in a frown of concentration. It was not the air of someone who merely played at business. Such was his absorption that he remained unaware of her presence. Good. She didn't want him to look up and see her—not yet.

She'd thought she'd prepared herself, but the meeting of her imaginings had been rather more formal. In this reality—when she'd come upon him quite alone, in the privacy of his own office—he wore no coat, and he'd rolled back his sleeves, baring his forearms. His shirt gaped open at the neck, revealing his throat and a tiny triangle of dark chest hair. Once, she might have crept forward and slipped her arms around him. She knew how that felt. She knew how his skin tasted.

When she pushed the door wide, he glanced up.

For several seconds, he didn't react. Then he sat up a little straighter in his chair, training his gaze on her with the same fixed intensity he'd shown the ledger. Her skin prickled with the remembrance of intimacies cut short, lusts unfulfilled, and opportunities missed. But how to bridge the chasm she'd created?

She could think of only one way to begin. "Hello, Jemmy."

He bolted to his feet.

For one mad instant, she thought he might leap across the desk at her—either that or run from the room.

"What are you doing here?" The question sounded like an accusation. No, worse than that. It sounded like an insult.

"I came to see you of course." She spoke in the light, airy tone she used for formal calls. She'd come a long way in the last two years, but when she felt cornered, she still fell back on her early training.

"Well, of course," he said, taking on the same polite tone. "How rude of me. It's wonderful to see you." But she knew how he sounded when he thought something was wonderful. Had time extinguished his feelings so utterly, or was he as nervous as she?

He rounded the desk, reaching for her hands, which she allowed him to take.

"Thank you," she said. "It's lovely to see you, too."

How embarrassing. He must know this wasn't a mere social call. If it were, she'd hardly pay it at Fleet Street. The only way to save face was to brazen it out. If she pretended she hadn't made a fool of herself, he'd have to pretend too. She met his look and hoped she wouldn't blush.

His gaze traveled over her, riveting on the top of her head. "You've forgotten your hat."

"I . . ." Withdrawing one of her hands, she reached up. What a stupid thing to do. As if he might be mistaken. As if she might feel it perched there after all. "Oh. I didn't realize. I left in something of a hurry."

He let go of her other hand as if her touch burned. "I heard about the verdict," he said. "You must be pleased."

"It wasn't the outcome I expected." It was so hard to keep looking at him. She turned and walked partway round the desk. Idly, she trailed her fingers over the open ledger, and then the papers scattered across the surface. "It's cluttered."

Glancing up, she saw that his eyes followed her hand's progress as it moved across his belongings. "Yes," he said, but it came out a croak. Clearing his throat, he tried again. "Yes. I know where everything is, but I daresay I should be more organized."

"Not at all. I like it. It's a real workplace." Obeying a sudden impulse, she sat down in his chair, leaned both elbows on the desk, and rested her chin on her hands. He didn't protest, though he gaped slightly. "I'm told you're Ashton's partner now."

"Yes." He perched on top of one of the ledgers. She hadn't left him much option, unless he sat in the visitor's chair. "I knew he needed the money, and it seemed like a good opportunity."

A charge crackled in the air between them. He wanted to reach over and touch her. She could sense it.

He stuck both hands in his pockets. "To be honest, I wasn't sure what else to do."

"Couldn't Mrs. Price help you?"

"I didn't ask her. After . . ." He frowned, and she felt the tenuous bridge she'd built between them shift beneath her feet. "Aunt Miriam wrote to me. She wanted to see me, but I told myself I'd go tomorrow. I put it off again and again for weeks. Even when I bought into *The Review*, I thought I'd go back to her eventually."

She was almost too afraid to ask. "And now?"

His eyes grew cold. "Now? Now I know I never will. And I know what you're thinking. It's not because she wouldn't have me."

"That isn't what I was thinking."

"No? Well, perhaps you think I've grown tired of money. I can't have you laboring under that misapprehension. Much as I'd love to inherit Aunt Miriam's wealth, I'm afraid it comes with far too many strings. And I find I like my independence. I will *never* regret my decision." His eyes flashed defiance.

"You're angry with me."

"Christ. You never know when to leave things alone, do you?" He stood and strode to the window but, when he got there, he faced her again. "Angry? Why ever would I be angry?"

Perhaps she'd been foolish to hope for forgiveness. He'd given up so much and received nothing in return. "I should go." She would try again another day. Perhaps write him a letter or a limerick. But, if she didn't leave now, her cheery facade would crumple.

As she reached the door, he was there, looming behind her. She'd opened the door a crack, but he slammed it shut. "We didn't talk about the verdict. I asked if you were happy, and I'm still waiting for an answer."

His breath stirred the hair at the nape of her neck. She didn't care that he was angry because she knew he'd never hurt her. It was easy to close her eyes and just savor his nearness, the warmth of his body against her back, the sense of rightness. "I will be."

He eased her around to face him. So close, close enough to kiss.

A pity he still looked furious. "You will be? How nice for you. Because, you see, I was happy or at least content, until about ten minutes ago. I was quite merrily, and literally, going about my business. And now you swan in and destroy my peace. You didn't just come here to pass the time, so I'll ask you again. What are you doing here?"

"I came to see you."

"Obviously." His hands encircled her upper arms. "Why?"

"I wanted to tell you how sorry I—"

He swallowed the words with a rough kiss. The touch of his lips, hot and demanding, after so long made her forget everything else. How had she lived without this? Why had she even tried?

He broke away far too soon for her liking. "You were saying?"

Had she been?

Oh, yes.

"I was a terrible coward that last day and for months since. I didn't believe you when you said—"

"Stop. Forgive me but I can't listen to this."

"I see." Oh God, he wasn't even going to hear her out. Just as she hadn't listened to him that day. "I'm sorry."

"You see *nothing*. Never apologize to me for your poor opinion then. I'd spent a lifetime earning it. Why would any sensible woman trust such a sudden change?"

"You are more generous than I deserve." She ducked her head, as determined now to avoid his gaze as she'd once been to hold it. "But, if that's truly how you feel, why are you still so angry."

"Do you have any idea how difficult it's been to respect your wishes and stay away? When I looked up and saw you standing there, I thought I'd fallen asleep at my desk. I have a very vivid imagination, but I confess I never could have envisioned this charming walking dress. Your shadow self spends most of her time flat on her back and invariably nude. Unlike you, she confines herself to evening calls. During the day I work hard—extremely hard—to keep her at bay."

"That's why I came here. I wanted—"

"It doesn't matter. I don't care what you came here for, unless you're here to stay forever."

"Yes." Her heart leaped. "Yes. That sounds perfectly lovely."

For several seconds, he looked thunderstruck. "I didn't offer you an extra biscuit."

She shook her head. "No, certainly not, although you did mention the possibility of my staying forever. If that's an option, if you'd like to make an offer to that effect, then I'd quite like to take you up on it."

His grip on her arms loosened, but only a little. "I said I wouldn't do this."

"Do what exactly?"

His touch gentled as he cupped her cheek, but his voice stayed hard. "I have nothing to offer you—no fortune, no estate, none of the things to which you're accustomed—only me, and whatever I can make of myself." He framed her face with his hands and, at last, he sounded like himself. "But I do love you, Fran. I'll always love you. You can trust in that. You can trust in me. I won't ever—"

She grabbed his shirtfront and hauled him even closer. His kisses, fierce and desperate, sent spirals of heat coiling through her. She reached for the top button of his shirt, but he pulled her hand away and leaned his forehead against hers.

"Marry me," he said. Soft words whispered against her skin.

She tried to speak and knew at once that she'd start crying like a fool if she did.

"Say something," he urged.

Her happiness felt too great for a single person to contain, as if she might break apart like light passing through a prism. "Oh," she said, voice breaking. "This proposal is a vast improvement on the last one."

"Is that a yes?" He didn't wait for a response. "When? When will you marry me?"

"The judge will pronounce the decree absolute in about six months. I'll marry you the very next day if you want."

"That's a long time to wait. Are you sure you won't change your mind? I know you wanted to be free—"

She brushed his lower lip with the tips of her fingers. "I will be. With you." When he relaxed against her, she knew he believed her. "I'm sorry I've been such a coward. I was afraid to trust in us, but I want you to know there's never been a moment when I haven't loved you."

"I may need more proof. If you'll accompany me home, I have shabby new lodgings I'd like you to see." As he spoke, he retrieved his coat from the hat stand.

"I cannot think of anything I would like more, except . . ."

"Except?"

"That's a very sturdy-looking desk you have there."

Somehow the coat slipped from his grasp. In his haste to get to her, he almost trampled it. She screeched as he picked her up and set her down again on top of the mass of papers. "I'd forgotten how this feels," he whispered.

She reached for his top button. "Let me remind you."

And she did.

EPILOGUE

London, Summer 1898

Rosamund gazed across Hyde Park at the small, dark-haired woman and wrinkled her nose in confusion. "She doesn't look particularly scandalous."

Ned, her younger brother, rolled his eyes. "What did you expect? They don't make them wear scarlet letters, you know."

"As if you'd know anything about it."

Ned had adopted that world-weary tone ever since he'd come home from Rugby, and Rosamund found it tiresome in the extreme.

Mrs. Francesca Standish, the subject of their discourse, stood in the shade of a tree with her escort, a tall well-dressed gentleman. Neither was precisely young—perhaps even as old as Papa—but something about the way the gentleman looked at the lady made Rosamund wistful.

Ned shrugged. "I think she looks nice."

Though Rosamund hated to admit it, she agreed. "She's not as pretty as Mama, though."

A hundred yards away, James risked another look at the boy and girl sitting on the grass.

Francesca waited. "Well? Are they still looking?"

He nodded. "But how can you be sure?"

"Oh, please! That boy is Edward's double." And the beautiful blond girl, with her proud bearing, was every inch a Thorne.

He set his hand on her shoulder and squeezed. "Do you want to go home?"

"No. I don't mind. If I were them, I'd want to get a good look too."

As one, they turned and followed the path toward the bridge.

"Do you ever think about him?"

For a second, she didn't know who he meant. "Who? You mean Edward? Goodness, no. Sometimes it's difficult to believe we were ever married." Standing here in the sunlight with James, those long, lonely days seemed insubstantial, like a bad dream.

She looked at the boy and girl again. "By all accounts, he did much better with Sylvia. I hear they're very happy."

He took her hand. "And us? Are we very happy?"

He knew the answer, but he never tired of hearing her say it.

"You tell me," she said, lips curving in a deliberately provocative smile.

Oblivious to the respectable throng out for an afternoon stroll, he pulled her close for a tender kiss. "I love you," he whispered.

And, as always, she knew it was true.

ACKNOWLEDGMENTS

Thank you first of all to the Bookends team, especially my agent Jessica Alvarez. Thank you to everyone at Union Square & Co., particularly my editor Barbara Berger, Kristin Mandaglio, Kevin Ullrich, Sandy Noman, Elizabeth Lindy, and Lisa Forde. And thank you to Vi-An Nguyen for my gorgeous new cover.

To Olivia Waite, even though we don't know one another, for that amazing *New York Times* review. What a difference you made!

To Ben, Sam, and Ollie for your love and patience.

To Dianna Stirpe. Your critiques were invaluable.

And to the people at BioWare for not releasing *Dragon Age 4* yet.

TOPICS AND QUESTIONS FOR DISCUSSION

1. As the story opens, James and the Thornes are all living their lives according to the conventions of late-Victorian society. When we meet them again ten years later, Francesca has rebelled entirely. What changes has she made? In what ways are she and the others still bound to convention?

2. James is heir to his rich aunt Miriam. What expectations and restrictions does she place on him? How do they differ from the expectations and restrictions placed upon Francesca?

3. Why do you think James agrees to mediate between Francesca and Thorne? How does the resulting encounter change things between James and Francesca? Between Edward and James? Between James and Miriam?

4. The trajectory of James's and Francesca's romance could be described as *friends to lovers*. To what extent do you agree with this designation?

5. Edward has been unfaithful to Francesca countless times during their marriage, but she is condemned for a single rumored infidelity with Tommy Trafford. To what extent and in what ways does each character subscribe to this double standard? What, in society's view, makes her behavior worse than his? Do you think the double standard still exists?

6. Miriam encourages James to court Sylvia Randle, a woman who seems like the perfect debutante—just like Francesca at the start of the story. What are the parallels between the two women? How are they different?

7. Virginia Kirkpatrick is, at first, presented as the archetypal "other woman": overtly sexual, dripping in diamonds, and apparently oblivious to the feelings of the wife she's usurping. How is Virginia different than she first appears? How did your idea of her evolve as you read? Are there parallels between her and Francesca? What about between Virginia and Sylvia?

8. "He won't give you the life you want. He won't like you or understand you. He won't let you paint naked men. He'll stifle everything that makes you unique and wonderful." Edward says this to Sylvia, but he's clearly talking about his

marriage to Francesca as well. To what extent is he redeemed at the end of the story? Did he deserve the ending he got? What, if anything, do you think he's learned?

9. To varying extents, the main characters are all trying to balance the rules of society with their wishes and desires. How successful are they in the end relative to when we first meet them?

10. In the epilogue, ten years on, Francesca and James have built a happy marriage but society still regards Francesca as a scandalous figure. How did you feel about this aspect of the ending?